ROSAMUNDE'S
Knight

**SILVERTON SERIES
BOOK 1**

HARPER BLACK

Copyright © 2024 Harper Black

All rights reserved.

No part of this publication in print or in electronic format may be reproduced, stored in a retrieval system, or transmitted in any form or by any means, electronic, mechanical, photocopying, recording, or otherwise without the prior written permission of the publisher.

This is a work of fiction. Names, characters, organizations, places, events and incidents are either the products of the author's imagination or are used fictitiously. Any resemblance to actual persons, living or dead, or actual events is purely coincidental.

Design and distribution by Bublish

ISBN: 979-8-9880768-3-4 (paperback)
ISBN: 979-8-9880768-2-7 (eBook)

WARNING

This book is intended for adults. It is a romance novel that contains scenes of violence and addresses suicide and mental health issues.

PROLOGUE

Rosamunde "Taylor" Sawyer had a love-hate relationship with early-morning flights. On the one hand, they were great because they got you where you were heading during daylight hours, but on the other hand, they were *so damn early*. She often slept poorly the night before because she was afraid she would oversleep. Then, once on board, she could never fall asleep no matter how tired she was because planes made her nervous.

"Excuse me, miss. Could I trouble you to reach up into the overhead bin and grab my bag?"

Taylor looked over at the man sitting next to her. He was an older gentleman whose features looked slightly pinched as if he were tired or not feeling well.

"Certainly," she said. "It's no trouble at all." Getting up, she grabbed the bag out of the overhead bin and handed it to him. He unzipped it and pulled out a pillbox. He opened the compartment marked "W am" and emptied its contents into his hand. He put the box back in his bag and handed it to her. Taylor returned the bag to the bin, retook her seat, then asked him if he needed water. He said he did. She offered him the unopened bottle of water in her bag, before telling him she could call the flight attendant if that's what he preferred. Not wanting to make a fuss, he accepted her offer.

She turned away and went back to the book she'd been reading to give him a semblance of privacy as he took his medication but found it hard to concentrate. Her flight companion thanked her again and asked if she was enjoying her book. Taylor replied, "It's okay." They talked a bit more about the book, then the conversation drifted to other topics. Before long, the plane began to prepare for landing. She found time had flown by quickly and that the man next to her was feeling much better, as evidenced by the sparkle in his eye and his relaxed appearance. He looked better, but she wasn't sure if he was 100 percent, so she asked the flight attendant to arrange for a wheelchair for him upon landing.

The wheelchair turned out to be a great idea. Though the man was feeling better, he was still a bit weak. Taylor walked beside him as the attendant wheeled him to the ground transportation area. After the attendant left, she offered to get him a cup of coffee while he waited. She had an hour before her connecting flight and wanted to make sure he was okay. When Taylor returned with the coffee, he told her he'd received a text from his son saying he would be late due to a bad accident on the highway. She didn't feel right leaving him, so she decided to wait with him until his son arrived, even though it meant she would probably miss her flight.

His son and daughter-in-law arrived two hours later, one hour after her original connecting flight had taken off. They eyed her curiously as they approached. The father greeted the couple and then introduced Taylor. He told them how she'd helped him on the plane and that she'd kindly kept an old man company until they arrived. They thanked her for her assistance and spoke for a few more minutes. Taking his father's bag, the son told them he'd meet them outside, thanked Taylor again, and left. After his son's departure, Taylor turned her attention to her new gentleman friend she'd spent the last few hours with. She lowered herself until she was face-to-face with him and told him what a pleasure it had been to have met him and that she was truly glad he was feeling better. She then placed her hand on his shoulder, leaned forward, and kissed his cheek. Standing, she smiled, said goodbye to him and his daughter-in-law, gave a little wave, and headed toward security.

With a smile on his face, the man watched her walk away, then turned to his daughter-in-law and told her he was ready to go. She turned the wheelchair toward the automatic doors and headed outside to wait for her husband. When he arrived, she got in the back seat and the man's son assisted him into the front passenger seat, went over to the driver's side, got in, and eased into the traffic lane toward the airport exit.

"So, Pop, what's up with you picking up women on the plane? Didn't we have the 'don't talk to strangers' talk before you left?" PJ smiled as he looked over at his father.

"We did. But what can I say?" The man smiled. "I'm charming." They all laughed. "She really was sweet. She never let on that she knew I was having some discomfort. She just took care of me. When she found out you guys were going to be late, she told me she'd wait with me. She went and got us coffee, and we sat and talked while we waited. I was glad for the company, but I think she may have missed her flight."

"I'm glad she was there too. I was worried when we found out how late we were going to be. Now I see we didn't need to, since you were in good hands and working your magic," Cheryl, his daughter-in-law, said from the back seat.

"What's that about magic?" PJ asked.

"Your father was in rare form. She kissed him on the cheek when she said goodbye."

"Check you out, Mr. Smooth. How are you feeling now?"

"I'm fine. I took a pain pill on the plane, and it didn't take too long to kick in. I'm glad I got ahead of it." The remainder of the ride back to the ranch was filled with talk about the older man's trip.

Back in the airport, the ticket agent told Taylor the next flight to Milwaukee, Wisconsin, would not be leaving for another two hours. She wouldn't get home until 11:00 p.m. After getting her new boarding pass, she went through security and walked to her gate. She hoped there was an open bookstore on the concourse. She only had a few chapters left in the book she'd brought with her, so she wanted to get another one, to keep her company while she waited. She also needed to call her brother to let him know she would be coming in on a later flight.

chapter 1

The morning had come particularly early. A night spent tossing and turning made for a groggy rising—a common occurrence in the life of Rosamunde Taylor-Sawyer, known as Taylor to friends and family. As she headed to the kitchen, all she could think about was getting that first cup of coffee, which usually helped to clear her head. She grabbed a coffee pod from the cabinet, placed her favorite mug in position, and hit brew. While she waited, her phone rang.

"Hello?"

"Hello. May I speak to Ms. Taylor-Sawyer?" a male voice asked.

"This is she."

"Ms. Taylor-Sawyer, my name is Jackson Edwards. I'm an attorney, and I'm calling from Silverton, Wyoming."

"Silverton, Wyoming?" she asked, wondering why he might be calling her.

"Yes. I represent the estate of Preston Knight. I don't know if you remember, but the two of you met on a flight about six months ago."

"Six months ago? Yes, I remember him."

"Mr. Knight passed away a few weeks ago."

"I'm sorry to hear that." Taylor was genuinely sorry to hear this.

"He had cancer. He was a very sick man when the two of you met."

"Oh, wow."

"Your kindness left a big impression on him. So much so, that he mentioned you in his will."

"Wait. What?" She thought she'd misunderstood him.

"He mentioned you in his will, which brings me to the reason for this call. The reading of the will is scheduled for next week. Mr. Knight requested you be present for the reading. If you agree, I'll have my assistant make your travel arrangements."

"I'm sorry. Can we back up a minute? Did you just say a man I met on a plane left me an inheritance of some kind?"

"Yes, that's correct."

"Um, I don't know what to say. Would it be okay if I get your number and call you back later?"

"Certainly." He gave her his contact information, including his email address, and ended the call.

What in the world? Taylor stared at her phone as she tried to process the conversation she'd just had with Jackson Edwards the attorney. *Was he for real?*

She grabbed her coffee cup, added half-and-half and a dash of cinnamon, then went to her home office and sat down in front of her computer. She googled Jackson Edwards, and sure enough, he appeared to be just who he said he was. She then searched for Preston Knight and found his obituary. It seemed he had died after a short battle with pancreatic cancer. His wife had preceded him in death two years prior. He was the father of three sons, Preston Jr., Michael, and Denton. He was a Vietnam Veteran who became a rancher and was well-loved by the local community as well as his family and friends. Taylor teared up as she read about his life. She'd only known him for a few hours, but it felt much longer.

Later that day, she stopped by her parents' home for lunch and told them about the phone call she'd received that morning. Lily and Daniel Sawyer had adopted her when she was ten years old, after the death of her biological parents. She'd known them all her life leading up to the adoption and was very close to them. In addition to getting new parents, she'd also gotten two brothers—Daniel Jr., called "Blue" by family and friends, who was three years older, and Grant, who was two years her senior.

She'd told them about meeting Mr. Knight and how nice he'd been. She'd thought his discomfort might have been due to his age or the long plane ride. She would never have guessed how sick he was. Her parents asked her if she was planning to go to Wyoming. She hadn't yet made up her mind, so she told them she didn't know. Having researched the lawyer and finding him to be legitimate, she was giving serious consideration to making the trip. However, she'd be lying if she said she wasn't worried about attending the reading with Mr. Knight's family. Her father told her to take some time to think about it but suggested that, in the meantime, she could call the attorney back for more information. She thought that was a good idea and asked if he could be on the call with her. He assured her he would be happy to.

Driving home, she thought about the time she'd spent with Mr. Knight. He'd been a very charming man. He was tall, with a head full of silver hair and dark-brown eyes. He had kind of reminded her of the actor Sam Elliott, except he'd been taller and had more bulk. From her time with him and seeing the passing glances he received from some of the women on the flight and in the airport, others seemed to have noticed as well. Preston Knight Sr. had been a silver fox; he must have been downright lethal in his younger years. Hmmm.

Midmorning the next day, Taylor arrived back at her parents' home. Her mother was heading out the door just as she pulled up. She hugged Taylor and told her there were fresh cinnamon rolls in the kitchen and that she'd be back later that afternoon. Taylor returned her hug, thanked her for the rolls, and went into the house and straight to the kitchen.

Poppy, her father, was in the kitchen pouring a cup of coffee when she entered. He raised the pot, and she nodded. She took a cup from the cabinet and handed it to him. She then took two cinnamon rolls from the cooling racks, plated them, and took a seat next to her father at the table.

"You know Mimi doesn't want you to eat too many, right?" she asked with a smile, knowing what his answer would be.

"I know. But she shouldn't have made them if she didn't want me to eat them." He returned her smile. Taylor couldn't blame him. Her mother's cinnamon rolls were made from scratch and were delicious.

"So, you still want to call the lawyer this morning?"

"Yes, I do. I think after hearing more about Mr. Knight, I'll be able to make up my mind as to whether I'll attend."

"Okay. Whenever you're ready, we can make the call."

"I was going to wait until I finished eating, but I think I want to do it now and get it over with."

"Okay, Tay-Bay," he said. "Tay-Bay" was her family's nickname for her. When she was adopted, she added her new last name—Sawyer—to her existing last name, becoming Rosamunde Taylor-Sawyer. Her brother Blue started calling her Tay-Bay, and the name stuck. She also began introducing herself as Taylor instead of her actual first name.

Taylor grabbed her phone and the paper on which she'd written the lawyer's contact information. She dialed the number and put the phone on speaker. When it was answered, she identified herself and asked if Mr. Edwards was available. She was placed on a brief hold before Jackson Edwards came on the line. Taylor greeted him and told him she had him on speaker and that her father was there as well. She introduced the two of them. She then asked him to tell her a little more about Preston Knight.

He readily agreed, and she could hear the love in his voice as he spoke. He and Preston Sr. had grown up together and had been best friends from as far back as he could remember. They'd gone to school together, were drafted, and joined the Marines. They'd gone through boot camp together but received orders to separate battalions. When they were discharged, they came back home and went to college using the GI Bill. After graduation, Preston married his high-school sweetheart, and Jackson went on to law school and married a woman he met in college. Both men eventually went back to Silverton, where Preston took over his family's ranch and Jackson joined one of the firms in town before later opening his own practice.

Jackson was godfather to two of Preston's three sons, Preston Jr. (PJ), and Denton—the oldest and the youngest. Mike was the middle son, and his godfather was Jared Hawkins, or "Hawk," who'd served with them. Jackson then went on to talk about some of the work Preston had done in the local community. He'd been a board member for many land conservation organizations and was instrumental in getting the farmers market started, as well as a county pantry where excess produce was canned and preserved and available to those in need. Jackson said that more than anything else, Preston was a family man. He also told them about the death of Preston's wife two years prior, when he had received his diagnosis of pancreatic cancer, and his subsequent death.

Jackson asked Taylor if she had any other questions or needed any more information. Needing some time to think about it, she told him she'd call him back in the next day or two with her decision. He said that would be fine and surprised her when he asked Poppy if he had any questions. Her father said no, but depending on Taylor's decision, he may have a few later. Taylor thanked him for his time and reiterated her promise to call.

After the call ended, Taylor looked over at her father.

"What do you think?" she asked him.

"It seems like this is a legitimate thing, but I think this is a decision you'll have to make on your own. Either way, you'll have our support."

"Thanks, Poppy. In the meantime, though, I think I'll have one of these rolls. Care to join me?"

"I'd love to."

Friday arrived, and Taylor, having made her decision, called Jackson Edwards, and told him she would come. They spoke for a few minutes more before he put her through to his assistant, who spoke with her about travel arrangements. After confirming she would email the itinerary as soon as it was ready, she asked Taylor to contact her if she had any questions or needed any additional information. Taylor thanked her and ended the call.

Taylor sat for a moment thinking about what was to come. She had a lot to do between now and Wednesday. First, she needed to call her parents, and then she needed to pack. What did one pack for a trip to Wyoming in the summer? What was the weather like? What were the people like? Would she be the only Black person in the whole town? Maybe she hadn't thought things through as much as she should have. In any case, it was too late to back out, since she'd said she would go.

chapter 2

"Are you sure you want to go through with this?" Her mother, who was sitting in the front seat, asked. "It's okay if you change your mind."

"I am, Mimi." Taylor had planned on taking an Uber to the airport, but her parents insisted on driving her.

"She's got her mind made up, Lily. You know how stubborn she is once she sets her mind on something."

"I'll be fine. And I don't want you to worry. I'll call you as soon as I get settled. I'm only going to be gone a few days."

"I know. But I'm your mother, and it's my job to worry about you."

"Well, worry or not, Lily, we're here." Her dad pulled alongside the curb at the departure terminal and got out. He grabbed Taylor's suitcase from the trunk and set it on the sidewalk. Taylor hugged her mother and told her she loved her and not to worry. She hugged her father and told him the same, grabbed the handle of her suitcase, and wheeled it around. She reminded her parents she'd call them as soon as she got settled, then walked through the sliding glass doors toward the security checkpoint.

During the ride home from the airport, Daniel Sawyer tried to calm his wife's fears.

"Lily, she's going to be okay."

"I know, I just worry. I mean, she's going to Wyoming. What Black people do you know go to Wyoming? What if she's the only one in the whole town? What if they don't treat her right?"

"Lily, Taylor is a forty-five-year-old woman. If she doesn't know how to take care of herself by now, we did a piss-poor job as parents. Don't you think you're going a little overboard?"

"You're right. I'm blowing this all out of proportion."

"It's okay," Daniel smirked. "Besides, you know if they hurt my Tay-Bay, I'll *eff* them up."

Lily laughed, grabbed his hand, and said, "I know you would, baby."

"I'm here." Taylor smiled as she spoke to her parents. They'd insisted on FaceTime and were speaking to her via their iPad. "I'm safe and sound. Mr. Edwards had a court date and was unable to meet me, so he had one of the sheriff's deputies pick me up."

"The police picked you up?"

"It's a small town, Poppy. It's not like they have Uber or Lyft. Anyway, it was kind of funny. The deputy had a sign with my name on it. I don't think he was expecting someone who looked like me. When I approached him and told him I was Rosamunde Taylor-Sawyer, he looked a bit surprised. He even looked at his sign and looked back at me. 'What's the matter?' I asked. 'Expecting someone else?' He said, 'Yes,' then quickly said, 'No, I mean no. I was just about to ask if you need help with your luggage.' He seemed genuinely sorry for his gaffe. I told him I just had a carry-on and if he was ready to go, I was too." After he got over his initial embarrassment, he turned out to be nice, albeit a bit goofy. The airport is about an hour's drive from here. He pointed out a lot of the scenery and told me a bit about the area. Then he dropped me off at this cute little bed-and-breakfast, and here I am."

"We're glad you made it safe. Have you spoken with Mr. Edwards since you arrived?"

"No. I did meet his wife though. She was here at the B&B when I arrived. She's a very nice lady. She's going to come by tomorrow and take me to Mr. Edwards's office."

"That's nice of her," her mother said. "It sounds like they're going out of the way to make you comfortable."

"It does, doesn't it? I wasn't expecting all of this. But then again, up until a few months ago, I'd never heard of Silverton, Wyoming. It certainly wasn't on my list of places to visit, but here I am." They spoke a little longer, and Taylor promised to call them tomorrow after everything was done.

After talking with her parents, Taylor decided to do a little exploring. It was early afternoon, and Angela, Jackson Edwards's wife, had told her about some of the shops. She decided she'd check out some of the local spots, grab a bite to eat, and head back to her room. She'd told her parents all was well, but in reality, she was a little nervous and out of her element. Grabbing her sweater and her camera, she placed them in her backpack along with her room key, and walked out the door.

Silverton was a quaint Western town that managed to be modern yet hold on to its roots. It was not big enough to be a city, but it wasn't a traditional small town either. Her B&B was on the edge of the Old Town area that was centered near the town square and covered a few city blocks. There were quite a few businesses—clothing and jewelry stores, art galleries, bakeries, a genuine old-fashioned general store and mercantile (or so the sign said), restaurants, a wine bar, saloons, etc. Hearing her stomach grumble, she decided the first order of business should be to get some food. The breakfast sandwich and coffee she'd had earlier that morning were a distant memory. The question was, where to go?

Taylor passed a few restaurants as she made her way around the square. She viewed the menus but didn't find a place she wanted to check out. She was reading the menu in front of the Red Buffalo Saloon when she heard a voice say, "I hear the food here is pretty good. The drinks aren't bad either."

She turned to the right and saw a tall man standing next to her. Like her, he was staring at the menu.

"Is that right?" she asked.

"Yes," he said, turning toward her and smiling, "I have it on good authority that *everything* is good here."

"Well, I guess I better check it out," she said eagerly. He moved toward the door and shifted the box he was carrying to his other arm.

"After you." He stood aside and opened the door. Taylor hesitated for a minute before she walked across the threshold.

The man followed her in, placed the box he was carrying on a nearby table, and extended his hand to her.

"Hi," he said. "I'm Mike. Full disclosure, I own the place."

Taylor looked up at him and laughed. "I'm Taylor," she said, shaking his hand. There was something about his rich-brown eyes that seemed a bit familiar, but she couldn't think why.

"Nice to meet you, Taylor." He continued holding her hand while he asked if she minded sitting at the bar. He explained they'd just finished the lunch rush and were technically closed until later that evening.

"Oh, I didn't know you were closed. I can go somewhere else."

"I wouldn't hear of it," he said, smiling again as he released her hand and walked with her to the bar. After grabbing a bottle of water and a glass, he set both in front of her, before turning and pointing to the chalkboard menu hanging on the wall. He told her to take a look at it and that he'd be right back, before going to pick up the box he had placed on the table.

What just happened? Taylor thought. This man had walked up to her from seemingly nowhere, and now she was sitting in his saloon. Said man was also tall, tan, and had some seriously sexy brown eyes. He reminded her of the town itself—a bit modern, a bit rugged, old-school cowboy. His hands were those of a man who worked with them on a daily basis. They looked big and strong. Just like the rest of him. At a few inches over six feet, he was solidly built, not necessarily muscular, but not fat either. His hair was thick and light brown in color, with silver strands appearing at his temples and throughout, and he sported what looked to be a day's growth of beard. His jawline was strong and looked as chiseled as the mountains on the horizon, and he had a scar that ran diagonally across his chin from left to right, which, in truth, added rather than detracted from his good looks.

Mike had seen her standing near the entrance of the Red Buffalo as he walked toward it. He'd been on his way back from picking up a few things from the office supply store. He guessed her height to be about five foot nine, which made her taller than most women he'd been around. Her skin was the color of honey, and her hair looked like it was in braids, with red and gold highlights peeking through. *She's probably a tourist*, he thought. Silverton, while a progressive town, wasn't very diverse. There *were* people of color there, but not many. What caught his attention was the way she filled out the jeans she wore. They seemed to hug her hips and ass as if they'd been custom-made for her. *Yup, a tourist,* he thought. No one around there had hips or an ass like that. The next thing he knew, he was standing next to her, inviting her inside, where he got an even better look at her. Her skin was smooth and really did look like honey. She had a tiny, sparkling nose stud and gold hoop earrings peeking through what he'd thought were braids but were actually locs. She was pretty, but there was something different about her. He didn't know exactly what it was, but he kind of liked it—so much so he'd invited her in, knowing they were closed. He hoped Caleb, his chef and best friend, was still around and hadn't shut the kitchen down yet.

Mike went to his office and set the box on his desk, then headed into the kitchen in search of Caleb, who thankfully was still there.

"Hey. You shut down yet?"

"No. I was about to fix something. You hungry?"

"Yeah, but can you hold up a minute? I, ah, let a customer in and told her she could order something."

Caleb turned and looked at him. "Oh, really? *Customer* or *guest?*"

"Customer." Mike turned and walked out of the kitchen. Caleb, being curious, followed him.

"Where are you going?" Mike asked.

"I'm the chef." Caleb smirked. "A good chef always greets his customers."

"Yeah, right."

Taylor was scrolling through her phone when Mike returned with a tall, handsome, Native American man wearing a white chef's jacket.

"Hi," he said, extending his hand. "Caleb Hawkins. I'm the chef here."

"Nice to meet you. I'm Taylor." She smiled, returning his greeting.

Mike asked her if she knew what she wanted to eat.

"I'm not sure. I was thinking about trying the bleu buffalo burger. Is it possible to get it with a side of chips instead of fries?"

"Certainly. We do them in-house, so they're freshly made."

"That sounds great. That's what I'll have then."

Caleb smiled and went back to what she guessed was the kitchen. Mike moved to the beer taps and asked if she was a beer drinker.

"On occasion," she answered.

"Would you like to try the house brand?"

"Sure." She watched as he reached for a small glass and placed it under a beer tap that had a red buffalo on it. She thought again how big and strong his hands looked and briefly wondered what they'd feel like if they were wrapped around her like they were wrapped around the glass he was holding. He placed the drink in front of her, telling her it was called "Red Buffalo Ale." At least that's what she thought he'd said. Taylor was watching his mouth but hadn't didn't quite hear him, so she had to ask him to repeat what he'd said. He gave her a slightly amused look and told her the name again as his phone began to ring. He looked at it, excused himself, and answered it as he walked toward the kitchen.

Get a grip, Taylor told herself. She was a bit stressed from being out of her element, which she told herself was the reason she was feeling Mike, a man she'd literally just met. She shook her head as she took a sip of the ale he'd placed before her. She hoped her food didn't take too long. She needed to eat and get back to her room. She had a big day ahead of her tomorrow and needed to keep her focus on it instead of Mike's fine ass.

Caleb prepared Taylor's food as well as something for Mike and himself while he waited for Mike to get off the phone.

"What?" Mike asked as he ended his call.

"Nothing. I'm just curious about your guest."

"My guest? She's a customer."

"No, she's a *guest*. You rarely, *if ever*, let anyone in when we're closed. Although, I can see why you invited her in."

"She's a tourist. I was just being nice."

"Sure you were. I don't blame you though. She's got that whole artsy, sexy thing going on. Couldn't resist it, could you?" Caleb teased and reached his fist toward him.

"She's got *something* going on." Smiling, he fist-bumped Caleb. Caleb plated their food. He picked up a plate and handed it to Mike. He grabbed the other two and followed him back to the bar.

"How do you like the ale? Would you like to try a pint?" Mike asked as he set a plate in front of Taylor.

"I like it. And yes, I would."

Caleb put one plate to Taylor's left, then put the other to her right and sat down. "I'd like a pint as well, Mike." He winked at Taylor as she spoke.

Taylor noticed her reaction to him was very different from her reaction to Mike. Caleb came off as a harmless flirt. Mike had a kind of grumpy, rugged demeanor that intrigued her. After pouring their beers, Mike sat down, and they began to eat. Taylor swore it was the best burger she'd ever eaten and told Caleb so. They talked while they ate. They told her a little about themselves and the saloon and invited her to check it out one evening while she was in town. She told them a little about herself and where she was from. She knew they thought she was a tourist, and she was fine with that. This wasn't a very big town, and they might know Preston Knight's family. She didn't want to start any unnecessary speculation as to why she was there.

After she finished eating, she lingered over her beer for a bit before deciding to head back to her B&B. They refused to let her pay for her meal. She thanked them and told both that she'd think about coming back one evening. She wondered if Mike was married or otherwise involved. A quick glance while they were talking showed a bare ring finger. *Damn*, she thought. She would have liked to stick around and talk to Mike a little longer. His voice was a baritone with a bit of a rasp. He probably sounded sexy in the morning, on the phone, or when he was balls deep in some lucky woman. *Hell, he sounded sexy now.* She sighed as she left.

When she got back to her room, she pulled out her sketch pad and began to draw. Her hobby and side business was designing jewelry. She'd gotten a few ideas while walking through town and wanted to get them on paper while they were still fresh in her mind. As was common, once she got started, time got away from her. It was 9:30 p.m. by the time she set the pad and pencil down. She pulled a T-shirt and a pair of boxer shorts out of her suitcase. Both were old, soft and faded. She'd brought them with her as a security blanket of sorts—a carryover from her childhood. When her parents died, Mimi had made a square for her, which she'd created from clothing belonging to her birth parents. She said she'd made it for Taylor as a reminder that her parents would always be with her. Taylor no longer carried the square, but she kept it in a special keepsake box. She liked to keep familiar items around for whenever she was feeling anxious or depressed. Just as the square had given her comfort, so had the T-shirt and shorts she'd put on before climbing into bed.

chapter 3

Today is the day, Taylor thought as she lay in bed, staring at the ceiling. Not knowing what to expect, she knew she needed to get up and get ready for it. She reached over to the nightstand and grabbed her phone to turn off the alarm. It was set to go off in an hour, but she knew she wouldn't be able to get back to sleep. Pulling the covers back, she sat up on the side of the bed and began to pray as she placed her feet on the floor and headed toward the bathroom. She had a feeling she was going to need every bit of her faith today.

An hour later, Taylor stood in front of the room's full-length mirror turning first left and then right to check her appearance. She put her locs in a low ponytail and decided on her usual enhanced natural look, which consisted of concealer, powder, soft eyeliner, and a bit of bronzer. She brushed on mascara and finished the look with soft, matte lip color and her diamond nose stud. Dressed in a rose-colored sheath dress with a matching cardigan and neutral-colored leather pumps with a three-inch heel, she took one last glance at her reflection. Satisfied with how she looked, she put on her jewelry: earrings, a watch, rings, and her favorite bracelet.

Two hours later, Taylor met Mrs. Edwards outside the B&B as planned. When she got in the car, Mrs. Edwards asked her how she was.

"I'm a little nervous, but I'm okay."

Mrs. Edwards looked at her and placed her hand on Taylor's, which had a death grip on the strap of her purse.

"I understand you being nervous. That's why I offered to pick you up and take you to the office myself. Preston was a good man, and his sons are some of the finest men I know," she assured her before squeezing Taylor's hand and pulling out of the parking lot, en route to the law offices of Jackson Edwards. Taylor tried to take Mrs. Edwards's words to heart, but her nerves wouldn't let her.

It was a short drive to their destination, and ready or not, they had arrived. A young, friendly receptionist greeted both Taylor and Mrs. Edwards when they entered. Mr. Edwards, who was sitting behind his desk, stood up when they walked in. He introduced himself to Taylor and shook her hand, then greeted his wife with a kiss. He apologized for not being able to meet Taylor the previous day and asked if she'd gotten settled in okay. She assured him she was fine. Mrs. Edwards stated she had an errand to run but would return in about an hour or so to take Taylor back to her B & B. Mr. Edwards excused himself and walked her out. In their absence, Taylor looked around the office and tried to calm her nerves.

When Mr. Edwards returned, he wasn't alone. He was accompanied by two women and three men. She recognized one man and woman as the son and daughter-in-law she'd met at the airport with Preston Sr. Walking in after them was a shorter man who bore a strong resemblance to the first man. She guessed they were related. Next to him was a red-haired woman who was pregnant. Taylor drew in a breath when she saw who followed. It was Mike, the man from yesterday. Judging by the look on his face, he was as surprised to see her as she was to see him. Mr. Edwards made the introductions: Preston, or PJ, and his wife, Cheryl. Denton and his wife, Lorraine, and Michael.

"Taylor?" Mike asked, smiling.

"Yes, it's me." Taylor smiled and gave a nervous little wave.

Mr. Edwards asked if they knew each other. Mike told him they'd met yesterday when Taylor had lunch at the saloon.

"Small world," Mr. Edwards said.

Taylor greeted the others as a group and offered her condolences. Mr. Edwards led them to their seats and began to tell them about the video Preston Knight had left for them. He would answer any questions they might have afterward.

Shock was the word to describe what Taylor felt after viewing the video. Preston Knight had left her a house. It was hers to do what she wanted with, as long as she lived in it for a year. After the year, she could keep it, rent it out, or sell it. During the video, Preston Knight also said he was grateful for her kindness. He hoped she would enjoy spending time in a new place where she could maybe create jewelry as beautiful as her smile. Taylor didn't know what to say as she looked over at his family. They didn't seem to be as stunned as she'd been when she heard the news. *Maybe they already knew,* she thought.

"Mr. Edwards, I don't know what to say. This is quite a surprise." Mr. Edwards chuckled.

"If you knew Preston, you wouldn't be surprised at all. He was always doing things like this. It's almost as if he had a sixth sense about people. I know this is a lot to take in, but would you like to see the house? I have the keys and can take you over after we finish up here."

"Um, yeah, I guess."

"Ms. Sawyer, please know that my father did this with good intentions. He was very much impressed with you." PJ smiled as he spoke to Taylor.

"Please, call me Taylor. I guess I'm just dealing with the shock of it all. When Mr. Edwards called and said I was mentioned in the will, I had no idea it would be something like this. It's a lot to take in. However, I do appreciate your father's generosity, and I'm glad I was able to help him when he needed it." Taylor looked over at Mr. Edwards and asked if he could direct her to the restroom. He pointed to a door on the other side of the room. She rose from her seat, excused herself, and walked out.

"So," Denton, also known as "Little D" or "D," said, "Why in the world did Pop decide to give someone a house? How'd she get him to do it?"

"D, honey, I don't think that's what happened. I think Pop just really wanted to repay a kindness," Lorraine, his wife, said. "Besides, she was just as surprised as we were. I think she's nice."

"Me too," said Cheryl. "She seems the same as she was when we met her at the airport. What do you think, Mike? Sounds like you spent a little time with her yesterday." They all looked at him as they waited for him to answer.

"I thought she was nice. Funny too." He didn't think it was a good time to mention that the only reason he'd spoken to Taylor in the first place was because of the way she looked in the jeans she'd been wearing. Hell, she was looking pretty good in that dress she had on today too. She might have been going for a more conservative look, but with the nose stud, the rings, and the hint of a tattoo he saw peaking from under the sleeve of her sweater, she wasn't quite able to pull it off. Instead, that sexy, artsy vibe Caleb had mentioned was on full display. He liked seeing her this way as much as he liked seeing her in her jeans. And now that he'd seen a little of the tattoo, he wondered if she had just the one or if she had others. Not the most appropriate thoughts to be having, but he couldn't seem to stop them.

Taylor walked over to the sink as soon as she entered the restroom. She turned on the water and looked at herself in the mirror as she waited for the water to warm up. A man who hardly knew her left her a house because he thought she needed a change of scenery. How did he know this? How had a complete stranger gotten such a complete read on her in such a short period of time? Was she that transparent?

The fact was, she *was* sad, and in the last year, she'd just been going through the motions and pretending to be okay or, as her brother Grant said, "phoning it in." It had started with her boyfriend. After three years together, he up and ghosted her. All the time they'd been together, and he just stopped all communication. He wouldn't return her calls or texts, and when she went to his house, he was either not there or he refused to answer the door. He even blocked her number. She later found out he'd been in a relationship with another woman the whole time he'd been with her. Taylor had been devastated. She spent months trying to figure out what she'd done to deserve that. She'd never been one to give her heart easily, but to her, he was "the one." Three months later, he called her out of the blue, tried to apologize, and said he wanted to give them another chance. She'd stopped him before he could even get all the words out, giving him a firm no, and ended the call.

The more she thought about her current situation, the more she knew she might be overreacting out of fear. Yes, it was a surprise that Preston Knight thought enough of her to remember her in his will. It was an even bigger surprise to find out the man she'd met yesterday—and was sort of crushing on—was his son. That was a bit awkward. Whatever the case, she needed to get back in there.

Later that afternoon, Taylor stood in a small yard next to Jackson and Angela Edwards. They walked up the path leading to what turned out to be a small, cute, ranch-style home. The yard was well-groomed, with beautiful red rose bushes planted in front. The porch had a swing on one side and two chairs on the other. Inside was an eat-in kitchen with an open floor plan that flowed into the living room. There was a small half-bath in the hall that led to the back of the house.

The home had two bedrooms, each with a connected bathroom, and a smaller space that looked to be an office or a den. At the rear of the house was a porch enclosed in glass that could be raised to lowered for fresh air to flow through. It also had a skylight. In the back of the house was a fenced-in yard with a grill and colorful outdoor furniture. On the side of the house was a garage, which Mr. Jackson said held a truck for her use.

At the end of the house tour, Mrs. Edwards asked her how she liked it. Taylor said she thought it was very nice. The artist in her loved it. She could see herself working in the back office or on either of the porches. The lighting was great, and the atmosphere was tranquil. It was close enough to town not to feel isolated but far enough away for peace and quiet.

"Now that we got all the official business out of the way, would you care to join Jack and me for a late lunch? We'd love to talk with you more, and we could tell you a little more about Preston and this area."

Taylor smiled and accepted the offer. She was a bit of a loner, but they'd been so nice to her, she didn't have the heart to say no.

Lunch was nice. The Edwards were a sweet couple. They shared stories about the Knight family and the town of Silverton. Mr. Edwards, as he'd told her before, had grown up there, and Mrs. Edwards had been a city girl before their marriage. Moving there had been a bit of an adjustment for her because of the local single female population. Preston and Jackson were quite the catch. With Preston marrying Jemma, his high-school sweetheart, that left Jackson for them to pursue. The locals were not happy to see her come home with him to meet his folks during a school break one year. It was Preston's wife who befriended her and helped her make the transition. She'd said that since they got the "picks of the litter"—her words—they needed to stick together and look out for one another. The Edwards were also still very much in love. They never seemed to miss an opportunity to touch each other. Taylor thought they were lovely.

chapter 4

After returning to the B&B, Taylor sent pictures of the house and surrounding property to her parents so they could see them before they FaceTimed. She'd texted her mother earlier to tell her about the will reading and had promised to give her more details that evening after she'd seen the house. When she called, she was pleasantly surprised when her brother Grant's face appeared on the screen. Her brother was a former professional football player and was now the head coach of a college football team. They were close, but they didn't get to see each other often.

"Hey, Tay-Bay, what's up?"

"Hey, Grant! Good to see you. When did you get into town?"

"About an hour ago. I decided to come a day early. What's this about you being in cowboy country? You got a new boyfriend?"

"No, I do not. Mimi and Poppy didn't tell you why I'm here?"

"They were about to, just before you called."

Taylor went on to tell him what had happened and how she came to be in "cowboy country." He and her parents "oohed and ahhed" over the pictures she'd sent.

"So, what do you think you might do?" Grant asked.

"I don't know, but I'm thinking about doing it. It's not as isolated as I thought it would be, and I can work remotely. Also, I wouldn't be the only person of color in town, so there is that," she added with a laugh. "I think it might be a nice change, and I could use the time away."

"Taylor, are you sure?" her mother asked with a slight frown. "That's a long way from home."

"I'm sure. Plus, it won't be so far away if you come and visit while I'm here."

"That's true," said her father. "When do you plan to move?"

"I'll be home tomorrow. I'll need to pack up some things to ship, but I anticipate being back here in the next two to three weeks." They talked a little longer and eventually said goodnight. *Yes*, Taylor thought. *It might be good to get away.* A change of scenery would be good after what she'd been through. Maybe she could talk her best friend, Rae, into coming for a visit as well. Speaking of which, she needed to give her a call.

"I know this is not my supposed best friend who ghosted me," Rae answered.

"Girl, we are not dating, so why the hell would you say I've ghosted you?"

"You know what I mean. I was out on a research project, and you disappeared off the face of the earth. If Mimi and Poppy hadn't told me you were okay, I would have thought the worst. Would it have killed you to text the closest thing you have to a sister and let her know you were still walking among the living?"

"Don't you think you're being a little dramatic?"

"Yes, but so what? I was worried about you." She paused. "So, what's up?"

Rae and Taylor had been friends since they were children. Rae's family lived across the street from her parents. They'd met when Taylor moved in with the Sawyers. Rae was now a professor at the local university and had been out of the country on a research project for the last few weeks. Taylor had told her about meeting Preston Knight but hadn't given her the latest development.

"Rae, do you remember me telling you about that older man I met on the plane a few months ago? Well, I got a call from a lawyer last week about him. Preston Knight, that was his name, was very sick and recently passed away. The lawyer told me he mentioned me in his will."

"*What did you say?*" she asked her in disbelief.

"He mentioned me in his will," she repeated. "Long story short, I'm in Silverton, Wyoming. The reading of his will was today. Mr. Knight bequeathed me a house and a truck."

"Are you serious?"

"Yup. I could hardly believe it myself. I went by to see the house, and it is gorgeous."

"So, are you telling me you're moving to Wyoming?"

"Yes and no."

"What do you mean yes and no?"

"My stay is temporary. I have to live in it for a year. After that, I can keep it, rent it, or sell it."

"Wow. I don't even know what to say to that. When are you coming back?"

"I'll be here for two more days. Will you still be in town?"

"Yeah, let's plan to meet up so you can give me more details."

"Sure thing. And you can tell me how your project is going."

"All right. Love you. See you soon."

"Love you too. Bye."

Today had been some kind of day. She hadn't known for sure until she spoke with her parents that she would come back to Silverton. She knew her folks would worry, but she had a feeling it was the right thing to do. She opened her laptop and booted it up. She'd been there two days and hadn't touched it. She'd done quite a bit of sketching but no work. She needed to get busy. After all, she would be working remotely soon. She needed to come up with a work plan to submit to her manager.

chapter 5

Now that she was back home, Taylor needed to make a list of all the things she would need to get done before going back to Silverton. She had called her manager and emailed him her work plan for the next quarter. She would meet with him next week to discuss it and iron out the details. In the meantime, Rae was coming over for dinner, so she needed to finish cooking. Taylor knew she had enough food. She just wondered if she had enough to drink. She had a bottle of wine and a couple of bottles of sparkling water. She texted Rae and told her to bring whiskey or wine, her choice. Rae responded with a thumbs-up emoji and said she'd see her later.

"So, tell me about this place, Taylor," Rae said as they finished cleaning up after dinner. "Is it as exciting as it sounds?" she snickered.

"It's not bad. Grab the bottle, and let's go to the den. I'll tell you all about it."

Rae picked up the bottle of Blanton's Bourbon and two glasses. She poured a drink for each of them and handed one to Taylor before joining her on the couch.

"Start talking."

Starting with her arrival at the airport, Taylor told her about the trip.

"Back up. What about this Mike guy?" Rae held her hand up.

"What about him?"

"What do you mean, what about him? What's he like? Don't think I didn't notice you saying you had lunch with him *before* you found out who he was."

"There's not much to tell. He walked up while I was checking out the menu and invited me in. Turns out, he's the owner."

"What did he look like? Young? Old? Handsome? Hideous? What?"

Taylor felt her face grow warm as she described him. "He's a little on the rugged side, but he's nice looking. Why?"

"No reason," Rae smirked. "You just gave more details about everyone and everything else except him."

"Whatever."

"Whatever is right. Seems like he piqued your interest. I think I like him already."

"How can you like him? You haven't even met the man."

"Doesn't matter," she told her, shrugging her shoulders. "For the first time in a while, I see signs of life in you that have been missing. I'm guessing he has something to do with that."

Taylor busied herself drinking from her glass. She didn't want Rae to know just how true her words were. She hadn't been able to stop thinking about Mike since she returned home.

"Whatever. You know I'm right though." Rae rolled her eyes as she sipped her drink.

They continued to drink and talk into the early hours of the morning. Taylor helped Rae prepare the sofa bed in the den and went up to her room.

The two women hung out together for the rest of the weekend. Rae helped Taylor get organized and packed. On Saturday night, they went out for drinks at a local bar owned by one of their friends. It was kind of a dive, which was intentional and part of its charm. The drinks were good, and they had live music on the weekend. Liam, the owner, had purchased the bar when he retired from the Army. He, Rae, and Taylor had been friends since elementary school. He was the only boy in a family of five girls. Back then, Liam had been cute but shy, had worn glasses, and had been shorter than most of the other kids. The three of them became friends when they were assigned to work together on a class project. They'd been thick as thieves ever since.

Liam hit a growth spurt in high school and shot up to six foot four. His shyness and glasses disappeared. When they graduated, Taylor and Rae went off to college, and Liam joined the military to "get away for a bit and see the world." He ended up staying in for a twenty-year career. While on active duty, he'd invited them to visit him at a few of the places he'd been stationed. When they were able, they did, and it was during those visits that Taylor suspected Rae and Liam might have feelings for each other. Seeing them interact since he'd returned home, Taylor wondered if they'd taken their friendship to the next level.

Sunday afternoon, Taylor and Rae went over to her parents' house for dinner. Blue, Taylor's oldest brother, and his wife, Dasia, were there with their kids, Daniel III (DJ) and Addison. Grant, who was still in town, was there with his fiancée, Luna. Sunday dinner was a tradition in the Sawyer household when all the siblings were in town. Blue was a surgeon who traveled a lot, and Grant's coaching schedule didn't allow a lot of time home except during the offseason.

The conversation at the dinner table centered around Taylor and her recent trip to Wyoming. They were surprised about the will and teased Taylor about what *really* transpired during the plane ride to make Preston Knight leave her a house. Blue, the jokester of the family, winked at Taylor and whispered loudly, "Come on. You can tell me the truth. I won't tell," which caused the table to erupt in laughter. Taylor playfully gave Blue the side eye and reminded them her plan was to only stay the required year, but she hoped they each would have time to visit her.

chapter 6

Five days later, Taylor stepped off the plane in Wyoming and went straight to baggage claim to wait for her luggage. Jackson Edwards had told her someone would meet her at the airport. She guessed it would be him, his wife, or both. She saw she had guessed wrong when Michael Knight walked in wearing loose-fitting jeans and a faded green T-shirt that showcased his wide shoulders and muscular arms. The five o'clock shadow he sported, combined with the well-worn ball cap, gave him a rugged, sexy appearance. *That's a very good look on him,* she thought. Other women in the area apparently thought so too, as they eyed him appreciatively as he walked past them.

"Hi, Taylor," he smiled as he walked up to her and greeted her with a hug.

Surprised and a little rattled, she managed to respond, "Hey, Mike."

"How was your flight?"

"It was okay. I didn't know you were going to meet me. I hope it was no trouble."

"No, it's fine. I had business in the area, so I told Uncle Jack I'd pick you up. I hope that's okay."

"Oh, it's *not* a problem. I mean, uh, it's okay." Taylor stumbled a bit over her words and couldn't quite look him in the eye. Her nearness to Mike was making her more than a little nervous, and judging by the amusement she saw in his eyes, he was aware of it.

"Has your luggage come out yet?" he asked looking in the direction of the carousel.

"It's just coming around now," she told him, eyeing the conveyor. "I have the two large blue bags."

"Let me grab them, and we can get going."

"Thanks." Taylor watched his muscles move as he reached over and grabbed her suitcases. He turned toward her after getting the last bag and caught her staring and smiled.

"Ready?"

"Um, yes. Lead the way."

They exited the airport, and soon they were settled inside his vehicle and entering the on-ramp to the freeway.

"So, are you looking forward to your time here?"

"I am. I think it'll be a nice change of pace and allow me to get a better work-life balance. I'll be working remotely, and I'll also have more time to work on my hobbies."

"Oh, yeah? What are some of your hobbies?"

"I sketch, design jewelry, and sew. I also do some painting when the mood hits."

"Sounds like you're a modern-day renaissance woman."

"I guess you could say that," she told him with a smile. "I come from a line of creatives, so it's in my blood. Other than taking sewing lessons, I don't remember ever not knowing how to paint or sketch."

"I'd be interested in seeing some of your work while you're here if it's not an imposition."

She held up her wrist and showed him the bracelet she was wearing. "Here's one of my first pieces." It was a brown leather cuff with a bronze butterfly laced on it.

He took his eyes off the road for only a moment to admire the beautiful bracelet before he faced forward again. "I noticed it earlier. You made that?" He looked over at her, a little awed.

"Yes. I've had it for a while. I've had to replace the lacing on it a couple of times because I wear it so often, but it's held up."

"That's really nice. My daughter buys craft kits a lot. She likes to make jewelry."

"You have kids?"

"Yes, ten-year-old twins."

"Identical?" Taylor asked.

"Fraternal. What about you? Do you have any children?"

"No, I don't. I have a niece and nephew. If you count some people I work with who are like my children, then yes I do."

He laughed. "I can relate to that. My niece Dana works at the saloon. She's sweet and works hard, but she's young and a bit of a drama queen. If she wasn't so good at her job, I would fire her."

"Really?" she remarked, looking over at him. "Wouldn't that cause problems with your family? I mean, that's the kind of stuff that gets you placed at the kids' table during the holidays."

"You say that like that's a bad thing," he said with a chuckle. "The little people in my family are much more interesting than the adults." He went on to share a few stories about his nieces and nephews. The niece he mentioned earlier was his older brother's daughter. He and his wife also had three boys. His younger brother had two children, a boy and a girl, and was expecting another girl soon. He mentioned that the deputy who'd picked her up at the airport was his youngest brother's best friend. He and his family, which included a boy and two girls, were close to them and their children.

They continued to talk as the ride went on. The time passed quickly, and before long, he pulled into the driveway alongside her new home for the next year. They both got out of the truck and went into the house.

"Just to let you know, some packages arrived for you earlier this week. I hope you don't mind, but Aunt Angie had us put them inside. She and Cheryl, PJ's wife, also did some shopping so you'd have some basic necessities when you got here."

"Oh, thank you." *That's a nice surprise*, she thought to herself. "Please tell them I said thanks as well. I appreciate what you all have done."

He looked down at her and smiled. "You're very welcome. The keys to the truck and the remote for the garage are on the counter," he said, his gaze lingering on her.

Her face grew warm, and she smiled, turning away before things got awkward. He picked up a sheet of paper lying next to the keys on the counter. It was a list of contacts, he told her—the Edwards, both his brothers and their wives, and his. With his, he added his cell and office number at the Red Buffalo.

"Lastly, there's going to be a live band at the saloon tomorrow night. If you find yourself bored and want something to do, let me know, and I'll save you a spot at the bar."

"Thanks, I may just do that."

"Okay then," he told her, dragging his departure out. "I'll let you get situated. I need to head to work. Don't hesitate to let one of us know if you need anything."

"I won't. Thanks again."

"Bye, Taylor."

"Bye, Mike."

After closing the door behind him, Taylor shot off a group text to Rae and her family to let them know she'd arrived safely. She rolled her suitcases into her new bedroom and took the boxes to the den. She unpacked her clothes and put her toiletries in the bathroom, then moved to the den. She unpacked two of the five boxes she'd mailed to herself. Soon, she found herself getting hungry and decided to check the contents of the kitchen to see what she could put together for a meal. After a quick meal, she finished unpacking the remaining boxes. Since she planned to go to town the next day, she made a list of items to be picked up.

Mike was glad he'd volunteered to pick Taylor up from the airport. When he walked in, he spotted her right away. It hadn't been hard to do in the small airport. He saw Native Americans and Hispanics whose skin color was similar to hers, but to him, her beauty and her height made her stand out, and everyone else fade into the background. She wore a copper-colored maxi dress paired with a blue denim jacket and a scarf around her neck. Large gold hoop earrings were visible between her locs, and a small gold hoop had replaced the nose stud he remembered. A light-brown lipstick covered her full lips. He liked the way she looked. The dress' color complimented her skin.

As he walked toward her, he noticed she was looking at him as intently as he looked at her. She seemed surprised. *Hmmm*, he thought. *She must have been expecting Uncle Jack or Aunt Angie. They must not have told her I'd be the one picking her up.* He'd volunteered after overhearing his uncle talking to her on the phone. He had a lot going on with the saloon and out at his ranch, but he willingly rearranged his schedule to pick her up. After seeing her, he was glad he did.

He enjoyed the drive back from the airport with Taylor. She was funny and, judging by the bracelet she showed him, very talented. He also liked the light floral fragrance that accompanied her into the cab of his truck when she got in. It reminded him of jasmine. He knew she had things to do, and he needed to get to work, but he found himself lingering when it came time to leave her. He didn't know if she'd show up tomorrow night, but he hoped she did. He wanted to see her again.

chapter 7

Midmorning on Saturday, Taylor got in her truck and drove the short distance to the town square. She could have easily walked, but she needed to pick up a few things while she was there and thought they might be too much to carry. The first stop was the post office to get a P.O. box for the duration of her time there. Next, she went to the local market to pick up some additional cleaning supplies and groceries. She ran into Caleb, the chef from the Red Buffalo, in the checkout line. He was there with a woman who looked like she might be related to him.

"Hi, Taylor. Welcome back." He smiled and hugged her.

"It's good to be back." She returned his hug.

"This is my sister, Mary. Mary, this is Taylor. She's new in town and is going to be with us for a while."

"Nice to meet you," Taylor said.

"Likewise. Hope you don't find it too boring here." Mary smiled.

"I think it will be just my speed."

Caleb asked if she had plans for the evening.

"Mary's band is playing at our place tonight. If you're not doing anything, you should stop by."

"Yeah," Mary said. "It'll be fun."

"Mike mentioned there'd be live music at the saloon tonight when he dropped me off yesterday."

"Good. Hope you'll come out," Caleb responded as he paid for his food and grabbed his purchases.

"If you decide to come, we'll see you there," Mary said.

"Okay, great. See you later."

"Bye!" Caleb added.

After leaving the market, Taylor made stops at the arts and crafts store and the wine bar. She made a few purchases in each and then went home. Once she got her stuff put away, she took a moment to text Mike to let him know she was coming to the Red Buffalo that evening. Instead of responding in the same manner, he called her when he received her text, asking her to let him know when she was on her way. Taylor told him she would, and they ended the call.

Having no clue what she would wear, she put in a FaceTime call to Rae.

"Rae, I'm glad you're home. I need your help. I'm thinking about going to hear live music at one of the local bars tonight, and I have no idea what to wear."

Half an hour later, they settled on an outfit. Taylor laid her clothes out on her bed and thought about other things she needed to take care of before she headed out. First, she went to the kitchen and made a late lunch. When she was done eating, she washed her dishes and headed to the bathroom to take a shower and get ready for the evening.

With Rae's help, she'd decided on dark-washed jeans with a black, fitted V-neck T-shirt and sandals. The jeans fit like a second skin. The top showcased her curvy frame, as it hugged her waist and showed more than a hint of cleavage. Except for her watch, she accessorized with some of her creations: a black leather and silver wrap bracelet, a silver necklace with a teardrop onyx stone, and large silver hoop earrings. She wore her locs down and added a few pieces of jewelry to them. She kept her makeup simple: light foundation, bronzer, eyeliner, and a bold fuchsia lip color. *Well, she thought, this should be interesting.* She grabbed her phone to check the time and saw it was 8:15 p.m. Mike had told her the best time to get there would be around 8:30 p.m., so she grabbed her bag, and a black cardigan and headed out the door. Since it was warm outside and the sky was clear, she decided to walk the few blocks to the saloon. Besides, the area was well-lit, and she had her pepper spray.

She felt herself starting to get a little nervous the closer she got to her destination. She'd spent evenings out on the town solo before, but not like this. Before, she could get lost in the crowd, but here, not so much. Yup, she was bound to stick out. *Well,* she told herself, *I'll just stay an hour. If I'm not feeling it by then, I'll leave.* She was so caught up in the inner dialogue that she arrived at the Red Buffalo Saloon sooner than she had expected.

There was a sign outside with a picture of Caleb's sister's band. They were called Fire Lake. There were people hanging outside the saloon, some talking and some smoking. Based on their attire, she knew she'd made the right fashion choice, which made her feel slightly better. She took a deep breath and walked to the door. One of the bouncers smiled at her and asked if she was Taylor. After confirming her identity, he introduced himself as Steve and told her he'd take her to Mike. She nodded and nervously looked around before following him into the saloon.

The place was fairly crowded inside. Music was playing, and there were people on the dance floor in front of a stage that was set up with the band's equipment. As they approached the bar, she saw Mike talking to a tall, slender, blonde woman. Judging by their expressions, they seemed to be in a serious conversation. The bouncer must have noticed as well because instead of walking towards Mike, he took her over to Caleb, who was standing beside the bar. She'd been so focused on Mike and the woman he was talking to, she hadn't even noticed Caleb. The bouncer spoke to Caleb, then turned to Taylor and with a wink and a smile, wished her a fun night before turning and going back to the entrance before she could thank him.

Many of the saloon's patrons noticed the tall African American woman as she walked past them. One cowboy sitting at a table near the bar smiled appreciatively as he observed her. He nudged his friend and tilted his head in her direction. The other man gazed where his friend indicated and gave a slow nod. "Damn, she must be new in town."

"Probably a tourist."

"I wonder if she needs someone to show her the lay of the land?"

"I'd be happy to show her the lay." He tracked her with his eyes as she took a seat at the bar.

"I'm sure you would." His friend snickered.

Mike saw Taylor when she came in with Steve, one of the bouncers. He'd been looking forward to seeing her all day. Unfortunately, his ex-girlfriend had chosen that moment to show up and once again attempt to convince him to give them another chance. He motioned for Steve to take Taylor over to Caleb. He and Linda had been together for almost three years. In hindsight, he didn't know how they'd stayed together as long as they did. She wasn't a bad person, but over time, she'd become clingy and demanding. She'd also started to drop hints about making their relationship permanent. Mike had been married for ten years before it ended in divorce. He had two beautiful children he loved, but he wasn't in any hurry to go back down the road to matrimony. When Linda had given him an ultimatum to either get engaged or end it, he'd opted to end it. It hadn't been a hard choice for him to make. He didn't want to marry her, and he sure as hell didn't want to get back together. He told her as much before he left to join Taylor and Caleb at the bar.

Caleb greeted Taylor with a hug when she came up to him.

"Hey, Taylor. You're looking lovely tonight."

"Thanks, I wasn't sure what to wear."

"We're pretty casual in these parts, so it's practically anything goes. Let me get you a drink. What will you have? Wine, beer, or a cocktail?"

"How about bourbon?"

"Bourbon?"

"Yes, Blanton's neat, if you have it."

"Oh, you're serious about your bourbon, huh?" he asked, giving her a playful look.

"I am," she laughed.

"All right then. Blanton's coming right up."

Caleb turned toward the bar, pulled out a stool with a padded backrest, and invited her to sit down. He sat on the stool next to her and signaled to the bartender. He ordered two bourbons, neat. Mike walked up at the same time and changed the order to three.

Taylor turned around and found Mike standing behind her. "Hi Mike," she said, suddenly feeling a little shy. His hair was tousled as if he'd been running his hands through it. He wore a black button-down shirt and a pair of jeans that fit him very nicely. She didn't look, but she guessed he had on cowboy boots as well.

"Hi, Taylor. Glad you could make it." He smiled.

Damn, he looked good.

"Glad *I* could make it?" Caleb asked just as the drinks arrived, and all three laughed.

Mike made a toast. "Welcome to Silverton and new adventures. May the adventures be many and fun." They clinked glasses. Mike kept his eyes on Taylor as he sipped his bourbon. Taylor wanted to look away but found she couldn't. Caleb cleared his throat, offered up his seat to Mike, and said he was going to check on the band. He looked at the two of them, smiled, and left.

Heading toward the back, Caleb saw Mike's ex Linda, the blonde woman Mike had been talking to earlier, sitting at a table with some of her friends. They'd been broken up for a while now, but based on the way she was dressed and the conversation she and Mike were having earlier, it was evident she was looking to get back together. As he passed their table, he noticed they were looking at Mike and Taylor sitting at the bar. "Ladies." He interrupted their ogling and nodded as he continued on his way, choosing not to stop to chat with them. The three of them were beautiful women who reminded him of a coven of witches. From what he'd just seen between Mike and Taylor, Linda was fighting a losing game. *Things are about to get interesting*, he thought to himself.

Taylor ended up staying at the Red Buffalo longer than she expected. Her original plan had been to stay for an hour and leave. Between the music, dancing with Caleb and a few other men who'd asked—that was a surprise—and talking with Mike when he wasn't taking care of saloon business, she had a better time than she thought she would. The band was good, and Caleb taught her a couple of the dances. She had a few more drinks with both him and Mike, but around 10:30 pm, the activity of the last few days, and lingering jet lag, began to catch up with her. She was getting tired. She told Mike she was about to leave. He asked where she was parked and if she was okay to drive. She told him she'd walked, and he told her he would take her home. Caleb joined them, and she thanked him for hanging out with her. Mike reappeared and told Caleb he was taking her home and he'd be back.

The truck was parked in the back of the saloon, and just as they walked outside, Mike stopped and checked his pocket for his keys when he suddenly remembered they were back on his desk. He told Taylor he would be right back. As soon as the door closed behind him, her purse started buzzing, and she found she had a FaceTime request from Rae. She pressed the button to accept.

"Where have you been?!" Rae said, immediately. "I've been calling you for the last hour, girl! You said you were only going to be out for an hour or so."

"Yeah, that was the original plan."

"What happened? Did some cowboy throw you on the back of his horse and take you to his hideout?"

"Are you serious?" she asked her friend, laughing. "You *do* realize what century this is, right?"

"Yes. But I was worried about you."

"As you can see, there was no need to worry. I'm on my way home now. I'll call you when I get there."

"Okay, you better."

Taylor ended the call just as Mike walked up. He opened the door of the truck so she could get in and then went around to the driver's side. Once they were both strapped in, he pulled out of the small lot behind the saloon and drove to her house. After pulling into her driveway, he put the truck in park and cut off the engine.

"So, your friend is worried about some cowboy dragging you off to his hideout?"

"You heard that, huh?"

He nodded.

"Yeah, she has an overactive imagination." They both laughed. He opened the door to get out of the truck at the same time she did. Meeting at the front of his truck, he put his hand on the small of her back as they walked up the steps to the door.

"I'm glad you came out," he told her softly.

"Me too. Thanks for the invite."

He couldn't seem to take his eyes off her lips. Leaning forward, Mike kissed her on the cheek, said goodnight, and walked back to his truck. She stood in front of the screen door and waved at him once he was inside the cab. He waved back and drove off.

Taylor's phone buzzed again while she stood in the open doorway. She sighed as she closed the door and answered the phone.

"Hey, girl."

"Don't 'hey, girl' me." I want the details! All. The. Details."

"I don't have a whole lot, because not a lot happened."

"I don't care. Spill."

Starting with her arrival at the Red Buffalo, Taylor told her about the bouncer taking her to Caleb instead of Mike, who had been in what looked like a serious conversation with a tall blonde woman. She told her about the band and that it was pretty much a fun evening of laughing, drinking, and dancing.

"And, by the way, they had Blanton's. You know how hard that stuff is to find. So, all in all, I would call it a good night. That's why I ended up staying longer than an hour."

"So, did you meet any guys?" Rae asked.

"Not really. I danced with a few, but I mostly talked with Caleb and Mike most of the night, then Mike brought me home."

"Mike? That's the guy who owns the saloon, right?"

"Yes."

"Sooo . . ."

"Sooo, what?"

"Anything happen between you and Mike?"

"Didn't you just hear me say he was in a deep conversation with a woman when I got there?"

"Yes, but that doesn't answer my question."

"No, nothing happened. He brought me home, walked me to the door, and that was it."

"Oooh, he walked you to the door? What a gentleman," Rae teased.

"Yeah, that was kind of sweet. Anyway, that's it."

"Not bad for your first night out in town."

"It went better than expected."

"I'm glad. Now that I know all is well, I can sleep peacefully. After my booty call arrives, that is."

"Your booty call?"

"Yes. Don't judge. My best friend moved away, Liam isn't available, and I needed to be comforted."

"Don't put this on me. Just promise me you'll call me if you need me."

"I will. Talk to you soon."

"Bye." Taylor worried about Rae. She'd hoped Liam was the booty call, but she was almost sure it was her on-again, off-again boyfriend, Bobby. Every time they were on, the breakup that followed tended to take a harder toll on Rae. Her friend deserved better. She wished Rae would walk away from him, but until that happened, if it ever did, Taylor would be there for her.

Mike parked his truck and walked through the rear entrance of the saloon. He found Caleb locking up the front door. The servers worked quickly to collect glasses and get the place cleaned up so they could call it a night and head home. The bartenders worked in sync in their areas doing the same. When Caleb saw him, he walked over.

"So how was it?" he asked smiling.

"How was what?"

"The drive. You enjoy taking Taylor home?"

"It was a short ride," he said with a shoulder lift. "Nothing special."

"Hmmm." Caleb chuckled. "Linda sure didn't think so. I'm surprised you didn't feel her and her coven staring a hole in your back."

Mike laughed. "Coven?"

"You gotta admit, they are kind of evil."

"I'll agree with you there. Although, in my opinion, Linda shouldn't care what I do. We're not together anymore."

"Yes, well, you know she's trying to change your status on that."

"She can try all she wants, but it's not gonna happen."

Caleb laughed in his face. "Good luck with that."

"Whatever." Changing the subject, he asked, "Do you want to start staging the inventory tonight or save it for Sunday."

It didn't take long to finish up, and soon, everyone was heading home. Mike drove, thinking about the evening and how it had been better than he'd expected. Whenever they had live music, which they often did, he usually helped at the door, did some bartending, or made the rounds to speak with his customers, but tonight had been different. He'd invited Taylor and told himself it was because she was new in town. That was a partial truth. The whole truth was, that Mike was attracted to her. Inviting her seemed like a good way to see her again, until Linda and her coven, as Caleb called them, showed up. He knew there was a chance she might show up since the saloon was a popular spot, especially when there was live music. He was just hoping she wouldn't, but she did, and she decided to plead her case. He didn't want to be rude, but he did want her to go away. Especially when he saw Taylor walk in with Steve. That's why he redirected him rather than have her in the middle of the heated discussion he was having with Linda. He'd had a good time with Taylor, and after this evening, he knew for certain he wanted to get to know her better.

chapter 8

A week later, Taylor was doing a final review of a report she'd just completed when she got a text from Mike asking if she had time for a call. Curious, she replied yes. A few seconds later, her phone rang.

"Hey, Mike." Taylor smiled as she answered.

"Taylor. How are you?"

"I'm good. You?"

"The same. Look, I won't keep you, but I was wondering if you were busy Sunday."

"No, I haven't made any plans yet. What did you have in mind?"

He was quiet for a few seconds.

"I was wondering if you'd be interested in seeing some of the local area with me and maybe grabbing some lunch."

"That sounds nice."

"So, is that a yes?" he asked.

"It is. However, I'm only saying yes because you promised lunch," she joked.

"In that case, I'll pick you up at nine. Be sure to wear comfortable clothes and shoes you can walk or hike in."

"I will. And Mike?"

"Yes."

"Thanks."

"Sure. See you Sunday."

"You too. Bye."

Taylor looked at her phone. Hearing from Mike had been a pleasant surprise. She'd thought about him more than a few times this past week and wondered when she might see him again. She also wondered what his relationship was with the woman he'd been talking to the other night. He didn't mention her that evening, but that didn't mean there wasn't something between them. Although Taylor could admit she was looking forward to seeing him on Sunday, she didn't want to be included in anyone's relationship drama.

Not wanting to think much more about it, Taylor decided to call her mom. When she was back home, they talked regularly. While she could still talk to them often, she missed being able to see her parents whenever she wanted or needed to.

"Hey, Mimi! How are you and Poppy?"

"We're fine. How are you doing, Tay-Bay?"

"I'm fine. I've got everything in its place, and I've pretty much settled in."

"That's good to hear. Have you been getting out of the house and doing things, or have you just been working?"

"Is that your way of asking whether I've curbed my workaholic tendencies?"

"It is," her mom told her with love in her voice. "And I'm not wrong. You do work too much."

"Well, I'll have you know that since I don't have many distractions, I've been pretty much keeping standard working hours, and I've been getting out, and doing some sightseeing."

"It does my heart good to hear that. I worry about you overdoing it and not getting enough rest."

"I know, but I'm fine and I'm getting lots of rest. Now, enough about me," she said, changing the subject. "Tell me what's been going on with everybody. I miss you all so much."

"We're doing pretty good. Blue and his family are on vacation, and Grant is thinking about visiting you before training season starts."

"I hope he does. It would be great to see him."

"He's planning to call you so you guys can work out the details."

"Okay."

Taylor and her mother talked a little longer and then ended the call.

chapter 9

Sunday arrived, and from the looks of it, it was going to be a beautiful day, Mike thought as he got in his truck. He was headed to the Red Buffalo to pick up the lunch he'd asked Caleb to prepare. His friend had ribbed him a bit about his request after he told him what it was for, but he agreed to do it. Caleb was already doing the meal planning for the week, so preparing a lunch basket wouldn't take much effort. When Mike walked through the back door of the saloon, he found Caleb sitting at his desk, sipping coffee.

"Hey, Caleb."

"Mike." He raised his cup in greeting. "How's it going? Are you ready for your date?"

"I told you, it's not a date. I'm just showing her around."

"Sounds like a date to me," Caleb mumbled under his breath.

"Well, it isn't." Mike gave him a look.

"Whatever. Your lunch is in the kitchen. I added a few breakfast biscuits and some coffee."

"Thanks, I appreciate it."

"No problem. Where are you two headed today?"

"We're going to Canyon Ridge and stopping at a few local spots."

"Are you going to take her to the butterfly meadow?"

"I wasn't planning on it."

"I think you should. She likes butterflies."

"How do you know that?" Mike was curious to know how Caleb had come across that bit of information.

"She has a tattoo of one on her inner forearm. I saw it when we were dancing."

"Oh, you did, did you?"

"Yup. Hmmm, I wonder if she has more." Caleb looked questioningly at Mike as he spoke. "Think she does?"

"Do I think she does what?" Mike asked, even though he heard the question loud and clear.

"Have more than one tattoo."

"I don't know."

"Might be interesting to find out . . ."

"It might." Mike smiled, cutting him off, and walked out of the office. "I'll see you later. Thanks again for the food."

"You're welcome. Have fun!"

Taylor had gotten up early in anticipation of the day's outing and spending time with Mike. She didn't know his situation, or if he was even interested in her that way, or in women of color for that matter. He was rugged and rough around the edges, and his manner was a little gruff, but he was also sweet. He had that same charm she'd seen in his father during the short time she'd spent with him. Today would be an opportunity to get to know him a little better.

Not knowing exactly where they were headed for the day, she wondered if some hiking might be involved since he mentioned it. She mulled over what to wear and finally settled on a pair of her most comfortable jeans. They were soft and faded and while not tight, they fit her like a glove. They looked distressed, with a few rips that came from years of wear. She wore a gold, long-sleeve top that had a picture of a fairy with brown skin and an Afro reclining on a star. In addition to colorful wings, the fairy had on sunglasses, combat boots and was holding a glass of wine. Taylor wore the same trail shoes she normally wore for hiking and had just put her earrings on when she heard Mike's truck pull up. Instantly, butterflies took up residence in her stomach. She glanced out the window and saw him walk up the porch steps. He had on a gray long-sleeved henley that emphasized his wide shoulders, a pair of faded jeans, and boots. With the shades and cowboy hat he sported, he looked as if he was about to ride the range instead of chauffeur her around in his truck.

Mike heard music playing as he walked up the steps to the porch. He looked around and noticed changes to the house's exterior. On the porch were potted plants, colorful cushions on the chairs and porch swing, and a welcome mat. It gave the place a warm, lived-in look that hadn't been there before. He knocked on the screen door rather than ringing the bell. He smiled appreciatively as he watched her come to the open door. She paused as she stood facing him from the other side of the screen.

"Hey, Mike," she greeted him with a warm smile.

"Hi, Taylor."

She unlocked the screen door and opened it to let him in.

"How are you this morning?" she asked.

"I'm good. You?"

"Same."

They stood staring at each other.

"Are you ready to go?" he asked.

"Um, yes. Let me grab my stuff."

Mike watched Taylor walk toward the back of the house. He liked the way she filled out the jeans she wore. They looked as if they were holding and caressing her ass like a lover. Her body type was different from most of the women he'd been around or been attracted to. She was a full-figured woman with an hourglass shape. Mike's taste in women was mostly for those on the slender side. Her figure reminded him of the vintage pinup girl calendars his godfather, Jared Hawkins, or "Hawk" as everyone called him, used to keep at his shop when Mike was growing up.

His uncle Hawk was Caleb's father. Unlike Mike's father and Uncle Jack, Hawk wasn't a native of Silverton. He'd met the two men in Vietnam when he was a Navy corpsman. He'd saved both men when they were caught in an ambush and nearly killed. After the war, they kept in touch. Occasionally, Hawk sent postcards from the various places he traveled. One day, Preston invited Hawk to come for a visit. He accepted the invitation, and soon after, he arrived in an old black pickup truck, towing his Harley-Davidson motorcycle behind. Mike learned from his father that Hawk had not been doing so well when he'd arrived. He'd been a nomad of sorts since returning to the States. Living with PTSD, he rarely slept more than a few hours each night, due to reoccurring nightmares. Preston, seeing the condition of his friend, had been alarmed. After talking with Jemma, his wife, he offered up the guesthouse to Hawk to use as long as he wanted. Hawk accepted the offer and moved in.

Not long after he arrived, he started accompanying Jemma to the farmers market, where she sold her homemade jellies and preserves. She'd been pregnant with Mike at the time. He helped her with the canning, loading, and setting up for the market. It was there he met Rainbow, Caleb's mother. She sold honey and beeswax products in the booth next to Jemma's. Rainbow had been five months pregnant with Caleb at the time and had lost her husband in an accident a month earlier. Hawk would help her carry her items to her truck when the market closed for the day. That soon changed when he offered to pick her up on the way to the market so he could help her load up. Pretty soon, it was Hawk and the two pregnant women working side by side. He did all the lifting and watched their tables when they needed to take breaks. Romance blossomed between Hawk and Rainbow, and he ended up staying in Silverton, where he opened a mechanic shop repairing automobiles, motorcycles, and farm equipment. Preston and Jemma asked Hawk to be Mike's godfather. He agreed, and he later married Rainbow and raised Caleb as his own.

As children, Mike and Caleb had been in awe of Hawk. He was big, strong, and a little scary. He had no problem unleashing the crazy if you crossed him or hurt the ones he loved. Mike once asked him why he had the old-fashioned pinup girl calendar on the wall. Hawk had laughed and said, "Because they don't make women quite like that anymore." At the time, Mike didn't understand what he was saying, and Hawk didn't elaborate. Seeing Taylor in her jeans just now brought back to mind that conversation he'd had with his godfather, and he found himself wondering what she might look like if she was dressed like the women on the calendars—or with no clothes at all.

"I'm ready," Taylor said as she walked toward him.

She'd put on a jacket and had her backpack in her hand. Mike reached forward and grabbed it so she could lock the door. At the truck, he opened her door and helped her inside, then placed the backpack in the back seat of the cab before he walked around to the driver's side and got in. He pointed to the bag in the middle of the seat.

"I stopped by my place to pick up lunch," he announced, then he started the truck. "Caleb also made some breakfast stuff, and there's coffee in the thermos, so help yourself."

"Thanks, I will." She looked in the bag and caught the aroma of what smelled like fresh biscuits. She pulled one out, wrapped it in a napkin, and handed it to Mike.

"Would you like some coffee?" she asked as they headed down the street.

"Sure."

She poured a cup and placed it in the cup holder next to him. "Do you take it with anything?"

"Cream and a little cinnamon."

She looked back in the bag. Sure enough, along with the small half-and-half cups, there was a small container labeled "cinnamon."

"That's the same way I take mine." She added cream and a bit of spice to his coffee and stirred. Taylor poured a cup for herself, then reached back into the bag and grabbed a biscuit.

"Where are we headed first?" she asked between taking bites of the warm biscuit filled with honey butter.

"This might sound a little weird, but I thought I'd show you where we laid my father to rest. The cemetery sits on a plateau that is surrounded by mountains and overlooks a valley. It's a beautiful area, and I thought you'd enjoy seeing it."

"I'd like that."

Mike looked at her as she sipped her coffee.

"I'd like to get a chance to thank your father," Taylor said softly.

He turned his attention back to the road ahead. She centered her attention on his hands as they gripped the steering wheel. They were large and tan. His right hand had a scar across the back of it. She remembered shaking his hand when she first met him. She'd felt callouses as well as his strong grip. Now, she wondered about the scar as they continued to make their way to their destination in comfortable silence.

About twenty minutes later, Mike's voice cut into her thoughts. "We're here."

Taylor looked out the window and saw a well-maintained cemetery surrounded by mountains. Mike was right, this place was beautiful. He opened the back door of the cab, removed a bouquet of flowers, and walked over to the gated entrance. He undid the latch and held the gate open for her. She walked next to him as he began telling her the history of the area. This was the burial place for his family dating back to the late 1800s. As they made their way to his parents' graves, he said, "My dad found out he had cancer two years after my mom's passing."

"I remember Mr. Jackson saying you'd lost your parents close together. I'm so sorry."

"Thanks. I miss them a lot." He kneeled, removed the dried bouquet sitting in front of the headstone, and replaced it with the new one. They both stood there silently for a few minutes. "Ready?" he asked.

"Yes."

They walked back the way they had come. Mike secured the gate and threw the dried flowers in the trash receptacle next to it before they got back to his truck. Silence filled the cab as they rode along the highway.

"You were right," Taylor said, breaking the silence, "that place is beautiful. Thank you for bringing me."

"You're welcome."

"What else is on the day's agenda?"

"There's a canyon, a meadow, and a genuine ghost town."

"All in one day?"

"Yes. They're relatively close to one another. We're headed to the canyon now. Hopefully, you'll be able to see some of the wild mustangs that roam this area."

"I hope so."

"The canyon is also said to be the hideout of the notorious Benton Gang."

"The Benton Gang?" she asked curiously.

"They were outlaws in this area when it was still a territory."

"I guess Rae was right."

"Rae?"

"She's my best friend. She was the one I was talking to the night you drove me home."

"Oh yeah, I remember." He chuckled.

"Now I'll be able to tell her that a cowboy took me to an honest-to-goodness outlaw hideout. I need to make sure I get some good pictures to send her."

Once they arrived, they went to the welcome center, which also housed a small museum. According to the guide leading the tour, the canyon had been home to quite a few outlaws in its heyday. With statehood came more law enforcement, which helped reduce criminal activity in the area. They didn't see any wild mustangs, but they were able to go into some of the notable hideout areas that had been preserved.

Back inside his truck and driving toward the exit Mike asked, "Which would you prefer next? The ghost town or the meadow?"

"Hmmm. Let's go to the ghost town."

"Ghost town it is." He turned right onto the highway.

"I've been to a couple of ghost towns before. They seemed to have more tourists than ghosts though," Taylor said, laughing.

"This one is not as well-known as some of the others in the state, so it's not likely to be as crowded. Be warned though, the caretakers for the town are a little odd. You'd think it was because they're just doing reenactments like most historical areas, but that's not the case. They live as if this is still the nineteenth century."

"Really?" Taylor let her eyes drift in his direction. "Well, this should be interesting."

"It will. But don't say I didn't warn you."

Taylor looked over at Mike questioningly to see if he was kidding.

"You'll see what I mean when we get there."

She tried to get him to tell her more, but he remained tight-lipped. He would only say they were harmless and that she'd have to see for herself. She didn't know what to make of that cryptic response, so she decided she'd take her backpack with her in case she needed to use her pepper spray. Odd or not, if they came at her wrong, she wouldn't hesitate to give them a dose.

The sign at the entrance of the town read, "Welcome to Hammond, Wyoming." After parking, she grabbed her backpack and got out of the truck. She noticed there were a few cars and trucks in the lot, but for the most part, it was relatively empty.

"The church, schoolhouse, and library are on this side of town. The doctor's office and infirmary, post office, and general store are toward the middle, as well as the sheriff's office and courthouse. The other end of town is where you'll find the saloons; there were two of them and a brothel. There are a few other businesses as well, but those are the main attractions." Mike pointed out different sections of the town as he spoke. "Let's start here and hit the main buildings first. We can see the others on our way back to the truck."

"Sounds good," Taylor agreed.

The old church was the first building they stopped at. It looked to be in pretty good condition for being over one hundred fifty years old. When they walked in, a tall, thin man greeted them. He had a handlebar mustache and his clothes looked homespun. He was also wearing a cleric's collar.

"Hello and welcome to the Hammond Baptist Church. I'm Reverend Smith." He spoke with an interesting accent Taylor couldn't quite place. He shook Mike's hand, then Taylor's, giving her a wink as he held her hand a little longer than was necessary.

"All God's children are welcome here."

Taylor smiled back and removed her hand from his.

"Thanks," Mike grunted, not liking how the reverend looked at Taylor.

"This church was the first church built in the town of Hammond and the only one to remain standing to this day. My ancestor was one of the first pastors in this area, and there has been a Reverend Smith in each generation since. We practice keeping things the same now as they were during the very first service. We've had weddings, baptisms, funerals, and revivals here." Reverend Smith's eyes never strayed from Taylor as he talked about the church and a few other interesting anecdotes about some of the residents of the town who'd been members over the years. When Mike heard other people enter the church, he took the opportunity to thank Reverend Smith for the history lesson, grabbed Taylor's hand, and walked out.

"Okay, was it my imagination, or was the *good* reverend flirting with you the whole time we were in there?" he asked with a bit of irritation.

"No. It wasn't your imagination. You saw him wink at me."

"Yeah, I did. He must have thought angels had his back."

"Why do you say that?" Taylor asked, surprised at the comment.

"He didn't know our situation. It was pretty bold of him to flirt with you right in front of me," he responded. "He caught me on a good day. I'm a nice guy, but I'll fight in church."

Taylor laughed, and Mike joined her as he guided them to the next area.

They walked over to the schoolhouse, then down to the saloon and the brothel. Mike hadn't lied about the town's residents. The caretakers and docents of Hammond were a strange bunch. At first, she thought they were just bad actors, but she later learned from one of the bartenders that most of them were descendants of the original families who started the town. Some went as far as taking over their previous family members' roles in the town—everything from the doctors, shop owners, blacksmiths, and brothel employees, the latter of which seemed to clearly enjoy keeping the family tradition alive. One offered to show Mike *and* Taylor a good time. Mike declined the offer, saying he couldn't possibly share Taylor with anyone because then they'd want to be with her all the time.

"Really, Mike? That was the best you could come up with?" Taylor asked.

"Yup. How does that saying go? Once you go Black, you never go back." He smirked at her.

Taylor stopped, looked at him, and laughed. She shook her head. "You're something else, Mike, you know that?"

"I've been told that once or twice." Smiling, he asked if she was ready for lunch.

"I am."

"There's a picnic area by the meadow. If you're okay with it, we can eat there."

chapter 10

They pulled into the picnic area, where a man with wings on his back was walking between two little girls, holding their hands. Beside them, a little boy dressed as Spiderman pulled a wagon.

"Hey, Albee!" Mike called out as he grabbed the lunch basket out of the back of the truck cab.

"Hi, Mike! Kids, it's Uncle Mike."

"Uncle Mike!" the girls yelled, and they left the man's side. They ran to Mike, who kneeled to hug them.

"Hi, Matt." Mike gave him a hug and a high five. As Taylor walked around the truck, she was surprised to see the man with the wings was the deputy who'd picked her up from the airport when she'd first come to Silverton.

"Hi, Ms. Sawyer," Albee greeted Taylor.

"Hi. Please, call me Taylor."

"Hey, kids, this is Miss Taylor. She just moved here. Taylor, these are my kids. Angelica and the twins"—he pointed to the older girl and boy—"Matthew and Matilda. Say hi, kids."

"Hi, Miss Taylor," all three children replied obediently.

"Hi, Angelica, Matthew, and Matilda. It's nice to meet you." She smiled at them.

Mike lifted the basket. "We're about to have lunch. Looks like that's where you're headed as well. Care to join us?"

Albee looked at Mike and Taylor, then back at Mike. "If you're sure we wouldn't be interrupting anything."

"You're not interrupting anything," Taylor answered. "But I have to say, I'm interested to hear the story behind the wings you're wearing."

"Let's get situated, and I'll tell you all about it. Come on, kids, let's get over to the table so we can eat."

Lunch was a lively affair. The meadow they were visiting was one of the places butterflies visited during their migration. The wings were Albee's daughters' idea. Once, while visiting their grandparents, they'd watched the animated movie *A Bug's Life*. One of the characters was a male ladybug. The girls decided if there were male ladybugs, there had to be male butterflies, hence Albee's wings.

"What about Spiderman?" Taylor asked.

"He's always Spiderman," Albee replied, smiling.

Angelica, Albee's youngest daughter, was convinced Taylor was a fairy princess. She told her she was pretty and looked just like one of the fairies in her book. Plus, she had a fairy on her shirt. The other two children asked her where she was from, if she'd been scared to move away from home, and if she liked it there. They were sweet kids and well-mannered. It was clear Albee was a hands-on father. He seemed comfortable wearing butterfly wings on his back as he fed his children lunch and carried on a conversation with Mike and Taylor. When the meal was finished, Matilda asked her dad if Miss Taylor could take them into the meadow to see the butterflies.

"I don't know, honey. You'll have to ask her."

With her father's encouragement, Matilda walked over to the other side of the table to stand next to Taylor.

"Miss Taylor, can you take us into the meadow? We'll show you the best places to see the butterflies," Matilda asked with a hopeful smile.

"If it's okay with you, Albee, I'd be happy to. Why don't you two fellas stay here and talk, and I'll take the kids."

"Yay!" Matthew grabbed his dad's sleeve. "Dad, maybe you should give Miss Taylor your wings since you're not going in."

"Okay." Albee took the wings off and gave them to Taylor. Mike helped her put them on.

"Ready, kids?" Taylor asked with a big smile.

"Ready!" they shouted.

"Okay, since this is my first time going into this meadow, I'm going to need you to hold my hand."

"You only have two hands, and there are three of us. How're you gonna do that?" Matthew asked.

"How about going in, I hold Angelica's and Matilda's hands, and Matthew holds Angelica's other hand. When we come out, I'll hold Angelica's hand and your hand, Matthew, and Matilda can hold Angelica's other hand. How's that sound?"

"Great!" all three children yelled at the same time.

"All right, here we go!" Taylor laughed and looked over at Mike and Albee, who waved at her as she was pulled toward the meadow entrance by three energetic and surprisingly strong kids.

"You're just going to let her go off into that meadow with your kids and not warn her about them?" Mike asked Albee as they waved at Taylor. His children were sweet, but they were also rambunctious. When they weren't in school, they spent a lot of time running around their ranch getting into anything they could. The twins were two years older than Angelica, but you'd never know it by the way she kept up with them. And when they got together with Mike's niece and nephew, his brother Denton's kids, it was like they all became little hellions who fed off each other's bad behavior.

"Yup. If she's gonna be here for a while, she should learn now," Albee laughed.

"Man, that's just mean."

"No, that's me catching a break after having to wear wings."

"I don't know, you look pretty comfortable in them," Mike laughed.

"Well, I wasn't. You know how it is having girls. It's hard to say no to them. Although Matthew doesn't seem to suffer from that affliction. He flat out refuses to do anything he considers remotely girly."

"Yeah, well, that won't last long. My boy was the same way. However, nerd that he is, the girls love him. He won't admit it, but he likes the attention. His sister is the same. She's as smart as her brother, but the boys are a little intimidated by her. I'm secretly glad of this, and I tell her the right boy will appreciate how smart she is. I'm not looking forward to them becoming teenagers. You're going to have your work cut out for you when yours get older."

"I'm *not* looking forward to that," Albee replied as they walked back to the picnic table and sat down. "So, you and her?" Albee moved his head in the direction Taylor and the children had gone.

"No. There's no me and her."

"Why not?"

"I'm just showing her around."

"You should think about it. I mean she's nice *and* she's pretty."

"Yeah, so?"

"All I'm saying is you're single, and maybe if she is, you should ask her out." Albee raised his hands as if surrendering.

"You sound like Caleb."

"That's because brilliant minds think alike." Albee raised his eyebrows as he looked at Mike.

"Now see, that's where you're wrong. I don't recall brilliant ever being applied to you or Caleb."

"You can joke all you want, but I know you like her. I think she might like you too if you showed a little interest."

"I get what you're saying, but she's not going to be around long."

"She'll be around long enough. Nobody said you had to marry her. Just take her out. Have a little fun. Do something besides work and hang out with your kids."

"Okay, just stop. Not only are you sounding like Caleb, but you're starting to sound like Aunt Angie."

"Just think about what I'm saying."

Mike didn't have to think about it. He *was* planning to ask Taylor out again. He hadn't expected today to be as enjoyable as it had been. Not only was Taylor easy on the eyes, but she was also sweet and funny. But Albee didn't need to know that.

After about a half hour of talking and catching up, Albee and Mike decided to go rescue Taylor from the kids. When they found them, they were standing in the meadow surrounded by flowers. The forest ranger standing near them clapped his hands, and the butterflies appeared, flying all around them. Mike looked at Taylor, who was laughing as she slowly turned in a circle to watch them as they flew around her. He pulled his phone out and quickly snapped a picture. If he forgot everything about the day, he would remember this moment. The butterflies seemed to be drawn to her, as if they too knew how sweet she was. He watched as she joined Angelica, Matilda, and Matthew, who were chasing butterflies. The park ranger smiled and said something that caused her to stop and move closer to him. She laughed as she listened to him. Mike didn't know what he said, but now that he could see who the ranger was, he wasn't sure he liked him standing that close to her. As if Albee could read his mind, he said, "Seems like you got some competition, Mike."

Mike grunted, then walked over to where Taylor stood next to the ranger. He saw the ranger handing her a card as he approached them.

"I see you enjoyed the butterflies."

"I did!" she exclaimed. "Ranger Davis was telling me all about the migration and the different species and fauna here. It's pretty cool." She smiled at the ranger as she spoke.

"It was my pleasure," Ranger Davis said, returning her smile. He smirked at Mike and Albee. "Hey, Albee, Mike." Both men returned his greeting.

Bastard, Mike thought, though he had no right to be jealous. He'd known Davis Baker, aka Ranger Davis, since they were kids. Growing up, they'd attended school together and later college. During that time, they'd always seemed to compete with each other for one thing or another. Davis wasn't a bad guy, but he was an ass. While he could piss you off to no end, he was a guy you could count on if you ever needed help or got in a fight. In Mike's opinion, those were his only redeeming qualities. Women and girls thought he hung the sun every morning and couldn't get enough of him. Taylor appeared to be no different.

"Come on, kids. Let's head to the car. We need to get back and get the chores started." They ran to Albee, racing to see who would get to him first.

"Bye, kids. Taylor, I hope to see you soon," Ranger Davis told her.

"I'll look forward to it. Thank Ranger Davis, kids," Taylor said.

They thanked him as they walked past. Matthew and Matilda frowned slightly, and even little Angelica gave him the side-eye. They seemed to be feeling the same way Mike did. Maybe he needed to rethink his opinion of Albee's children. Mike and Taylor followed them back to the path that led them out of the meadow toward their vehicles, where he helped Taylor remove the fairy wings.

"What did you think of the meadow?" he asked as they got in the truck.

"It was beautiful. I loved the butterflies." Taylor looked out the window and waved to Davis as they drove by.

Mike suppressed the urge to spin his tires and send a little dirt and gravel his way.

"It's another one of those locals-only places."

"I can see why you'd want to keep the tourists away. They could ruin it. Thank you for bringing me."

"No thanks needed, but you're welcome."

"Well, I'm thanking you anyway. I've always wanted to visit a place like this but never seem to find the time."

"You love butterflies, huh?"

"Oh yes. I've always loved them. My father made a keepsake box for me when I was little. It has a large butterfly carved on top of it. The sides have flowers and butterflies that appear to flit and dance over them."

"Flit and dance?"

"Yes. That's what they looked like to me. My father was a very gifted craftsman."

"Was?"

"Yes, he was killed in Vietnam."

"I'm sorry, Taylor. I didn't know."

"Thanks."

Mike didn't quite know what to say after that. Before he could think of an appropriate response, Taylor spoke.

"Remind me sometime to show you the box. I take it with me wherever I go."

"I will. I'd love to see it."

They continued with the small talk, and Taylor told him a little more about her jewelry-making hobby, revealing she kind of fell into it but the love of working with her hands was in her blood, inherited from her parents. The talk eventually returned to the meadow.

"Did you have fun with the kids?"

"I did. They're sweet and very smart. They told me the names of some of the flowers they recognized, and Angelica told me a story about a butterfly princess. I was also told you were a fun uncle and that you had twins like them."

"Like them? Fraternal?"

"Yeah, they couldn't remember the word, so they said 'like them,' as in a boy and a girl." Taylor laughed as she repeated the conversation about the first time they'd met Mike's children.

"I remember that. Matthew was smitten with my daughter, Kay. He still has a crush on her to this day."

"They told me their Uncle Denton's kids are their best friends."

"More like their partners in crime."

"They seem to be good kids."

"They are when they want to be. Other times, they are straight up bad, especially when they're with D's kids."

"I'm glad I missed that side of them."

"I think they like you. By the way, how did you meet Davis?" He winced inwardly the moment the words came out of his mouth. He hadn't meant to ask that question.

"Ranger Davis? He came over and spoke to the kids, and they introduced me. He offered to give us a tour of the meadow, but the kids said they couldn't stay long and had just come to see the butterflies."

Mike grunted.

"How do you know him?" Taylor asked.

"He's a local. He, Caleb, and I went to school together."

"He's nice. The kids seem to like him. Matilda and Angelica thought he was cute but not as cute as their Uncle Mike." She looked at Mike as she spoke. "Matthew said he probably wasn't as strong as you either. Seems like you have quite the fan club."

"Smart kids." They both laughed.

"Here we are. Back safe and sound. You can tell your friend you got to see a genuine outlaw hideout and lived to talk about it," Mike said when he cut the engine and got out of the truck. He walked around to the passenger side and opened the door as Taylor grabbed her backpack and then walked her to her door. After she pulled her key out of her pack and unlocked the door, she turned to face him.

"Thanks for a wonderful day, Mike. I had a lot of fun."

"My pleasure. Maybe we could do it again sometime."

"I'd like that." Taylor hitched her backpack on her shoulder, reached up, and kissed Mike on the cheek. "Thanks again." She opened the door and quickly walked in. She looked at him as she locked the screen door. "Drive safe."

He smiled and walked down the steps to his truck. She watched him through the screen as he drove off.

Two thoughts were at the forefront of Mike's mind as he made his way home. One, he had liked Taylor before today, but now he was intrigued and found himself wanting to know more about her. And two, there was no way in hell she was going out with Davis Baker. He found himself smiling as he thought about what their next date should be.

Later that evening, Taylor sat in the den and looked at the sketches she'd just finished. Today's outing had inspired some ideas. The sketches were essentially rough drafts of what she hoped to create. Once she fleshed them out and added the colors from the pictures she'd taken, she would make mock-ups. She got up to fix a cup of tea when the phone rang.

"Hi, Taylor. It's Angie Edwards. How are you?"

"I'm fine, Mrs. Edwards."

"Oh, none of that Mrs. Edwards stuff. Please, call me Angie. Do you have a few minutes to chat?"

"Sure, Miss Angie."

"Are you busy next Saturday? Jackson and I are having a party, and we'd love for you to come."

"Thank you. I'd love to."

"Great. It's a barbecue. There'll be plenty of food, so you don't need to bring anything other than yourself."

"Oh no, I'd like to bring something. Maybe an appetizer or a dessert?"

"Either one will be fine. I'll text you the time and address."

"Thanks, I look forward to seeing you then."

"Okay. See you Saturday. Bye."

chapter 11

Taylor was on a call with Mimi when she found out her brother Grant was on a business trip and was planning to stop through for a quick visit before he went home. Taylor was looking forward to seeing him. She called Angie Edwards to tell her that since her brother was going to be in the area, she wasn't going to be able to make the party. Miss Angie told her she was more than welcome to bring her brother along, and she hoped she would still come. Taylor told her she'd ask Grant, and if he wanted to, they would be there. After talking with Miss Angie, she decided a trip to the market was in order. She had enough food for herself, but her brother was a coach and former professional athlete with a big appetite. She grabbed her purse, keys, and reusable grocery bags and headed out the door.

"You didn't tell me how the date went." Caleb walked into Mike's office with two cups of coffee. He handed one to Mike and sat down.

"That's because it wasn't a date."

"You can call it what you want, but how was it?"

"It was good."

"Just good?"

"Yes, good." Mike found himself smiling at the memory.

"Where did you take her?"

"I took her to the cemetery to see Pop's grave, and then we went to Hammond and the butterfly meadow."

"Sounds like a pretty full day."

"It was."

"Did that pervy preacher behave himself?"

"Nope. He was *quite* enchanted with Taylor."

"Not too enchanted, I hope?"

"No, but only because he wasn't sure if we were a couple or not."

"Is it just him or was the whole family line of preachers that way? I mean, I've heard stories, and I'm beginning to think it's a family tradition," Caleb laughed.

"You might be right."

"Did she like the meadow?"

"She did. By the way, thanks for telling me about that. She liked it a lot. When we got there, Albee and his little hellions were there. We had lunch with them and then they went with Taylor into the meadow."

"How could you let that happen? Those kids are bad as hell."

"They asked to go in with her and show her around. After they'd been gone a bit, Albee and I decided to go and rescue her. When we got there, she was talking to Davis. He gave her his card."

"What are you going to do about that? You can't let her go out with him. If you do, you'll never get a chance to go out with her again and you'll never hear the end of it."

"There's nothing I can do about it. She's a grown woman, and she can do what she pleases." Mike didn't tell Caleb that he'd already decided she wasn't going out with Davis.

"You should take her to the party on Saturday. That way, he'll know she's with you."

"In case you forgot, this is a bar, a place of business. I'm working Saturday."

"You're the boss. You can take a little time off and go in late. I can't believe you're willing to let Davis' cockblocking ass steal your girl."

"She's not my girl, and I'm not letting him steal anything."

"So, you're taking her to the party?"

"No, I'm not. But according to Aunt Angie, she'll be there, so I'll see her then." Mike looked at Caleb over the rim of his coffee cup. "You know, for someone single, you seem to have a whole lot of relationship advice."

"I do, don't I? But I'm rarely wrong, so heed my words."

Taylor was pulling the last batch of cookies from the oven and had set them on the rack to cool when she heard the doorbell ring. She walked to the door and saw her brother Grant standing on the porch, holding a duffle bag. With a big smile on her face, she quickly opened the door.

"Grant!" she shouted excitedly.

"Hey, Tay-Bay!" He dropped his duffle, enveloped her in a big hug, then lifted her and twirled her around.

Grant was six foot four, two hundred thirty pounds of pure muscle, with smooth caramel skin. Bald and sporting a goatee, he had a beautiful smile and an easygoing manner that immediately put people at ease; unless you were opposite him on the football field. Then, it was a different story.

"It's so good to see you," she said.

"You too." He sniffed the air. "Smells good in here."

"I'm baking your favorite cookies."

"Couldn't ask for a better welcome than that."

"No, you can't. Are you hungry?"

"I'm always hungry."

"Yes, you are. I'll show you where you'll be sleeping. After you put your bag down, you can join me in the kitchen."

"Tay, this is a nice place," Grant said as he walked into the kitchen a few minutes later. "It's a lot bigger than it looks from the outside."

"I thought the same thing when I first saw it and was pleasantly surprised. Especially when I saw the back room. It has a lot of natural light and is perfect to use as a studio."

"This kitchen is pretty big too. And speaking of kitchens, what are you cooking?" He looked at the food she'd placed on the counter.

"I'm making salad bowls, or rather a bowl for me and a platter for you. I also have some flatbread in the oven."

"What's in the bowls?"

"Arugula, brown rice, quinoa, tomatoes, artichokes, cucumbers, chickpeas, grilled chicken, and feta cheese. I also made a vinaigrette. You can use it as a salad dressing or a dip for the flatbread."

"That sounds pretty good."

"It is good. I bet you're surprised I remembered you're in training." Taylor smirked.

"I am. You need any help?"

"Sure. How about you take care of the tomatoes and cucumbers? I'll shred the chicken. By the time we finish, the bread should be done, and we can eat."

"Show me where you keep your knives, and I'm on it."

Taylor pointed to the block on the counter where the knives were kept. Grant washed his hands, grabbed a knife, and got started.

After they had eaten, Grant wiped his mouth on a napkin and said, "That was good, sis, thanks."

"Did you get enough? If not, I can fix you something else."

"No, this is good, thanks."

Taylor got up to refill both of their glasses with iced tea. Grant took a drink and looked at Taylor.

"What?" she asked, noticing his look.

"You, that's what. How are you doing out here in cowboy country?"

"I've only been here for a few weeks, but I'm doing good."

"That's good to hear. From what I see, looks like you are doing well. I haven't seen you this rested and relaxed in a long time. It's a good look on you."

"Thanks, Grant. Please don't tell me Mimi and Poppy had you come out and check on me."

"I came because I wanted to see for myself that you were okay. I'm not gonna lie and say they aren't worried about you, because you know how they are. And your friend Rae isn't helping matters. Her dramatic ass told Mom she's been having a hard time reaching you."

"As you can see for yourself, I'm fine. Rae knows this. There's only been one time couldn't reach me when she called. I was out at one of the local bars and stayed longer than I had planned. And please tell Mimi and Poppy not to worry—Blue also. The way all of you are acting, you'd think this is my first time away from home."

"*It kind of is*, Tay. You rarely go anywhere that's not work-related or one of my games. Of course we're going to worry about you."

"As you can see, there's nothing to worry about."

"That remains to be seen, but I'll take your word for it for now."

Taylor spent the rest of the afternoon telling Grant about the people she'd met since she'd been in Silverton. She showed him the pictures she'd taken from her outing with Mike and the sketches she'd made. She also told him about the Edwards' party the next evening and asked if he wanted to go. He said he did. He wanted to see what the people of the town were like. She told him since he was coming, he could help her with the appetizer and dessert she was planning to take. He tried to balk at that until she bribed him with a few dozen of his favorite cookies.

"So, what's the appetizer and what's the dessert?"

"For the appetizer, I'm making bacon-wrapped dates stuffed with goat cheese and giving them a balsamic glaze. The dessert will be a sock-it-to-me cake."

"Sock-it-to-me cake? That'll probably be a first in this town." Grant laughed.

"You might be right."

"What's next—mac and cheese, banana pudding, potato salad?"

"I'm planning to introduce them to all of those, one party at a time." They both laughed.

chapter 12

"Are you sure you know where you're going?" Grant looked out the window at the passing scenery. "I haven't seen nothing but grass, cows, and horses. Not a road sign in sight. *You know you're directionally challenged.*"

"Just because I got lost one time does not make me directionally challenged. And yes, I know where I'm going."

"For the record, you've been lost *many* times. The fact that you would lie about it makes me even more worried."

"Not true. But anyway, we're here." Taylor exited right off the highway.

"How do you know? I don't see any signs. We could be anywhere."

"Because that big stone over there has a circle and an E painted in the middle of it."

"And?"

"That's the landmark where I'm supposed to turn. We're coming up to the gate now." Taylor drove down the road toward the large ranch-style home. It sat in the middle of a circular driveway. She parked off to the side.

"If you're done whining, let's get out, and I'll introduce you to Mr. and Mrs. Edwards."

"I wasn't whining. I was just voicing concern over your poor navigational skills."

She grabbed her purse and the appetizers from the back seat of the truck. Grant grabbed the cake and followed her to the front door.

"Are we going to be the only Black people here?"

"Yes, but not the only people of color."

"Good to know. I like to know the potential ladies I might meet."

Taylor rolled her eyes and rang the doorbell. Jackson answered the door.

"Hi, Taylor! Welcome to our home! Come on in."

"Hi, Mr. Jackson. Thanks for having me. This is my brother-"

"Grant Sawyer! A pleasure to meet you!" Jackson smiled and shook Grant's hand. "I'm a big fan!"

"Nice to meet you, Mr. Edwards. Thanks for having me and for looking out for Taylor."

"Call me Jackson. Taylor is a sweetheart, and we're glad she's here. This is my wife, Angie. Honey, meet Taylor's brother, Grant Sawyer."

"It's nice to meet you, Grant."

"You as well, Miss Angie." Grant shook Angie's hand and gave her the full force of his megawatt smile.

"Oh my, aren't you something?" she said breathlessly. "Jackson, why don't you take Grant to get a drink and introduce him to everyone? Taylor, come with me." She took the cake carrier from Grant and walked with Taylor to the kitchen. "Your brother is one *good-looking* man," Angie said as she set the cake on the counter.

Taylor laughed. Grant had a way of charming women. It didn't matter who they were, he always seemed to make them smile.

Caleb, Mike, and Davis were in the yard unloading bags of ice from Mike's truck when Taylor and Grant arrived.

"Isn't that Taylor?" Davis looked over as he saw her red pickup park next to the house.

"Looks like her." Caleb stood next to Davis and looked at the truck. "Mike, who's that with her?"

Mike stopped what he was doing and watched Taylor walk with a tall Black man to the front door of the Edwards house. She had on a peach-colored dress, and her auburn locs were pulled back into a ponytail. She was laughing at something the man had said. She'd never mentioned having a significant other. He wondered who he was.

"I don't know."

"Don't you want to know?" Caleb asked.

Mike grunted and went back to unloading the ice.

"I'd like to know. I was planning on asking her out, but that dude is big." Davis put a bag in the cart they were using to carry the ice.

"That never stopped you before," Mike commented as he watched Taylor and the unknown man enter the house.

"True. But since I've gotten older, I pick my battles a little more wisely."

"So, you two aren't even a little bit curious?" Caleb looked from one man to the other.

"No. Let's get this ice to the backyard and get a drink." Mike turned the cart around and pushed it toward the house.

After filling up the coolers, silver galvanized tubs, and ice buckets, they put the remaining bags in the outdoor freezer. Mike noticed that the man who had arrived with Taylor was with his uncle Jack. Davis grabbed some beers out of one of the tubs and handed one to Mike and Caleb each.

"Cheers." Raising his bottle, Davis took a swig after twisting the top off. Caleb and Mike did the same.

"Uncle Jack is walking around with that guy Taylor came with. He looks familiar," Caleb observed.

"Now that you mention it, he does. If I didn't know any better, I'd swear that was Grant Sawyer," Davis said, squinting to get a better look.

"Looks like they're coming this way, so I guess we'll find out who he is," Mike said.

"Hey, boys, thanks for taking care of the ice. I got someone I want you to meet. Grant, can you come over here for a minute?" Uncle Jack asked.

The man who'd come with Taylor was talking with two older women who looked starstruck. They followed him with their eyes as he walked away from them.

"Mike, Davis, Caleb, meet Grant Sawyer. Grant, these are my nephews."

"Wow, Grant Sawyer! Nice to meet you, man." Caleb reached out to shake his hand.

"I thought you looked familiar." Davis smiled as he spoke.

"Uncle Jack, I didn't know you knew Grant Sawyer," Caleb said.

"I just met him. He came with Taylor."

"So, she's who brought you to our little town."

"Yup. Had to come check on my little sister."

"You're Taylor's *brother?*" Caleb smirked at Davis and Mike. "Hopefully, she's been enjoying her time here."

"She seems to be."

They talked a little more, and Mike asked Grant how long he planned to stay.

"I'll be here until Monday."

"If you have some time, have Taylor bring you by the saloon. We're doing brunch tomorrow. Caleb is the chef there," Mike said.

"Sounds good to me. I'll ask her."

"I'm going to introduce Grant to a few more folks. Have a good time and *behave* yourselves." Jackson looked at each man as he and Grant left.

"Grant Sawyer's little sister. Who knew?" Davis took a swig of his beer.

"Definitely not us. Is it me, or does he seem a whole lot bigger in person than he looks on television?" Caleb looked at Grant, who was now standing next to Jackson, Hawk, and Rainbow.

"He's pretty big, but from the look on his face, he suffers from the same affliction as every other man who comes in contact with your mother, Caleb," Davis laughed.

Rainbow, Caleb's mother, was as beautiful now as she had been in her younger years. In fact, except for the steel gray that mixed with the black strands of her shoulder-length hair, she appeared not to have aged at all. She was tall and curvy. Her copper complexion was smooth, radiant, and clear. Growing up, she'd been the crush of all Caleb's friends, Mike and Davis included. Men were envious of her husband, Hawk, and women wanted to hate her, but her sweet nature made it difficult. Along with Aunt Angie, she'd been Mike's mother's best friend.

"Yup, looks like he's under her spell," Mike agreed.

"That's my mother you're talking about, you bastards."

"We know." Mike and Davis said, laughing and clinking their bottles together.

Angie walked out of the house, followed by Taylor, who was holding a bright yellow serving platter. She sat the platter on one of the food tables and placed a stack of cocktail napkins next to it. Mike quickly excused himself and joined her.

"Hi, Taylor."

Taylor turned toward him when he spoke. She looked beautiful. She had little to no makeup on. Her full lips were lightly glossed, and gold earrings hung from her ears. A colorful butterfly tattoo decorated the inside of her left forearm, and a bronze cuff circled her right wrist.

"Hey, Mike."

He was so caught up in looking at her that he almost didn't hear her.

"How are you this evening?" he asked.

"I'm fine."

"You definitely are."

"Excuse me?"

"You look lovely."

"Thanks." They stood looking at each other. "Um, would you like to try one of these? I just took them out of the oven."

"Sure."

Taylor picked up a napkin, plucked one of the dates off the platter, and held it up to Mike's lips. He bit down on the savory appetizer, his lips grazing her fingers. Taylor's eyes widened in surprise. She felt a rush of heat from where his lips touched her fingertips. More than a little bothered, but unable to look away, she handed him the napkin.

"Can I have another one?" he asked, his eyes not breaking contact.

"Yeah, uh, sure." Taylor nervously picked up another date, intending to hand it to him, but he opened his mouth and she fed him a second time as he bent slightly to take the treat.

"Thanks. Care for a drink?" he asked.

"A drink would be good." She needed something cold to decrease the heat he was generating.

"Damn, Davis. Did you see that?" Caleb smacked Davis on the arm.

"Yeah, I saw it." Davis sounded slightly annoyed.

"You still thinking about asking her out?"

Davis glared at him. Caleb chuckled.

"Sorry man, I'm just giving you shit. If it makes you feel any better, I thought about asking her out too."

"So why didn't you?"

"I was there when they first met. It was clear even then there was something between them. Mike swears he was just being nice since she's new in town and all, but his actions said otherwise. If I thought she would've said yes, I'd have asked."

"I'm surprised. She's not his normal type."

"No, she isn't, which makes whatever it is between them all the more interesting."

"It does at that."

Changing the subject, Caleb asked Davis if he was planning to come to brunch the next day, and the conversation drifted to the upcoming rodeo. The rodeo signaled the beginning of tourist season, which was a busy time for the saloon as well as the national parks and historical landmarks. Both men would be busy in the coming months. Brunch the month before the first rodeo of the summer was a tradition for Mike, Davis, and Caleb that had started in college and continued with each passing year.

After arriving back at her house, Taylor handed Grant a bottle of water and sat down next to him on the sofa.

"Did you enjoy the party?"

"I did." Grant nodded his head. "Everyone was nice. The food was good too."

"You should know. It seems like every time I looked your way, some woman was bringing you another plate."

"What can I say? Ladies love me." Grant smirked at her. "So, what's up with you and Knight?"

"What do you mean?"

"You know what I mean."

"No, I don't." Taylor knew exactly who he was referring to, she just wasn't willing to answer the question, because she wasn't sure of what was going on herself. Grant gave her a blank stare.

"Yes, you do."

"Okay, fine. Nothing's up. He's just been nice to me, that's all."

"*That's* what you think? This man gave you a free lunch at his bar, drove you home from a night out, and then showed you around the area. Oh, and don't think I didn't see you feeding him. I'd say he was more than just 'being nice.'" Grant did air quotes. "He likes you."

"No, he doesn't." She scoffed. "He just got out of a relationship, and from what I've seen, the other half of that relationship is not ready for it to be over."

"Well, she might not be ready to move on, but from the sparks I saw between the two of you, he is. And for the record, I'm not the only one who thinks so. Jackson and Knight's uncle Hawk think so too."

"Is that right? Does Mike's uncle Hawk know about you drooling over his wife?"

"Hey, I couldn't help it. That woman is a goddess. And from what Jackson said, Hawk is used to it. I'm just another sucker in a long line of men who become completely smitten when they enter her space." Grant and Taylor laughed. "Seriously though, when I was talking with PJ, he said that growing up, all of them had a crush on Rainbow Hawkins. But back to *you*. Knight invited us to brunch tomorrow at his bar. Do you want to go?"

"Sure, if you want to."

"Oh, I *want* to. I need to check him out in his natural habitat."

"Whatever, G. I'm going to bed. How about eleven in the morning for brunch?"

"Sounds good."

"Good night. Love you."

"Love you too, Tay-Bay."

chapter 13

Taylor and Grant walked into the Red Buffalo at 11:45 am the next morning. Taylor had overslept. She'd fallen asleep thinking about Mike and had multiple vivid, erotic dreams about him. When she woke, she was aroused and a little sweaty. She looked at her phone and saw it was 10:30. They were supposed to leave at 11:00. She got out of bed and headed to the bathroom to get ready. After searching her limited wardrobe for something that wouldn't need ironing, she found a black tank dress she paired with a denim jacket and black Chucks. She put on a multicolored headband, silver disk earrings, and added a couple of rings to her fingers, before putting on her favorite berry-colored lip gloss. Done, she went into the living room, where she found Grant on the sofa, talking on the phone. He finished his call and stood up when he saw her.

"Still slow, I see. I thought I was going to have to come in there and light a fire under you."

"I'm not slow. I forgot to set my alarm." She sneered, making him laugh.

"I'm surprised you don't have a rooster crowing in your backyard. I thought that was the way most folks around here wake up in the morning."

"This might be the country, but this is not a farm."

"No roosters in the backyard then?"

"Not yet anyway."

Grant chuckled. "You look nice. Ready to go?"

"Yes. You want to walk or ride?"

"How far away is it?"

"About six blocks."

"Walking's fine."

Mike was standing at the bar, talking with Davis, when Taylor and Grant arrived. He had extended the invite to brunch last evening, but he wasn't sure whether they would come.

"Look who's here." Davis nodded toward the entrance. Mike turned his head and saw Taylor at the hostess stand.

"Talk to you later, Davis." He heard Davis laugh as he walked over to where Taylor and Grant stood.

"Hi, Taylor, Sawyer."

"Hey, Mike." Taylor smiled.

"Knight. How's it going?" Grant asked.

"Pretty good. Glad you guys could make it. I'll take you to your table." He grabbed a couple of menus and led the way. "We have a standard brunch menu and then we have the Red Buffalo special, which is whatever Caleb feels like cooking. The drink menu is in there as well. If you like them, the Bloody Marys are pretty good. They're a little spicy and come with a strip of bison bacon." While he spoke, a waitress came up to the table. She had strawberry-blonde hair and a big smile. "Dana here will be your server."

"Oh my goodness! You're Grant Sawyer! My dad said he met you last night, but I didn't believe him! I thought he just happened to meet someone with your same name. Who knew it was you? Wow! Welcome to the Red Buffalo Saloon." Dana seemed to not breathe as the words rushed out with her excitement at meeting Grant.

"Dana is also my niece. Take a breath, sweetheart, and get these nice people's order."

"I got it, Uncle Mike."

Mike excused himself and left.

"Can I start you out with something to drink?" Dana asked Taylor and Grant.

Taylor ordered a coffee and a Bloody Mary.

"I'll have a coffee and water please, Dana."

Grant rarely drank during training or football season. Grant smiled at Dana. Dana looked at him with a dazed expression on her face. After realizing she'd been staring, her face turned pink. A little flustered, she punched the order in on her tablet.

"Wow. Um, okay. Two coffees, a water, and a Bloody Mary. I'll go get your coffee and come back to take your order," she told them, then walked away.

"Looks like Dana's a fan," Taylor said.

"She's cute."

"She is, and she seems sweet." Glancing at the menu, she asked, "See anything you want?"

"Not sure yet. How's the food here?"

"I've only eaten here once, but it was pretty good. I think I'm going to have the special."

"Do you have any questions about the menu, or are you ready to order?" Dana asked as she placed their coffee on the table a few minutes later.

"She's ready to order, but I have a question. What would you recommend?" Grant asked.

"We do farm-to-table here, even the meat. Everything is pretty good, but I'd recommend the special. It's kind of a brunch sampler platter. It has a frittata, roasted red potatoes with tomatoes and feta cheese, bacon, French toast muffins, and fresh fruit."

"That sounds good. Tay, you ready to order?"

"Yes. I'll have the special," she said.

"And, I'll have the same," Grant added.

"Okay, anything else?"

"No, I'm good." Grant looked at Taylor.

"No, that's it."

Another server brought Taylor's Bloody Mary to the table as Dana left. Taylor looked at the drink, which was garnished with a celery stalk, olives, and a strip of bacon. She took a sip and found it spicy, just how she liked it.

"How is it?" Grant asked.

"This is good. Nice and spicy." She snapped a piece of the bacon off and put it in her mouth. "This bacon is good too. I might have a couple of these."

"That good, huh? Let me try it."

She gave her glass to Grant, who moved the garnish and straw to the side and took a sip. "Damn, that is good." He handed the glass back to Taylor.

She laughed. "Told you."

"You did. I hope the food is as good as the drinks."

"I think you'll be pleasantly surprised."

"I hope so."

"Trust me, you will."

"You're basing that opinion on one meal?"

"No. When Mike took me around last week, he brought a basket with lunch and biscuits that Caleb made. It was all good."

"Hmmm."

"What do you mean, 'hmmm'?" Taylor looked at him.

"You're still in denial about him."

Rather than respond, Taylor picked up her drink and wished their food would hurry up so Grant could do a little more eating and a little less talking. Truth was, she was into Mike. It had been a while since she'd been in the dating game, so she was out of practice on the social cues that Grant was insisting were evident in Mike's actions. As if the kitchen staff had heard her wish, she saw Dana and another server walking toward their table with their food. By the amount they were carrying, it looked like there was a little extra thrown in for Grant. *Good,* she thought. *Maybe the arrival of the meal will provide a change of subject.*

"Okay, you're right. The food here *is* good." Grant wiped his mouth with his cloth napkin and sat back in his chair, his plate now empty.

"Yes, it is. I've never had French toast muffins before. I wonder if Caleb will give me his recipe."

"If you ask him nicely, he might consider it," Caleb said, wearing a grin as he came to their table. "How was everything?"

"It was delicious," Taylor said.

"Glad you liked it."

"We did. And thanks for the extra-large portions," Grant told him.

"When I heard you were here, I wanted to make sure you didn't go away hungry."

"After that meal, I won't, that's for sure."

Dana, their waitress, came up and asked if they wanted more coffee. Grant requested a refill, and Taylor ordered a third Bloody Mary.

"So, what are your plans for the rest of the day?" Caleb asked.

"I'm going to show Grant around the town square, and then we're heading back home," Taylor said. "He has an early flight tomorrow."

"Make sure you take him by the Historical Society Museum. For a town this size, it has some pretty good exhibits. It's usually open for a few hours on Sunday."

"We'll do that. Thanks for the tip."

"You're welcome. Now, can I interest you in some dessert?"

"It depends. What is it?" Taylor asked, feeling a little buzz from her drinks.

"Bread pudding with bourbon sauce."

"I don't know about Grant, but if I could get it to go, that would be great."

"Make that two, please," Grant was quick to add.

"Sure thing."

"Caleb, what time do you guys close?" Taylor took another sip from her drink.

"We close at two."

"Do you mind if we come back and pick up the desserts after we check out the museum?"

"Sure, no problem."

"Thanks."

Dana returned with Taylor's drink and Grant's refill. Mike was with her. Grant asked for the check and was told their meal was on the house. Grant thanked her and left Dana a tip that equaled the price of their meal. As they were finishing their drinks, Grant noticed a woman staring at Taylor. She'd been doing so off and on since they'd sat down. She was seated at a table with Davis Baker, whom he'd met yesterday and two other women. At first, he thought she might be a fan, but the pissed-off look on her face was directed at Taylor suggested otherwise.

"Tay, there's a blonde lady a few tables over giving you the stink eye. Do you know her?"

Taylor looked over and saw Mike's ex glaring at her. She was sitting with Davis, who raised his glass and smiled at her. Taylor smiled back at him.

"She's Mike's ex. I don't know her, but I've seen her around."

"Was she at the party last night? I don't recall seeing her."

"No, she wasn't."

"The way she's looking at you, somebody must've told her about you feeding him, and him being all up on you," he told her with a smirk.

"I did not feed him." Taylor denied his statement a little too quickly, causing Grant to laugh. "I let him sample the appetizers I made. And he was *not* up on me. We had a couple of drinks and talked. I'm surprised you even noticed."

"With the heat you two were generating, it was hard not to." He glanced back over at the table.

Taylor excused herself after that last comment and went to the ladies' room. Davis and the other two women were laughing, but the blonde continued to look their way. When Mike came back to the table, she rose from her chair as if she was coming over to join them. Davis grabbed her arm before she could get too far and shook his head at her, and she sat back down. Grant decided to stir things up a bit. From what he knew of Knight so far, he liked him, but if he was trying to get with Taylor while he was in a relationship, well, that wasn't going to happen.

"Friends of yours, Knight?" Grant looked pointedly at the table.

Mike looked in the direction of his glance. "Two of them are. Not that it's any of your business, but one of them is my ex."

"Let me guess, the one with "resting bitch face"?"

"That's the one." Mike laughed. "And again, she's my ex."

"Thanks for clarifying that. Taylor's my sister. I know she has your interest. I just wanted to know if it was genuine, or if you were playing games."

Both men seemed to be in a stare-down when Taylor got back to the table. Mike nodded his head at Grant, who returned the gesture. She wondered what that was about.

"I hope you enjoyed your meal." Mike looked at Taylor as he spoke.

"I did. We're going to go over to the museum next and then circle back and pick up dessert."

"I think you'll like the museum. And you came here on a good day."

"Oh yeah, why is that?"

"Caleb doesn't make bread pudding often, but when he does, it's the most popular item on the menu. No matter how much he makes, it always seems to run out."

"I'm glad I'm not missing out then."

"I guess we'll head out," Grant announced, and he rose from his chair. "See you in a bit." He shook hands with Mike.

"See you soon." Mike smiled at Taylor and watched her as she left with her brother.

"I guess maybe now that they're gone, you have time to talk to me."

Mike turned and saw Linda standing next to him. He inhaled and exhaled slowly.

"What do you want, Linda?"

"I want to know why you've been ignoring me."

"I haven't been ignoring you. We're over. Remember?"

"I thought we were going to talk this through."

He could see the tears welling up in her eyes. *Here we go.*

"Look, Linda, I'm sorry things didn't work out between us the way you wanted them to. We've been over this a million times. I can't give you what you need."

"Can't or won't?"

Mike remained silent.

"It's her, isn't it? It's that woman. You don't even *know* her."

"It's not anyone. We just didn't work out."

Hearing Linda cry, people at some of the tables near them turned their way.

"I can't believe you're doing this to us, Mike, after all this time." She pouted as her crocodile tears flowed.

Linda's best friend, Shayla, walked up to where they stood. She glared at Mike as she put her arm around Linda.

"Come on, sweetie, let's go. He's not worth it."

She guided her back to their table, where they gathered their things, and then they left. Mike hoped that would be the last he saw of her. But being that Silverton was a small town, he knew that wouldn't be possible. He was bound to run into her again. Hopefully, when they did, she would have accepted the fact that they were over.

"That seemed to go well." Davis joined him.

"You think?"

"I do. I told her you're seeing Taylor and nice guy that I am, I offered her my condolences on your relationship."

"You're an asshole, you know that?"

"Yeah, but that's one of the reasons you love me." He laughed. "Me and Sis tried to talk her out of coming over here, but Shay was like, 'Go get your man.' As you can see, we have no influence with her. I don't think you've seen the last of her though. I don't know if she was more pissed about you moving on, or that you moved on with Taylor. I'm guessing it's Taylor."

"You know her pretty well, Davis. Why don't you go out with her?"

"That will be a hard no. I'll take my chances elsewhere. Ever since I've known her, the sound of her voice has gotten on my nerves."

Davis's sister, Mina, had been friends with Linda and Shayla since childhood. To Davis, Shay was bitch and Linda had always been a whiney brat. Mina was a sweetheart, and he couldn't figure out how the three women remained friends.

"Chicken."

"Yup." Davis smiled.

chapter 14

Taylor sat across from Grant as he ate the breakfast she'd prepared for him. She'd enjoyed her time with Grant during his short visit. He'd teased her about living in cowboy country, but she could tell he'd enjoyed his time here as well.

"Do you want any more coffee?" she asked.

"No, I'm good. Thanks for breakfast. It's early, and you didn't have to."

"No thanks needed. Besides, I didn't mind. I wish you could stay a little longer."

"Aww, you gonna miss me?"

"Little bit." She held her hand up, with a little space between her thumb and forefinger.

Grant laughed. "At least I can put the folks at ease when I tell them you're doing fine."

"Thanks for that. I know they worry. I can hear it in Mimi's voice every time I talk to her."

"You know how she is. She worries about all of us, but especially you—being the only girl and the baby and all."

"I'm a little old for her to be thinking of me as a baby, don't you think?"

"You know how it is. No matter how old you are, you're always your mama's baby. *Although*, I think she'd worry less if you were married."

"I don't think that'll happen anytime soon."

"I don't know about that. That forest ranger and Knight both seem interested in you. The ranger seems like he might be a player, but Knight seems to be a straight-up dude. Just saying."

"Yes, well, I'm only here for a short time. After that, I plan on giving this place back to their family and going home."

"You've only been here a handful of weeks, but this place looks good on you. You also seem rested, so I'm guessing you're not having bad dreams. *And* you're back at your hobbies. You may feel differently when the time comes to make your final decision."

"Maybe, but I'm not counting on it."

Grant rose from the table and put his plate in the sink. He hadn't been lying when he said Silverton had a good effect on her. Taylor's childhood had not been easy. When his parents adopted her, they all went out of their way to ease her transition and help her heal. She'd done well, but she often had trouble sleeping. Whenever she couldn't sleep, she'd draw or sketch designs for the jewelry she created.

Her therapist said the creative outlet was her way of managing her sleeplessness and depression. Grant remembered that both Taylor's parents had been gifted creatives. The Sawyers had some of the furniture pieces Taylor's dad had built. Both had been skilled in their crafts. Daniel and Lily often told Taylor that her creative ability was a gift from her parents. Grant hoped that after all this time, Taylor would truly be able to find some peace.

"I guess it's time for me to get on the road and let you get back to bed."

"I'm glad you came."

"Me too, Tay-Bay." He walked over to the door, where his duffle bag sat. Taylor followed him. He turned around and hugged her. "Love you."

"Love you too, G. Drive safe."

He picked up his bag and walked to the car, and after setting the back seat, he turned to wave at her. Taylor, watching him through the screen door, waved back.

Taylor watched Grant drive away, closed the door, and went back to bed. It had been good to see her brother. And he was right, she had been sleeping better since moving here. The pace was slower, and the surrounding mountains were both majestic and peaceful. Spending time with Mike had also been nice. Something about the vibe of Silverton soothed her. Maybe it was a combination of all those things. Luckily, she still had time to find out.

Taylor grabbed the grocery list from the table, along with her phone and keys. She planned to do some baking and needed to pick up a few things. She also wanted to stop by the craft shop. Angie had called yesterday and told her the farmers market would be opening soon and that she was going to help Cheryl Knight get her preserves and jellies ready. Cheryl had a table reserved for the weekend and had invited her to join them. Taylor wasn't sure what all was involved in getting ready for the market, but she told her she would go. Cheryl had invited her out to their ranch when she'd talked to her at the Edwards' party, telling her that the place was in desperate need of more estrogen. She and PJ had four children—Dana, whom she'd met, and three sons.

Taylor had learned to bake from Mimi. Mimi loved to bake and always had some sweet treat in the house to give the postman, the neighbors, or to take to a party, cookout, etc. Taylor didn't keep baked goods around like that, but she had developed a love for making them. Today she decided to do a mix of sweet and savory croissants: plain, ham and cheese, spinach and feta, and chocolate. She hoped she'd be able to find everything she needed at the market in town. When she'd been there last, it seemed to be well stocked. Pulling into a parking space, she made a mental note to stop at the wine store. Other than good whiskey, Pinot Noir was her favorite alcoholic beverage. She always kept both on hand, because one never knew when a glass of wine or a good stiff drink might be enjoyed or needed.

Taylor had been able to get a good parking spot that wasn't too far from the shops she needed to visit. She hit the craft shop first, picking up a few sketch pads and ordering a packet of leather sheets, hooks, closures, and other supplies for some new jewelry pieces. After, finishing up at the craft shop, she headed over to the wine store. When she entered, she saw Mike at the bar in the rear of the shop. He smiled at her and he waved her over.

"Hi, Taylor." He leaned toward her and kissed her on the cheek.

"Hey, Mike," she responded nervously. His kiss sent a little jolt through her. Thankfully, he seemed not to notice.

"I'm glad you're here. I was just doing some wine tasting. We're making some changes to the menu and wine list. Josh here was about to pour some options. If you're not in a hurry, I could use your help. I'm more of a whiskey and beer guy, and all the stuff Josh tells me about the wine never makes much sense to me."

"Um, sure. I'd be happy to."

"Great. Josh, this is Taylor, she's new in town. Taylor, this is Josh, and this is his place."

"Nice to meet you, Josh."

"I've heard about you. I was wondering if I'd get the chance to meet you." Josh smiled as he lifted her hand to his lips.

Taylor smiled back and felt her cheeks grow warm. Josh reminded Taylor of Sonny Corleone, Taylor's favorite character in *The Godfather* movie. He was a hothead, a little crazy, but he was also kind of charming. Josh didn't seem dangerous, but he did seem a little edgy.

"Are you going to get the lady a glass, or are you going to keep gawking at her?" Mike asked.

"Give me a minute. That's a tough question. Make a sale, or gawk at the pretty lady?" He laughed as he reached for a wineglass and coaster, and set them on the bar in front of Taylor. "Let's do a little wine tasting."

"That was fun!" Taylor said as she left the wine store with Mike.

What had started as a quick errand to pick up wine had morphed into an hour-long wine-tasting session. The wines Josh poured were excellent. In addition to giving them the flavor profiles, he also included the history of the varietals and the vineyards that produced them. Some of the stories were funny, and some were a bit on the macabre side, making her wonder what he'd done before he got into the wine business. With Taylor's help, Mike selected three new wines for his bar.

"And you got free wine," Mike said.

"I did get free wine." She laughed. "You know what goes well with free wine?"

"No, what?"

"Free ice cream."

"Free ice cream?"

"Yeah. Free ice cream that you're going to provide in exchange for me helping you with the wines."

"You say that like it was a hardship or something."

"Oh, it wasn't a hardship. It did, however, put me behind schedule for my errands today. I figure you can return the favor with some ice cream."

"You're in luck. I happen to know the best place to get ice cream."

"Lead on."

Turned out, the town of Silverton had a genuine old-fashioned ice cream parlor. It looked to be a popular place, judging from the line that extended out the door. Mike assured her it was worth the wait. When they finally got to the register, Taylor ordered a scoop of lemon custard topped with fresh strawberries in a cup. Mike ordered a scoop of chocolate in a cone. They walked over to the benches on the green in the town square and sat down.

"This is good." Taylor enjoyed the tart-but-sweet mix of lemon and strawberries on her tongue. "How's yours?"

"It's good. Would you like to try it?"

"Sure. Would you like to try mine?"

"I would."

Taylor scooped the custard and fruit mix with her spoon and held it to Mike's mouth, watching as his lips closed around the spoon.

"I like that." He held his cone to her lips and watched as she licked the chocolatey goodness.

"Ohhh, that's good. I need to try that one next time."

With little to no warning, Mike moved toward her, dipped his head, and kissed her. After the initial shock of his lips on hers, Taylor sighed as her lips opened under his, before closing her eyes and kissing him back. The rush she felt made her body heat up and had her wanting more. If he could kiss like that, she wondered what else he could do. Maybe this was why his ex was unwilling to let him go. Too soon, he pulled away and leaned back against the bench.

"I like that too." Heat filled his gaze as he looked at her.

Taylor didn't seem to be able to come up with a response, so she dug into her custard. The frozen custard did nothing to cool her down from the kiss they'd just shared. Mike chuckled and turned his attention back to his cone.

Mike didn't have a reason why he kissed her other than he just knew he wanted to. He probably would have waited to do it if he hadn't seen her lick the ice cream. After that, he couldn't resist, and he was glad he didn't. Her lips were as soft as they looked. They tasted like the chocolate ice cream she'd just had. He could have kept kissing her if he hadn't remembered where they were. He couldn't wait to do it again. He looked over at Taylor. From the way she was going at her frozen custard, he was pretty sure the kiss affected her as well. He gave her a sideways glance.

"Have any plans for Sunday evening?" he asked.

"No."

"How about dinner? I'll cook."

"You'll cook?"

He nodded. "I will. Believe it or not, I do know how to cook."

"Okay, sure."

"Good. I'll pick you up at six."

They sat in silence now, both wondering about their next kiss and what it would be like.

"I'd like to sit here a little longer, but I need to get to the saloon," he said. "Can I walk you to your truck?"

"I need to get going myself. I have to go to the market. I'm doing some baking later." Taylor was still feeling the effects of the kiss they'd shared.

Mike stood up and reached for her empty cup and her shopping bag. He tossed the cup and his napkin in a nearby trash can. He noticed she hadn't answered his question. She was also avoiding looking at him. *Good*, he thought. He was glad to know he wasn't the only one who'd been shaken by their kiss.

"I hope you're making something good."

She rose from the bench and walked beside him. "I am. At least, I hope so. I'm going with Angie to Cheryl's tomorrow, and I thought I'd make some croissants to take with me."

"Croissants?"

"Yes, I'm doing a mix of sweet and savory. I hope they like them."

"I'm sure they will. What's the sweet one?"

"Chocolate."

They'd arrived at her truck, and she got in. He handed back her shopping bag, leaned in, and gave her a quick kiss on the lips.

"I hope you save me a couple."

"If you want."

"Oh, *I want*." He winked at her, closed the door, and walked back toward the Red Buffalo. Taylor sat for a few minutes to calm her nerves and then started the car. Mike was giving her all the feels. It had been a long time since she'd been interested in a man like she was with him. She wasn't very good at relationships, and the few she'd had ended with a broken heart. Rae always said the men she tended to get involved with never really understood her but the right one would. Taylor didn't think there was a "right one" for her. Given her history with men, she didn't know if she'd be able to recognize "the right one" if he appeared right in front of her. She no longer trusted herself when it came to relationships. Mike scared and thrilled her all at the same time.

Mike was whistling when he walked through the back door of the Red Buffalo. He spoke to the staff on his way to his office. He'd had a very pleasant afternoon with Taylor. He was still replaying the events in his mind as he booted up his computer, and was deep in thought when Caleb entered with two cups of coffee. He hadn't even noticed he'd come in until he set the steaming cup down on his desk.

"Oh, hey. Thanks."

"You're welcome. How'd it go at Josh's?"

"Pretty good. I got the wine you asked for and picked out two others to replace the two we talked about."

"Thanks. So, what else did you do this afternoon?"

"What else?"

"Yeah. What else?"

"Not much."

"Interesting. Dana said she saw you going into the ice cream parlor with Taylor."

"Yeah, so?"

"That's not a place you frequent. In fact, you're not a big sweet eater at all."

"What's your point, Aunt Angie?"

Caleb laughed. "How was the ice cream?"

"If you must know, it was good. We got ice cream and then went to the green on the square."

"I know. I was driving in when I saw you put a lip lock on her. How was it?"

"Are you serious?"

"Yup. Inquiring minds want to know. Since my last breakup, I've been pretty much living vicariously through you, hence my question."

"Don't you have something you should be cooking?"

"Nope."

"Well, I'm not telling you shit, so unless you want to talk about something else . . ."

"Okay. Keep the details to yourself. But answer one question."

"What?"

"Do you like her, or are you just playing with her?"

Mike was starting to get annoyed with Caleb's questions. "Why are you asking me that?"

"It's just something my mom said. She thinks Taylor is nice, but she seems a little sad."

"How so?"

"She didn't say. She just said it was something she felt when she met her. You know how Mom is."

Mike thought about his words. Rainbow, Caleb's mother, often sensed things in people that others missed. Mike's mom had once told him Rainbow was an empath. He didn't know if she was or not, but she did have a gift for reading people.

"Let's just say I find her very interesting."

"Good. I like her too." Caleb took a sip of his coffee. "Now, let me tell you about some of the new items I'm adding to the menu next week."

When Taylor got home, she put her bags on the kitchen table, pulled her phone out of her purse, and called Rae, who answered immediately.

"What's wrong?" Rae asked quickly, concern in her voice.

"Hey, girl. How're you doing?"

"I'm fine. What's wrong?"

"Why does anything have to be wrong?"

"Don't make me repeat myself. You never call me in the middle of the day unless it's an emergency."

"That's not true."

"Yes, it is, and you know it. Hang up. I'm gonna FaceTime you."

Taylor huffed when Rae ended the call. A few seconds later, she received a FaceTime request from her.

"Okay, what happened?"

"Nothing happened."

Rae stared at her.

"If you must know—"

"Don't leave out any of the details. I want to know everything." Rae interrupted her.

"All right. The last time I talked to you, Grant and I were going to that party."

"How was it? Any other people of color there or just you two?"

"It was good. There were even a few other people of color there. Grant seemed to enjoy himself. He charmed all the women, as usual."

"Well, he *is* fine as hell."

"Moving on . . . At the party, Mike—"

"Mike is the guy who owns the bar, right?"

"Yeah, that's him."

"What did he do?"

"He didn't do anything. I mean, he did, but nothing bad. I think he might like me or something," Taylor finished lamely.

"Or something? Taylor, either he does, or he doesn't. What did he do to get you all hot, bothered, and confused?"

"I'm not hot, bothered, and confused."

Rae responded to that comment with another blank stare.

"Maybe I'm a little confused. He talked to me quite a bit at the party. Then, he invited us to brunch at his bar, which was really good, by the way. Today, I ran into him at the wine store."

"Sounds like there might be some interest there."

"Yes, but you should see the wine store though. It has a bar in it. The guy who owns it reminds me of James Caan when he was in *The Godfather*. Remember when we snuck and watched it when we were little?"

"I do, but what does that have to do with Mike."

"I'm getting there. Anyway, when I walked in, I saw Mike at the bar. He was getting some wines for his place. He waved for me to come join him and when I did he kissed me on the cheek."

"It sounds like a friendly greeting."

"It was. The wines were good, and Josh, the owner, gave me a free bottle."

"What happened after that?"

"We got ice cream. Well, he got ice cream, and I got frozen custard. Then, we, uh, um went to the square and sat down on a bench."

"Did he do something he *shouldn't have* while you were with him?" Rae asked with concern.

"No. He was the perfect gentleman, right up until I offered him some of my custard."

"What did he do?"

"He offered me a taste of his ice cream."

"He what? How dare he!" Rae replied, faking outrage, and then she laughed.

Taylor hesitated and looked away from the screen.

"Hey! Why are you looking away? What else did he do?"

"He kissed me."

"He kissed you? What kind of kiss? Was it a kiss on the cheek like he gave you at the wine bar? A quick touching of lips?"

"No, it wasn't either of those. It was a full-on kiss. A meeting of the lips, open mouths, tongues, chocolate . . ." Taylor looked away from the screen.

"Ohhh, sounds kind of hot. Wait. Did you say chocolate?"

"I did. He had chocolate ice cream."

"So, what's the problem? Do you not like him?"

"I like him well enough. It's just, well . . . I like him, but I…"

"I know you're scared, sweetie. And I know it's hard for you to trust. But this Mike seems like a nice guy."

"He is. He asked me out to dinner on Sunday."

"Did you say yes?"

"I think I did. To be honest, that kiss kind of messed me up."

"Yeah, but in a *good* way, right?" Rae laughed.

"I guess."

"Good. I'm glad you're getting back out there. And I expect to hear all the juicy details afterward."

"I don't know how juicy the details will be, but I'll let you know how it goes."

"Taylor, hear me when I say this: Make. Them. Juicy." Rae winked. "Now that that's taken care of, what else is going on in the cowboy capital of the world?"

"Not much. I'm going to help Mike's sister-in-law Cheryl get her preserves and stuff ready to go to the farmers market on Saturday."

"That should be fun. I'm guessing they probably have a nice market there."

"I think they do. From what Miss Angie said, it's been around for a while and draws people from all over the state."

They talked a while longer, with Rae making Taylor promise to keep an open mind about Mike before they said their goodbyes.

chapter 15

Taylor arrived at Miss Angie's at 8:00 am the following morning. Miss Angie was waiting out front with Mr. Jackson, who was holding a tote bag and a wooden box. Taylor got out and walked over to the couple. Each greeted her with a hug.

"Good morning, Taylor. How are you?" Jackson asked.

"I'm doing pretty good. How are you two doing this morning?"

"We're doing fine. Nothing to complain about."

"We've got a lot to do today, so I guess we'd better get going," Miss Angie said as she started walking toward Taylor's truck.

Opening the door, and moving the seat forward, she stepped back to allow Jackson to put the tote bag and box on the back seat. Taylor went around to the driver's side and grabbed a plastic container from the back seat, then handed it to Jackson.

"I baked some croissants last night. Some are plain, and some have ham and cheese. I brought you a few."

"Thanks, Taylor. That was mighty sweet of you. I'll have one with my coffee."

He pushed the seat back into its original position and stepped back so Miss Angie could get in. Once in, she put her seat belt on, and he leaned in and kissed her. "See you, ladies, later." He stepped back and closed the door. Taylor and Miss Angie waved at him as she turned down the drive to head back to the highway.

Miss Angie gave her directions to the Knight ranch. It wasn't too far from the Edwards' home so it was a short ride. When they arrived, Dana came out to meet them.

"Hi, Aunt Angie! Hi, Miss Taylor!" Dana took the box from Angie. "Come on in. We've got everything set up. Mom's got coffee ready and was about to make breakfast for us."

"I hope she hasn't done too much. I made croissants." Taylor held up the container.

"You made croissants? Wow!"

"I hope you like them."

"I'm sure we will. Let's get inside so we can eat."

Going into the kitchen Taylor saw PJ, who introduced her to his and Cheryl's other children: fourteen-year-old Preston Knight III, whose middle name was James, so everyone called him Jamie; ten-year-old Chase; and Stevie, who was nine. PJ and the boys were going to help Denton, his younger brother, repair some fencing. As they were leaving, Denton's wife, Lorraine, who was affectionately known as "Red," arrived.

"Hey, ladies!" She walked over to the table and sat down.

"How are you doing today, Red?" Cheryl asked.

"Now that the morning sickness has gone for good, I'm fine."

Dana hugged her. "That's good because Miss Taylor made some goodies for us. We have coffee. Do you want that, tea, or milk?"

"Tea is fine, Dana." She looked at the croissants in the center of the table. "Those look yummy!"

"They are," Miss Angie said as she took another bite of hers. "I've got the spinach one, but I'm planning to have one of those sweet ones next."

"There's plain, chocolate, ham and cheese, and spinach and feta. Taylor made them," Dana told her aunt.

"You made these from scratch?" Red smiled at Taylor.

"Yes, I made them last night. I didn't know how busy we'd get here, so I thought I'd bring snacks."

"That was sweet of you." Red bit into a spinach croissant. "This is good. My baby and I thank you. I swear, I just ate a little bit ago, and I'm hungry again. I may have to have another one."

Cheryl laughed as she sat down next to Taylor.

"Well, you are carrying a Knight. Those babies take all your food and energy whether they're in *or* out of the womb."

"Ain't that the truth!" Red laughed. Then she turned to Taylor. "Taylor, how have you been enjoying Silverton so far?"

"To be honest, I like it more than I thought I would. I thought I might be a little bit bored, but that hasn't been the case at all. My brother enjoyed his visit too."

"Miss Taylor's brother is Grant Sawyer, Aunt Red! Can you believe that?" Dana added.

"Grant Sawyer is your brother?" Red looked at Taylor for confirmation.

"He is."

"Wow. Besides being an amazing football player, he is one fine man!"

"He sure is! He came into the Red Buffalo. Uncle Mike sat him and Taylor in my section. He looks even better in person, and he's super nice."

"I heard he was at your party, Aunt Angie," Red said. "I sure hate I missed that. I would have loved to have met him."

Angie laughed. "I'm not sure if you would have had the chance, Red. Seems like every woman there was in his face at one time or another."

"Even Aunt Rain?"

"No, she and Taylor were probably the only two women who were immune to his charm and good looks. He, on the other hand, like most men, fell right under Rain's spell."

"I teased him about that," Taylor said. "He was quite taken with you too, Miss Angie."

"Ha! That's only because I rescued him a time or two from some of the women, and I kept giving him plates of food whenever something new came out of the kitchen."

Cheryl got up and refilled their coffee cups. "So, Taylor, I hear Mike's been showing you around."

"He has. He took me to a couple of places in the area."

"Where'd you guys go?"

"We went to visit Mr. Knight's gravesite, Hammond, and to the butterfly meadow."

"Did that creepy preacher try to hit on you?" Dana asked.

"He did," she said, shaking her head. "He flirted and threw out a few hints."

Red reached for another croissant. "Albee's twins told my kids, Denny, and Amanda, that they got to hang out with a fairy princess at the butterfly meadow. I'm guessing that was you?"

"I had a shirt with a fairy on it, and they gave me the fairy wings they'd made their dad wear."

"I bet he was a sight in those wings!"

"He was."

"Matilda said she thought Davis liked you because he gave you his card."

"Those kids are pretty observant."

"Yes, they are—sometimes too much. I swear, when they get together with my kids, they can sometimes make me want to pull my hair out."

"They can definitely be more than a handful," Cheryl added.

"Ranger Davis gave you his card?" Dana looked at Taylor. "Are you gonna go out with him?"

"I hadn't thought about it."

"You hadn't thought about it, Miss Taylor? What is there to think about? Ranger Davis is handsome and sweet. He's got a nice body and the cutest dimples. And he always leaves a nice tip when he sits in my section."

"I think you've thought about it," Angie said over her coffee cup. "I just think Mike distracted you."

"Distracted me?" Taylor asked.

"Yes, distracted you. I saw you feeding him those stuffed dates at the party."

"You saw that, huh?" Taylor felt her face grow warm.

"I did. It looked kind of hot. Sort of like that kiss he gave you in the park yesterday."

"You saw that too?"

"I did. And so did a few others. I think I saw one lady cover her kids' eyes."

Everyone laughed.

"I don't know what to say," Taylor murmured.

"I'm just teasing. I'm glad Mike's spending time with you. It's good to see him smiling again."

They continued to talk, and after Red finished her second croissant, they cleared off the table so they could begin working. Getting ready for the market involved putting special labels on the jars of jellies, jams, and preserves, and preparing small gift baskets. Dana, Red, and Taylor placed the labels, and Cheryl and Angie made the gift baskets. While they worked, the women told Taylor a little more about Silverton, Mike, and his ex. The ladies were not a fan of the latter. Cheryl told her that Linda, Mike's ex, had been after him since his divorce, and she pretty much chased away any competition. Red, who'd gone to school with Linda, said that since she couldn't say anything nice, she'd just keep quiet. Angie thought Mike could do better. Dana was also not a fan. According to her, every time Linda came into the Red Buffalo, she expected special treatment.

"It about killed her when she saw him talking to you the other day. After you left, she went up to him, crying and putting on something awful. Thankfully, Uncle Mike didn't cave," Dana told her. Taylor was secretly glad to hear that last part.

They finished up around 1:00 p.m. Cheryl made lunch, and the topic changed to the upcoming rodeo. From what Taylor could tell from the conversation, it was a popular event. In addition to the rodeo competitions, there was an expo and a party in the town square. During the three days it was in town, there were also nightly happenings at all the local bars and restaurants for the people who came in from out of town. Cheryl mentioned that Dana would be singing the national anthem at the opening ceremony.

"That's wonderful, Dana!" Taylor congratulated her.

"She has a beautiful voice." Proud mom Cheryl beamed at her daughter.

"I'm also going to be singing with a local band called Fire Lake," Dana added.

"I've heard them play at the Red Buffalo," Taylor said.

"I have one song I'll be doing and backup vocals."

"I've never been to a rodeo before. I'll have to check it out. I also want to hear you sing with the band."

"I'd love it if you came, Miss Taylor."

"Dana, honey, why don't you show Taylor the outfit you were planning on wearing to the rodeo." Cheryl looked at Taylor. "We have the basic outfit, but we haven't quite figured out how we want to accessorize it yet. Do you mind taking a look at it? Maybe you can help us out."

"Of course."

Dana hurried from the room and returned carrying a garment bag. She unzipped it and took out a pair of black jeans, a matching duster, and a red, white, and blue sequined top.

Taylor looked at the outfit. "What kind of look are you going for? Traditional? Conservative? Edgy?"

"I want a look that's sexy but not too much. And I don't want to it look like I worked too hard at it."

"So, you want a kind of effortlessly sexy, cowgirl look?"

"Yeah, I think that might be it."

"I think we can do that. You're going to be the center of attention when you sing, so might as well give them something to remeber. Are you wearing boots?"

"Oh yes. I have some nice ones."

"Do they have a heel?"

"Yeah, but not too high."

"Nice. We can get the look you're going for. If you're okay with it, I think the outside seam should be split a bit from the bottom up for a few inches. Then you could add a layer of bling like a tuxedo stripe along the outside seams. You can also consider adding a rhinestone star on the back of the jacket. I can help you with all of that if you like."

"That sounds great, Miss Taylor! Mom, what do you think?"

Cheryl nodded. "I think it sounds pretty good—better than what we came up with. Thanks, Taylor."

"Yes, thanks, Miss Taylor," Dana said.

"If you'd like, I can take this with me when I leave, and I can get started on it tomorrow," Taylor offered.

Dana carefully returned her outfit to the garment bag and set it on a chair at the end of the table. "I can't wait for my friends to see my outfit. They're going to be surprised when they see me in it."

"Would there be one friend, in particular, you want to see your outfit?" Red asked.

"Maybe, but he might not notice me."

"Trust me, sweetheart, he'll notice," Red told her. "Men tend to get a little more attentive when they have competition. Having all those rodeo cowboys around might serve to be a wake-up call for him."

"Ahhh." Taylor nodded. "So that's why we're going with the glamourous I-woke-up-this-way look. That young man who's been ignoring you will definitely take notice when he sees you in this outfit."

"Or he will take a number and stand in line." Angie laughed. She high-fived Red and they all started laughing.

chapter 16

It was Sunday. Mike was due to arrive in two hours, and Taylor still hadn't decided what she was going to wear. She'd showered and undid the two-strand twists she'd put her locs in earlier when she'd washed her hair and after drying they had formed into loose curls. She'd been standing in front of her closet for a full five minutes when the phone rang. Looking at at the screen she smiled before answering.

"You have excellent timing!" Taylor said excitedly.

"What? No hello for your best friend?"

She imagined Rae smirking on the other end. "Hello, best friend. You have excellent timing."

"Of course I do, I'm your best friend. And if I know you as well as I think I do, you're either trying to figure out how to weasel out of your date or you're still trying to decide what to wear."

"I hate you."

"I know you do, sweetie. Which is it?"

"I'm trying to put together an outfit. Mike's picking me up and taking me to dinner at his place."

"Oh, is he? Sounds like this evening is ripe with possibilities."

"No. No possibilities. I'm not trying to get caught up in anything when I'm not planning on staying here."

"Yup. Possibilities."

"Yup. Still hate you."

"What are you planning on wearing?"

"I was thinking about wearing a silver and black corset top with a black cardigan and black jeans."

"How are you wearing your hair?"

"I did a twist-out on my locs, and I'm either putting them in a high pony, half up and half down, or a messy bun."

"Sounds good. Based on what you just told me, sounds like you just might have some juicy details to share after all."

"Maybe. Maybe not. When I was over at Cheryl's place the other day, she, Miss Angie, and Red, the other sister-in-law, had plenty to say about Mike and his ex."

"Any red flags?"

"No. They seemed to dislike the ex-girlfriend quite a bit. They made a point to tell me that he was done with her."

"Really. Interesting. What else did they say?"

"There was a fair amount of teasing after that. Miss Angie saw Mike kiss me in the park."

"I don't know these women, but I think I like them. Like me, they seem to think he likes you. Try to keep an open mind this evening."

"I can't make any promises, but I'll try."

"That's a start. I'll let you get back to getting ready. Have fun tonight. Love you. Talk to you later."

"Love you too. Bye." Taylor got dressed and finished her makeup. She still had about twenty minutes before Mike got there. She decided to have a glass of wine while she waited.

"Are you sure you don't want me to make dinner for you?" Caleb asked Mike as they headed to the checkout line at the market.

"I'm sure." Irritated, Mike repeated the same answer to what seemed like Caleb's fifth time asking him the same question.

"I mean, it'll be pretty easy to do with what you have here in the basket."

"No, I got it. I *can* cook you know."

"Yeah, I know, but you might get distracted and ruin the meal." Caleb was sure that was exactly what would happen.

"I won't."

"How do you know you won't?"

"I *won't*. Plus, I'm not doing anything fancy. It's just steak, salad, and bread."

"At least let me pick the wine."

"Okay, if it will shut you up."

"I know what kind of bourbon she likes, but how is she about her wine?"

"She likes pinot noirs."

"They don't have a good selection here, so we'll need to go to the wine store."

"You're making this into a lot of work."

"I am, but Taylor's worth it."

"We'll see." Mike took his items from the basket and put them on the conveyor belt.

"Hello, Mike, Caleb. Will that be cash, credit, or debit?"

Sally, the cashier, was the mother of one of the waitresses who worked at the Red Buffalo. She'd been trying to get Caleb to go out with her, but he refused. Davis and Mike teased him about the creative ways she'd tried to entice him into changing his mind. Caleb thought she was a barracuda, and he wasn't willing to go out with her to put that theory to the test.

"What are you up to this evening, Caleb? Can I interest you in a movie?"

"Not much, just work."

"If you want to have the night off and go to the movies, I can help you with the paperwork tomorrow," Mike said, smirking when he met Caleb's glare.

"No, I need to take care of it today. Also, I need to finish the menu planning for next week. Sally, thanks for the offer, but I have to decline."

"Oh well, maybe next time. Consider it an open invitation," she replied, winking at him as she spoke.

"Uh, thanks."

"You boys have a nice afternoon." Sally tore the receipt from the register and handed it to Mike.

Mike and Caleb walked out of the market and crossed the street to go to the wine store.

"Was that necessary?" Caleb side-eyed Mike.

"No, but it was fun."

"Let's get your wine. You're going to need it in case you fuck up the meal."

"Will you stop saying that? *I'm not going to fuck up this meal!*" Mike felt himself going from irritated to angry. He wanted the evening to go well, but Caleb was right—the chances of getting distracted around Taylor were pretty high. But Caleb harping on that fact was *not* what he wanted to hear.

"Hey, fellas!" Josh greeted them as they walked into the wine store. "This is twice in one week, Mike. And you brought Caleb. What brings you two here today?"

"Mike has a date. He's making dinner and needs a good wine in case he fucks up the meal."

Mike huffed.

"Mike has a *date*? Anybody I know?"

"You might," Caleb said. "She was in here a few days ago."

"She was?"

"Yeah. You might remember her. She's a tall, curvy, honey-colored beauty with auburn locs that look like braids. Oh, and she has a nice smile."

Mike rolled his eyes as Caleb spoke.

"Oh yeah, I remember her. She came in the other day when Mike was here. That's a pretty good description of her. How did you get her to go out with you, Mike?"

"I *asked*, and she said *yes*."

Caleb snickered. "More like he cornered her when she first got to town and didn't give anyone else a chance."

"I don't blame you, Mike. I would have done the same thing if I saw her first," Josh said. "What kind of wine are you looking for? I want to make sure I get you a good one. That way, if you bomb the date, there's a fifty-fifty chance she might go out with me." All three men laughed.

chapter 17

Groceries and wine in the back seat of the truck cab, Mike pulled up in front of Taylor's house. He'd been looking forward to this date since he'd asked her out. He hadn't seen her since then, which was surprising, given the size of the town they lived in. As he walked up the stairs to the porch, he could hear music playing. He knocked on the door.

"Hey, Mike. How are you this evening?" Taylor opened the screen and stepped back to let him in.

"Hi, Taylor. I'm good."

He was planning on saying more but found his brain seemed to have slowed down when he allowed his eyes to take her in. She looked amazing. Her hair was pulled up into a messy bun that highlighted the structure of her face. Her brown eyes sparkled mischievously as if she held a secret, and her lush lips were covered with dark berry lipstick. Around her neck, she wore a choker that had a black stone in the middle, and on her ears were silver and black earrings. What tied his tongue was the top she had on. It looked like a corset, and it hugged her waist and made him want to reach out, pull her close, and kiss her. So, he did.

"I hope you're hungry, and I hope you're ready to go," he breathed out.

"I am. Let me grab my sweater, and then we can leave."

The drive to Mike's place was short. On the way, he told her that he and his father and brothers built the house and the barn.

"Do you have horses?"

"I do. I have four. Two belong to my kids. They like to ride when they're here. I can take you to the barn to see them after dinner if you'd like."

"I would, thanks."

Mike grabbed the grocery bags out of the back of the cab, and they walked toward the porch. The house was a single-story ranch style and was larger than a cottage but smaller than a mansion. The inside looked to be an open floor plan with hardwood floors. She followed him into the kitchen, which was large and modern. He set the bags on the counter.

"Have a seat." He pointed to the chairs on the other side of the counter. "Would you care for a drink?"

"I would. What do you have?"

"I have beer, wine, and whiskey, and I think there's some tea in the refrigerator."

"I'll have wine please."

He took a wineglass out of a nearby cabinet and placed it in front of her. Then he pulled a bottle of wine from one of the grocery bags, reached for a corkscrew in a nearby drawer to open it, and poured her a glass. He then reached into the refrigerator and grabbed a beer for himself. He raised the beer in toast after taking the top off.

"Here's to a great dinner and even better company."

"Here, here." She clinked her glass to his bottle and watched him raise the bottle to his mouth. She took a tentative sip from her glass as she saw the bottle touch his lips.

"How's the wine?" he asked.

Taylor swirled the wine around in her glass. "It's good."

"I remembered you mentioning Pinots. I'm glad you like it."

"I'm glad you remembered." She looked at him as she raised her glass for another sip. "What are we having for dinner?"

"A steak salad—blue cheese or cheddar crumbles optional—bread, and dessert. The dessert is courtesy of Caleb."

"Ooohh, Caleb made dessert?"

"He did. It's his mom's honey cake."

"I can't wait to try it."

"Hey, wait a minute. You didn't get this excited when I told you I was making dinner." He looked at her with a pretend frown.

"I know, Mike, and I can't wait to try your cooking. I'm *sure* it'll be good too."

"Okay, now you're just being patronizing."

"Is that what you think I'm doing?" Taylor tried to keep from laughing.

"Maybe. I'm not sure if I should feed you or not. I may even withhold the rest of this wine Josh gave me and let you walk home."

"Aww, Mike, don't be that way."

"After you just insulted my cooking, give me a reason not to." He gave her a heated look.

She walked around the counter and stood in front of him. "How about you refill my glass and fix dinner, and I'll feed you dessert."

He tried to look as if he were giving her words serious consideration, and then he smiled, which amped up his sexiness.

"I guess that'll be okay."

The game, it would seem, was on. Mike's signals were coming in loud and clear. So were hers.

They had just sat down to eat when it began to rain. What had started as a light drizzle had gradually increased to a summer shower. The conversation at dinner was light and funny. Taylor told him about some of the things she and her best friend had gotten into while growing up, and Mike told her stories about his brothers, Caleb, and Davis. They'd finished eating when Mike asked her about the meal.

"What's the verdict? Was it okay, or are you still hungry?"

"It was good."

"That's a relief."

"Why do you say that?"

"Caleb and Josh thought I was going to mess up the meal."

"Really? They thought you were going to mess this up?"

"They did. Excuse my language, but Caleb's exact words were, 'You better get a good wine in case you fuck up the meal.'"

Taylor found that funny, and after she stopped laughing, she said, "Well, you can tell them you did a good job and I enjoyed it."

"I'm glad you did. I was getting a bit concerned after your earlier comments."

"Hey now, we just had a good meal. Let's not drag up old stuff," Taylor said playfully. "How about we clean up and get to dessert."

"Sounds good to me."

They stood in front of the sink, doing the dishes. She washed and rinsed, and he dried them and put them away. The rain shower had turned into a downpour. It was not torrential, but it looked like it might change to that at any time. Taylor worriedly looked out of the window above the sink as she washed a plate.

"It's really coming down out there." She hoped it didn't turn into a full-on storm. She didn't like storms. They scared her and made her nervous.

"It does sound like it's getting worse," Mike agreed. "We get a lot of these late spring and summer storms that start quickly and end just as fast. This one looks and sounds like it may last a little longer than that. It might even turn into one of those storms the old-timers refer to as 'turd floaters.'"

"Turd floater?" Taylor looked at him. "Does that mean what I think it means?"

"Yeah, probably." Mike laughed. "There are a lot of colorful sayings around here. The longer you're here, the more you'll become acquainted with them." Mike's phone rang. He lifted it off the counter, saw who was calling, and answered.

"Hey, Caleb. Calling to gloat?"

"That depends. Did she like the wine?"

"She did."

"Then I'm calling to gloat. I'm also calling to tell you about the bridge over Sackett Creek."

"What about it?"

"It washed out. One of the columns collapsed. They're waiting for the rain to let up before they go in and assess the damage."

"Wow. The county was planning to work on that bridge this summer. I guess it was in worse shape than they originally thought. Was anyone hurt?"

"No, thankfully. I just wanted to let you know, so you'd know to take the back road when you head back into town."

"Thanks, man."

"No problem. I'll let you get back to your date. Remember, it if doesn't go well, you have the wine, and Taylor has the option to go out with me, Josh"—Caleb chuckled—"or Davis."

"Bye, fool." Mike ended the call. He turned toward Taylor.

"I have some bad news and some not-so-bad news."

"I'll take the bad news first."

"The bridge over Sackett Creek washed out."

"Was anyone hurt?"

"No. The not-so-bad news is that there is a back road that leads into town. The road is narrow and pretty rough on a dry day, but when it rains, it's a little more challenging to navigate. If you're okay with it, I'd prefer to take you home in the morning, instead of tonight. It will be a little easier going then."

"I'm okay with going home tomorrow if it's not too much of an imposition."

"It's not. Let's finish these dishes, and then I can put clean sheets on the bed."

"You don't have to do that, Mike. If you give me some linen, I can sleep on the couch."

"No, I was going to change them today anyway. I stripped the beds this morning and never got around to making them back up. I'll take the couch or make up one of the other beds."

"Okay, if you're sure."

"I'm sure."

When the dishes were done, Taylor followed Mike down the hall to his room. It was large, and the dark furniture looked heavy and solid. The walls were a smoky-blue color. The dresser held a wooden tray and a few framed pictures. The bed was a California king that sat on a platform, and just as he'd said, the bed was stripped with folded linens stacked at the foot. A picture flashed in her mind of her and Mike in the bed. They were naked, and he was –. She shook her head to clear it of the image. With the storm brewing outside, that was the last thing she needed to think about.

"Are you sure you want to give up this big bed for the couch?"

"I'm sure. Besides, the sofa's not bad."

"Well let's get this made up."

"Sure thing. And since you're staying over, how about we watch a movie after we get done with this?"

"A movie it is."

They made quick work of getting the bed ready, then went to the den just off from the kitchen. Mike grabbed the wine and the dessert so they could have it while they watched the movie.

"The remote is in the cabinet to the left of the TV," he told her.

Taylor stood in front of the cabinet, trying to decide what movie to watch when she saw some photo albums on a nearby bookshelf. Mike walked in and set the wine on the coffee table in front of the sofa before coming to stand beside her.

"Find anything you like?"

"Not yet. I was trying to decide when I saw your photo albums. Do you mind if I look at them?"

"That would depend."

"On what?"

"On how hard you plan on laughing at some of the pictures in there."

She smiled. "I'll try to keep the laughter to a minimum."

"In that case, help yourself. Grab a couple of the albums, and I'll get our glasses."

The next hour was spent laughing and drinking wine. Mike's mother had been a beautiful woman. Taylor had thought Preston Knight, Sr. was a silver fox when she met him and wasn't surprised to see he'd been a straight up hunk back in the day. There was a picture of him and Jackson in their Marine Corps dress uniform and Hawk, Mike's godfather, in his Navy dress uniform. They were each handsome men in their own right, but their uniforms made them even more so. There were pictures of Mike with his brothers and with Caleb and Davis. One was of Mike with the latter two when they might have been six or seven years old. They were carrying football gear and eating ice cream cones. They looked adorable. Other pictures in the albums were of a teenage Mike, followed by him with his children. There were pictures of him holding them as newborns up to what she guessed to be their current age. Both bore a strong resemblance to Mike. His son looked to be a carbon copy of Mike from some of the earlier pictures she'd seen. The rain continued to fall as they viewed the albums.

"I'm ready for cake now. How about you?" Taylor asked.

"That depends on whether you're planning to keep your promise to feed it to me."

"I always keep my promises, Mike." Taylor smiled.

He went to the kitchen and returned with two slices of cake and placed them on the coffee table in front of the couch. She put the album on the side table, then leaned toward the table and picked up a saucer and fork. She sliced into the cake and held a piece to his mouth. Mike smiled and opened his mouth to receive it.

"How is it?"

"Good as always. Keep it coming."

Taylor laughed. She went to feed him another piece, then at the last minute, ate it herself.

"Hey, you're supposed to be feeding that to me."

"I know, but it looked good, and you looked like you were enjoying it, so I wanted a taste. By the way, this is really good."

"I know. More please."

She laughed and fed him the entire slice.

"Thank you. Now I have a surprise for you," Mike said.

"Oh yeah? What is it?"

Mike got up from the couch and went into the kitchen. On the way back he said, "Close your eyes."

"Okay, they're closed."

Mike placed something near her lips, and Taylor opened her mouth, tasting that he'd added some fresh strawberries and cream to the cake.

"Ooohh, this is even better."

"I thought you might like it. That's how my mom used to serve it."

"Does that mean I need to feed you another slice so you can taste the strawberries?"

"No, you'll do," Mike whispered before he leaned over and kissed her. "Mmm, just like I remember."

Taylor was a little surprised by the kiss. They'd been flirting off and on all evening, but this was the first move he'd made. She wondered if it was because she was spending the night. As if sensing her confusion, Mike pulled away and leaned back.

"So, you ate a good meal, drank good wine, and got to see some of my more embarrassing life's moments in pictures. Other than being stuck here with me for the evening, I'd call it a win."

"I wouldn't call it being stuck, but I definitely would call it a win."

"I'm glad you think so. I would have had to try to change your mind if you didn't." He winked at her.

"How about we go ahead and pick a movie?"

They agreed on an action movie, but half an hour into it, Taylor fell asleep. When she woke, she saw the credits rolling and she was cuddled up next to Mike, covered by the throw that had been on the back of the couch. She slowly sat up.

"I guess I must have been tired. How was the movie?"

"I think it was good, although it was hard to hear over your snoring."

"Snoring? You're lying!"

He started laughing. "I'm kidding. Your snoring wasn't that loud."

"What?" she shouted.

"Sorry, I couldn't resist. The movie was good. And no, you weren't snoring. You did drool a little though." He was trying not to laugh when he added that last bit.

Taylor laughed and hit him with one of the pillows. He got up and held his hand out.

"Come on, let's get you settled so you can get back to sleep."

Mike held her hand as she walked unsteadily with him back to his room. He turned on the lamp next to the bed.

"There are towels in the cabinet next to the sink and extra toothbrushes in the drawer. There are also blankets in the hall linen closet if you need one." He walked over to the dresser and opened a drawer. "And here's something for you to sleep in." He handed her a T-shirt, boxer shorts, and a pair of socks.

"Thanks," she responded sleepily.

He leaned down and kissed her on the cheek. "Sleep sweet, Taylor."

"You too, Mike."

He left, closing the door behind him.

Taylor changed into the clothes he'd given her, then went into the bathroom, where she brushed her teeth and washed her face. She sat on the side of the bed and put on the socks, before turning the light off and getting under the covers. As she listened to the rain, her mind replayed the last few hours. She'd had a good time with Mike. He was funny, and his big, hard body had felt good as she lay against him on the couch. She could have stayed there all night.

She knew without a doubt that if she'd allowed it, they wouldn't have been sitting next to each other watching movies. Mike's kisses, desire-filled glances, and touch had awakened dormant feelings in her. Feelings she had tried to put to rest when she'd decided celibacy was needed after her last breakup. It had been so bad, she felt she needed a pause. She figured it would help her focus on herself and get a better perspective on what she wanted and how to make better choices when it came to men. The celibacy hadn't been much of a struggle until she came to Silverton and met Mike. Without knowing it, he'd put her no-sex status in jeopardy in just a few weeks.

chapter 18

The steady downpour had become a full-blown storm, complete with thunder and lightning. It was the sound of thunder that caused Taylor to wake up with a start. Her heart was pounding as she sat up and tried to get her bearings in the unfamiliar bedroom. She immediately started doing the deep breathing exercises she'd learned as a child to slow her heart rate. She hated storms. Her fear of storms and the bad memories that accompanied them had been with her since childhood. If she'd been back home, she would have lit up a joint or eaten a gummy to help her relax. Since she wasn't, she decided the next best thing would be to go check out Mike's liquor stash. Hopefully, he had something strong she could use to help dull the anxiety, pain, and sadness that always came with storms.

She turned on the bedside lamp, pulled back the covers, and got out of bed. She could hear the rain pelt the roof and sides of the house as she walked the short distance down the hall to the kitchen. If she was quiet enough, he wouldn't hear her rummaging through his cabinets. She opened the one she'd seen Mike put the glasses in. As soon as she had a glass in her hand, a loud clap of thunder sounded. Nerves already on edge, she let out a scream, and the glass slipped from her hand and shattered on the floor.

"Taylor? What's going on? Are you okay?" A shirtless Mike appeared in the doorway.

She looked at him, then down at the broken glass, and she began to cry. Careful to avoid broken glass shards, he rushed over to where she stood. He gently ran his hands up and down her arms in an effort to calm her.

"Hey. Hey now, what's all this?" he asked softly.

"I'm sorry. It's the storm. They, um, they make me nervous. I c-c-came in here to get something to drink, and the thunder kind of scared me."

Mike pulled her close and wrapped his arms around her. He rubbed her back in slow steady movements.

"Shh, it's okay," he said, trying to soothe her. "Storms out here can be pretty intense if you're not used to them." They stayed that way for long minutes until Taylor's breathing slowed and her tears slowed. "How about you go back to bed, and I'll fix something to help you sleep."

"You don't have to do that. I'll be fine." Embarrassed, she found herself unable to look up at him.

"I want to. I'll take you, so I don't have to worry about you stepping on any glass."

"What about you?"

"I'll be fine. We'll go around the other side of the kitchen to the back hallway."

With that, Mike effortlessly picked her up. Her arms went around his neck as he carried her back to his bedroom. Along the way, she noticed a few things about him. He was strong. She wasn't a small person, and he had no problem picking her up. His hair was sleep-tousled, and he was shirtless. The feel of his warm skin had a calming effect on her as she absently began to run her fingers through the hair at the nape of his neck and the back of his head. When they reached his room, Mike laid her gently on the bed.

"I'm going to sweep up the glass, then I'll be right back. Are you sure you're okay?"

"I'm fine. Really. Thank you."

He looked at her for a long minute before he turned and went back to the kitchen. After he disappeared, Taylor jumped out of bed and ran into the bathroom. She took a towel out of the linen closet and washed her face. As she stared at her reflection in the mirror, she saw the tear-stained face of a little girl who never quite got over her fear of storms. Mike probably thought she was a nutjob. He'd been sweet, but that didn't mean he thought her behavior was normal. For all she knew, he was probably wondering how fast he could get her back to her place before morning.

Mike had been dreaming about making love to Taylor when he heard her scream, followed by the sound of glass breaking. He got up from the sofa bed and ran into the kitchen to find a visibly shaken Taylor, in tears with broken glass on the floor in front of her. He immediately went over to her and thankfully managed to avoid stepping on any glass shards as he crossed the kitchen. Seeing her tears tugged at his heart, as he gathered her in his arms and held her until she calmed.

Without thinking about it, he picked her up and took her back to bed. Her arms went around his neck, and he could feel the smooth, soft skin of her bare legs as he carried her. He didn't think she realized she was playing with his hair. Both the touch of her skin and the feel of her fingers felt so good. He found himself wondering what it would feel like if he were taking her to his bed, touching every inch of her, and covering her body with his own instead of putting her to bed alone with a hot toddy.

Forcing himself out of that daydream, he swept up the broken glass, put his T-shirt back on, and waited for the kettle to heat up. When it was ready, he poured the hot water into a mug and added a decaf green tea bag, honey, and a shot of whiskey. When the tea had steeped enough, he removed the tea bag and carried the mug to Taylor.

Taylor was sitting up with her back against the headboard when Mike came back. He didn't say anything about what happened. He just handed her the mug and sat down on the side of the bed.

"Thanks," she said.

Her eyes were red-rimmed and a little swollen from crying, but other than that, she seemed okay. He also noticed she was avoiding eye contact with him. He reached out, cupped her cheek, and raised her head, forcing her to look at him.

"How are you feeling?"

"Better." She raised the mug to her lips.

"I should have told you about the storms. I didn't think this one would be more than a heavy downpour."

"You don't have to apologize. I have a long history with storms."

"You want to talk about it?"

"No, I don't want to bore you with my issues."

"Why don't you let me be the judge of that? Mind if I join you?"

Taylor shook her head, and Mike walked around to the other side of the bed and sat next to her. She took another sip of tea to stall for time, gathering her thoughts before she began to speak.

"Do you remember me telling you about being adopted?"

"Yes."

"Daniel Sawyer, the man I call Poppy, was my father's best friend. Poppy and my dad were both drafted and sent to Vietnam. Poppy was injured and sent home a few months before my dad's tour was over. While Poppy was in the States, my dad was killed in action." She paused and took a deep breath. "My mom and dad had known each other practically their whole lives, having met in elementary school. Mom used to tell me she loved my father from the moment she saw him building a house out of popsicle sticks in art class." Taylor laughed softly.

"Fast-forward, my dad grows up and becomes a carpenter. Poppy told me he was a true craftsman, and his work was always in demand. My mother was an artist. Mostly portraits done in charcoals and oils. Both were gifted with incredible talent. They had been married for four years before they had me." The tears started to flow again. Mike reached over and covered her hand with his.

"After Daddy died, my mom changed," she recounted in a soft voice. "She became really sad and started to spend more time in bed each day. Mimi and Poppy used to come over a lot to check on us to make sure we didn't need anything. One day, about six months after my father was killed, I came home from school, completely drenched. It had started to rain while I was on my way home. Storms always scared me, so I hurried. I walked into the house and noticed the lights weren't on. I thought maybe it was because the storm had knocked the power out." The tears began to increase. Mike handed her a few tissues from the box on the nightstand. "Thanks," she said, voice a little above a whisper. Softly, she continued her story.

"I went to see if Mom was in her studio, but she wasn't there. I don't know why, but for some reason, I decided to go to her room." She sobbed. "And that's where I found her. At first, I thought she was sleeping. I went over to the bed and tried to wake her up. She was so cold, and when I couldn't get her to, I got scared and ran next door to our neighbor's house to get help." She wiped her eyes. "But I was too late. Mama had taken a bottle of sleeping pills. She left me a letter saying she loved me, but she just couldn't live without Daddy. Afterward, Daniel and Lily Sawyer didn't waste any time starting the process of adopting me. My first name is Rosamunde, but no one calls me that. Taylor was my birth parents' last name. When the adoption went through, they hyphenated my last name to keep the connection to my parents, and I insisted everyone call me Taylor as a way to honor them," she gave Mike a sad smile.

"I know now that Mama was grieving and had slipped into a deep depression that she never escaped. But storms always remind me of that terrible day, and I sometimes struggle when the memories hit." She closed her eyes to try to stop the flow of tears.

Mike reached over, removed the mug from her trembling hands, and set it on the nightstand. Then he lay down and pulled Taylor down next to him. He held her and stroked her back as her head lay on his chest. They lay there in silence, listening to the rain intermixed with the soft sound of Taylor crying. From time to time, Mike would kiss her temple. His warmth and quiet strength settled over her like a blanket. His even breathing and the beating of his heart were a soothing lullaby to her senses. Taylor couldn't remember feeling so safe during a storm as she drifted off into a peaceful sleep.

A few hours later, Taylor woke up a second time that night, this time for a very different reason. She'd been sleeping with her back pressed against Mike's chest. His hands were roaming her body as he kissed her shoulder and the back of her neck. Feeling his breath against her skin as his hands touched her, her body started to react immediately. Her back arched as she shifted her body until she was face-to-face with Mike, and then she kissed him. Her hands moved along the contours of his body. He pulled her under him, and she could see the silent question in his eyes. Taylor stretched up toward him and kissed him.

"Yes," she whispered.

"Are you sure?"

She leaned back against the pillows. "Yes. I want this. But I need to tell you something first."

"Tell me what?"

"I've been celibate for a while."

"And?"

"And nothing. I just wanted you to know."

Mike opened the drawer of the nightstand, pulled out a condom, and smiled. "I guess I better make it worth the wait then, huh?"

Mike was surprised to hear Taylor was celibate. As beautiful and sweet as she was, he'd also been surprised she was single. It had been a rough night for her, and he was determined to make it better. He removed her T-shirt, then eased back and looked at her, taking in her smooth brown skin that reminded him of honey, her soft, lush lips, and her eyes that simultaneously held warmth and shadows. He gently brushed the locs back from her face, leaned forward, and took her lips in a deep, sensual kiss. His hands moved slowly across her shoulders and made their way to her breasts. He massaged them and teased her nipples into aching peaks, his powerful, work-worn hands increasing her pleasure. Lowering his head, he took one chocolate tip into his mouth and teased it with his tongue as he sucked vigorously.

Her breasts were very sensitive, and Taylor felt herself getting wet immediately at his touch. She began to explore Mike's body as he feasted on hers. Her hands glided along his back, tracing the solid muscles, then she trailed her fingertips along the curve of his firm ass. Feeling the hardness of his erection against her thigh, she reached between them and wrapped her hand around it. She heard a hitch in his breathing as she slowly slid her hand up and down his throbbing shaft.

Mike was enjoying Taylor's hands. Her touch was like silk on his cock. He would have loved to let her continue, but that would have to wait for a later time. This night was all about her. He slid the shorts down her body and gave her a wicked smile as he traced the landing strip on her pubic bone. Moving his hand farther down, he began to gently rub her already slick labia. His fingers rubbed her essence over her bud, and he tapped it gently, causing Taylor to buck forward. Then, he positioned himself between her legs and softly blew on her clit before covering it with a kiss and beginning a passionate assault with his tongue.

Taylor began to squirm. The sexy sounds she made were an encouragement to him as he made it as good for her as he could. He inserted two fingers into her drenched warmth, turned them upward, applied a bit of pressure, and was rewarded with a loud, long moan as an orgasm shook her body. He pressed another kiss to her, then reached for the condom and put it on.

Having a bit of trouble breathing as Mike's fingers and lips wreaked all types of havoc on her body, Taylor gripped his head and felt the silkiness of his hair as he made her body tingle. *Damn,* she thought, as her body thrummed with pleasure. *If he does this with his hands and mouth, what the hell is he gonna do to me with his dick?*

After sheathing himself, Mike moved up and plunged into Taylor's warmth. Her still-pulsating pussy was hot, tight, and slick. *Fuck, that's good.* He moved back and then thrust his hips forward, farther into her soaking wetness. With each stroke, he felt himself getting closer to the edge. He leaned down and gave Taylor a slow, hot, hungry kiss. Her passion matched his, kiss for kiss and stroke for stroke. He reached one hand between them and began to play with her clit causing an intoxicating wave to take over her body as she was hit with another orgasm. Mike watched Taylor as he felt the walls of her pussy clench around his cock. As she relaxed slightly, he whispered, "Taylor, open your eyes."

Taylor opened them but found it hard to focus. Looking at Mike as he slid in and out of her added another level of sensation to what she was already feeling. It was as intense as it was hot. He quickened his pace, and she heard herself call out his name loudly as she climaxed. Mike joined her in her release.

Damn, Mike thought as he kissed Taylor, then buried his face in the side of her neck. He wanted to collapse in her sweetness as he savored the moment before getting up to discard the condom and get a warm towel for Taylor. Back into bed, he pulled her close and moved her until she lay on top of him, wrapping her in his arms. The intimacy of the skin-to-skin contact seemed to forge a connection between the two of them as their breathing slowed and returned to normal.

chapter 19

"Morning, Rosebud." Mike's sexy voice woke her.
"Rosebud?"
"Yup, I'm calling you Rosebud from now on."
"Why?"
"Because I like it. Because of that rose tattoo I didn't know you had, and because you opened like a beautiful flower last night. Okay, that last bit was cheesy, but it's true."

Taylor laughed. "Good morning." She touched his face as she looked into his sleepy eyes. "Thank you for last night."

"No thanks needed. I'm glad I was here for you." He kissed her.

She kissed him back before moving away from him. "Much as I would like this to continue, I need to go to the bathroom."

"If you insist. But since you're up, how about I fix breakfast?"

"Sounds good."

They both got out of bed, and Mike slapped her on the ass as she walked past him. She let out a squeak of surprise.

"I'm hungry, so don't take all day." He smiled as he pulled clothes from a dresser drawer. He tossed her another T-shirt and a pair of boxers and left the room.

"I hurried, but I'm gonna be upset if there's no coffee," Taylor called out as she walked into the kitchen.

Mike was standing in front of the stove. He had on a pair of worn, loose-fitting jeans and an old T-shirt. She could see the movement of his muscles as he turned toward her, and his hair was still damp from his shower. She could see silver sprinkled throughout what looked like the start of a beard. He smiled and it stirred up the memory of last night. He'd thoroughly given her what she'd been missing during her period of sexual lockdown, and then some. He knew how to work what he had, and as promised, he'd made it worth the wait.

"Coffee's ready. The cups are in that cabinet over there. Will you pour me one too?"

"Sure." She smiled back at him.

They were sharing kisses and engaging in a little flirting after breakfast when they heard a knock at the door. Mike excused himself and got up to answer.

"PJ, D, come on in."

"Morning. How's it going?" PJ patted him on the back as he entered.

"Pretty good. You?"

"Good."

"I'm good. I'd be better if Red hadn't had me up all night complaining about her back hurting," Denton complained.

"You should be used to that by now. It's not like this is your first kid."

"I know, but she seems to be more demanding with this one."

"Well, hear me when I say this, little brother: don't let her hear *you* say that. You might not like the outcome."

"Yeah, yeah. Got any coffee?"

"Fresh pot in the kitchen. So what brings you two over this morning?" Mike asked as he led the way to the kitchen.

"We tried to call you, but with the power being out, the calls probably didn't go through. A tree fell on Uncle Jack's porch, and he needs help removing it. We stopped by to see if—" PJ stopped abruptly when he saw Taylor sitting on a stool at the counter. Her locs were loose, and she was holding a coffee mug. Denton, who was walking behind him, bumped into him. He was about to say something, but his surprise when he saw Taylor kept him silent. PJ cleared his throat.

"Um, good morning, Taylor."

"Good morning, PJ, Denton." Taylor smiled as she greeted the two men.

Denton continued to stare and nodded in response to her greeting.

"Help yourself to the coffee," Mike said as he walked over to Taylor. "I'm sorry, but we're going to have to leave a little sooner than planned. A tree fell on Uncle Jack's porch. I need to go help them clear it. We'll drop you home on the way."

"Okay, I'll go get dressed." She hopped down from the stool and went to the bedroom.

"You and Taylor, huh?" PJ patted him on the back as he watched Taylor leave the room. "I like her. Cheryl and the kids do too. Be warned though, Chase has a crush on her, so you may have some competition." He laughed.

Denton seemed to have found his voice after coming into the room and finding Taylor there.

"So, when did this happen? I thought you were taking a break from dating after all that drama with Linda."

"D, you're being awful nosy right now," Mike pointed out. PJ thought that was funny too, which caused him to keep laughing.

Denton took a quick look at PJ, then turned back to Mike. "I like Taylor too. She was nice to Pop, and she's been real sweet to Red. Somebody's got to look out for her."

"And that somebody has to be you?" Mike replied.

"Well, no, not necessarily but—"

"Let me stop you there. I like her, and we enjoy spending time together. And that's all I'm going to say on the matter."

"Just saying." Denton gave him a pointed look.

PJ drove and Denton sat in the front with him. Mike held Taylor's hand as sat close together in the back seat. She was a little disappointed that she and Mike couldn't go one more round before she went home. Taylor thought the ride back to her house was going to be awkward. However, the ride back was anything but. It was actually funny. PJ joked about the fact that Mike was going to have to have a talk with Chase, seeing as he kept Taylor out all night.

"He's a boy in the throes of his first crush. He may try to fight you for her. I wouldn't advise it though, because he's strong as a bull, and he might give your old ass a run for your money."

"If he fights anything like you did at that age, I got nothing to worry about." Mike countered.

Not to be left out, Denton chimed in. "Maybe you should just let Taylor talk to him and let him down easy. Taylor, tell Chase you chose Mike over him because you didn't want to hurt his feelings. You know, on account of him being so old and all."

Laughing, Taylor said. "How about I lead with, 'Messing with you is against the law and I don't want to go to jail'?"

PJ snickered. "That argument won't wash, Taylor. If that were the case, most would just congratulate him on having good taste in women."

The laughter and banter continued until they reached Taylor's house. Climbing out of the truck, she said goodbye to PJ and Denton before Mike walked her to the door. After opening the screen door and unlocking the main door, she looked up at Mike.

"Did you have any plans for today?" he asked.

"No. I was just going to work on some pieces."

"I'll give you a call when we get done."

"Okay. Be careful."

"I will."

With that, Taylor thought he was going to go back to the truck, but he didn't. He wrapped his arm around her waist and pulled her toward him.

"I look forward to seeing you later today." He kissed her. Not a cute, "see you later" peck on the lips but a kiss between lovers. She stumbled back a bit when he let her go. "Bye, Rosebud." He winked at her and sauntered back to the truck. He got in and lowered the window. All three men smiled and waved as they drove off.

chapter 20

A week had passed since the night of the storm, and since then Taylor and Mike had spent a lot of time together. She'd gone to the Red Buffalo to hear Fire Lake again and got a chance to hear Dana sing when she sat in with the band for a few songs. She had a beautiful voice, and judging by the response of the bar patrons, they thought so too.

Like last time, Taylor danced with Caleb, but this time she danced with Davis too. She was surprised at the end of the evening when Mike led her out on the dance floor. In addition to the evening spent at the bar, Mike had taken her horseback riding and to the farmers' market. While there, they ran into Linda, his ex. After saying hi to Mike and ignoring Taylor, she attempted to engage Mike in conversation, but he wasn't having it and quickly shut her down. Glaring daggers at Taylor, Linda angrily walked away.

One of the booths they visited was Hawk and Rainbow's. Mike told her that among many other things, Rainbow was a beekeeper. She'd sold honey and beeswax products for as long as he could remember. While at their booth, Taylor noticed Mike's face took on a flushed hue when he spoke to Rainbow. Taylor was wondering what that was about when his uncle put an end to the suspense when he laughed and said, "Damn, boy, after all these years, you'd think you'd be over that by now."

Curious, Taylor asked, "Over what?"

Mike looked like he'd rather be anywhere else but where they were.

"Mikey here has had a crush on my wife for pretty much his entire life." He continued to laugh. "He was a shy lad when he was younger, and whenever he was around Rain, he seemed to lose his ability to speak. Now he just starts blushing when he's around her. I can't blame him though. I was the same way when I met her, and I was a grown-ass man." Taylor found it hard to imagine Hawk as he'd just described himself. She couldn't see him as anything other than the rugged, sexy man she saw before her. Miss Angie had told her Rainbow was a beautiful woman with the ability to make everyone who came into her space feel special. Taylor agreed. It had happened with Grant, and he'd only met her once. It was also adorable to see Mike that way. She was learning a lot about him during the time they spent together.

Taylor sighed as she turned off the clothes steamer. She'd finished Dana's outfit for the rodeo and was smoothing out the wrinkles. The opening ceremonies for the rodeo were this coming Friday. She'd finished earlier than expected and called Dana to come over so she could make any last-minute changes. Dana would be arriving within the hour. Taylor decided to stop reminiscing about Mike and put the finishing touches on the bracelet and ring she'd made to go along with the outfit she'd worked on. The bracelet was a metal cuff she'd engraved with Dana's initials. The ring was adjustable and shaped like a clinging vine that would encompass the length of either her second or third finger and was accented with red, white, and blue crystals positioned to resemble flowers. She hoped Dana liked them. She was going to the room she used as a studio to get a box for the jewelry when her phone rang. She smiled when she saw who was calling.

"Rae! It's about time you returned my call. I was beginning to think you forgot about me."

"Hey, Tay."

"What's wrong? I can hear it in your voice, so don't try to lie to me."

"Liam's engaged."

"Liam is what? Did you say engaged?" Taylor wasn't sure she heard correctly.

"Yes."

"To whom?"

"Some woman he met right after you left."

"Aww, Rae. I'm sorry. I know how you felt about him."

"I was planning on telling him when I ran into him at a party the other night. She was with him. He introduced her and broke the news. And by broke the news, I mean broke my heart."

"I can't believe he just sprung it on you like that. After all this time, he had to have known how you felt about him. How you are holding up?"

"I'm okay, I guess. I mean I haven't cried today, so that's got to be progress, right?"

"It is. Not to change the subject, but what are you doing this weekend?"

"Let me check. Looks like I'll either be drowning my sorrows in weed or alcohol. I haven't decided which."

"Why don't you come here?"

"I don't know. I don't think I'll be good company."

"News flash! You're not always good company, but I still love you. Besides, the rodeo is in town. You should come."

"I don't know . . ."

"Oh, come on. The worst that could happen is you get to go to your first rodeo and meet a clown." Taylor laughed. Rae hated clowns. "The best that could happen, besides seeing your best friend, is getting away from it all, meeting real-life cowboys, and having fun." There was a long silence over the line.

"Okay, I'll come."

"Great. I have some frequent flyer miles we can use for your ticket. Can you fly out on Thursday?"

"I can. And thanks for the miles."

"Great. I'll get your ticket and text you the information. Be ready to have a good time!"

"Yeah, yeah. I have to go. Love you."

"Love you, too. Bye." Taylor was looking forward to seeing her bestie. She'd been hoping that Liam and Rae would get together, but that was no longer a possibility. She wished him well, but she wasn't happy that he'd broken Rae's heart and that he hadn't seemed too bothered about doing it. Yes, a trip to cowboy country might be just the thing for Rae, and it seemed to be perfectly timed. Taylor sat down, opened her laptop, and made Rae's flight arrangements. She didn't want to give her friend time to change her mind. When she was done, she emailed her the itinerary and texted her to let her know her travel had been booked and she'd see her in two days.

"Oh my, Miss Taylor! Thank you so much!" Dana turned from side to side as she looked at the outfit Taylor had fixed up for her. It turned out better than she'd expected. The jeans with the split seams and the rhinestone tuxedo stripe made her legs look long and lean. Taylor had cinched in the waist of the jacket, giving it a more fitted appearance. The star she blinged out on the back was simple yet sparkled brightly when the light hit it. Dana turned from her reflection in the mirror and hugged Taylor.

"I'm glad you like it."

"Like it? I love it! Look, Mom, Aunt Red! Isn't this great?"

"I agree with Dana, Taylor. It does look great." Cheryl looked at Dana. "You're going to look fantastic on the platform."

"How did you do all of that in such a short time?"

"It's kind of a hobby of mine, so it didn't take long. And speaking of hobbies, I have something else for you." She picked up a small, plain wooden box from the table beside the mirror and handed it to Dana.

"You made these?" Dana opened the box, then passed it to her mother and aunt. "These are gorgeous!" She tried on the pieces. "I love them!" She gave Taylor another hug.

The ladies stayed a little while longer before eventually announcing they needed to go. On the way out, Cheryl hugged Taylor.

"Thank you so much for what you've done for Dana. Ever since she was a kid, she's wanted to sing the national anthem at the rodeo. She was ecstatic when she found out her audition tape had been selected. Thank you for making it even more special for her."

"You're more than welcome," Taylor responded, her voice thick with emotion at Cheryl's words.

Later that night, after the Red Buffalo closed, Mike pulled into the driveway of Taylor's house. It was almost 11:30. The temperature was warm, and Taylor was sitting on the porch, enjoying the night air. He stood in front of her, smiling as he looked at her, then pulled her up and kissed her. She immediately felt the warmth that she'd come to associate with his kisses.

"Hey, Rosebud."

Taylor giggled. Something she seemed to only do around him. "Hi, Mike. How was your day?"

"A lot better now. I've been looking forward to seeing you all day." He briefly leaned his forehead against hers, then sat down with Taylor on the porch swing.

"Me too. A lot has happened today."

"Oh yeah?" He placed his arm around the back of her shoulders.

"Yes. Dana came to get her outfit for the rodeo."

"Did she like it?"

"She did. She was so excited, she almost had me in tears."

"She's a sweetheart. Has been since the day we met her."

"You mean when she was born?"

"No, I mean when we first met her. She was three years old when PJ met Cheryl. When things got serious between them, he started bringing them to family dinners and barbeques and stuff. We fell in love with her. Especially Pop. He used to take her for rides on his horse. They became pretty much inseparable."

"Well, her parents did a good job raising her. She is sweet and kind."

"That she is. So, what else happened?"

"Do you remember me talking about my friend Rae?"

"I do."

"I talked to her today. She sounded so sad. When I asked her why, she told me Liam had gotten engaged."

"Who's Liam?"

"He's a guy we grew up with. They had a friends-with-benefits situation, but Rae had feelings for him. They were at a party the other night, and Liam introduced her to his fiancée."

"Ouch. Is your friend okay?"

Taylor shook her head. "Not really. That's why I invited her to come here for a few days for a change of scenery. She'll be here on Thursday."

"Good. Maybe I can ask her why she thought you might get carried away to some hideout." Mike laughed. "Do you want to sit out here a little longer, or do you want to go inside?"

"Let's go inside."

"Go ahead. I've got a surprise for you in the truck. I'll go get it."

"What's the surprise?"

"If I told you, it wouldn't be a surprise, now would it?"

"You can tell me, and I'll act surprised when I see it."

"No, you'll have to wait and see. Now get in the house." Mike dropped a quick kiss on her lips, then turned her to face the door and smacked her playfully on the ass. "Get going."

"Ooohh, do it again"

He happily obliged her request. "Now go." Taylor laughed and went inside.

Mike walked into the house a few minutes later with a plastic container that held a favorite of Taylor's, chocolate-covered strawberries. Caleb had made them earlier that day as a favor to him. He put them in the refrigerator, went back into the living room, and locked the door. He called out to Taylor.

"I'm back here," she responded.

"Back where?"

"Come find me."

Mike walked to the back of the hall, checking the spare bedroom, the room she used as an office and studio, and finally her room. He immediately forgot about the surprise he had for her. The lights were low, and courtesy of the multiple candles placed around the area, there was a light scent of jasmine in the air. Taylor was standing next to the bed, watching him as she removed her clothes before climbing on the bed.

"Care to join me?"

"Why, yes. Yes, I would." Mike quickly removed his clothes and joined her. Seating against the headboard, he pulled Taylor close, so her back was leaning against his chest and his arms were wrapped around her.

"This feels incredibly good," Mike said as he trailed kisses along the side of her neck. He let his hands slide over her body, caressing her skin.

Taylor closed her eyes and gave in to the sensations she was feeling. With her body pressed into him, his lips and hands became a delicious, sensual assault on her senses, and she was loving every minute of it. Especially when one hand rubbed her breast and pinched and played with her nipples while his other hand slid between her legs. In between kisses, Mike breathed dirty whispers in her ear, which heightened her desire. She began to move and buck, as her orgasm began to build from his probing fingers. Mike held her body in place and continued to describe, in explicit detail, what he planned to do to her. His lips continued to heat her skin as he increased the speed of his fingers caressing her clit. Her body pulsed and shuddered as she felt a burst of intense pleasure. She was pretty sure she might have screamed. When her heart rate slowed and her breathing was almost back to normal, Mike loosened his grip and eased her around until she was straddling him.

Reaching up he removed the elastic band that had been holding her messy bun in place and ran his fingers through her locs as he smoothed her hair away from her face. Feeling a little shy, Taylor tried to look away from him. He cupped the side of her face and forced her to look at him.

"It's a little late to be shy isn't it, Rosebud? I mean, you were pretty loud a minute ago. I'm sure the neighbors heard you screaming and are wondering what's going on. We should probably wait a few minutes before we continue just in case the sheriff shows up. You know, with you disturbing the peace and all."

Taylor's mouth formed an *o*, and her eyes widened at his words, then narrowed. "I have no idea what you're talking about."

"Oh really? Is that your story?" One side of Mike's mouth went up in a lopsided grin.

"Yes, that's my story, and I'm sticking to it."

"We'll see about that."

He cupped the back of her neck and pulled her down to meet his lips. He traced her lips with his tongue, teasing her, as she opened to receive his kiss. He then devoured her warm and willing mouth and set her senses aflame once more. He grabbed a condom from the night table and handed it to her. Taylor used her teeth to tear open the wrapper, removed the condom, and quickly slid it onto Mike's rock-hard cock. She bit her lip as she felt his length fill her. For someone whose primary love languages were quality time and words of affirmation, physical touch—specifically, Mike's touch—was challenging that notion. The more time they spent together, the more she wanted him.

Mike watched Taylor as she rode his cock. He smiled, then closed his eyes to savor her sweetness. She fit him like a glove. As her body began to move over him, his hands kneaded the mounds of her breasts and tweaked her nipples. He gripped her hips and stilled her movements before rolling over and pulling out of her luscious body.

Taylor had been on the verge of cumming when he pulled out, flipped her over, and raised her so she was on her hands and knees. He reached in and began to stroke her bud. He bent down, gently turned her head toward his, and gave her a searing kiss that stole her breath away before entering her from behind. Taylor let out a loud moan as his cock slammed back into her.

Mike felt Taylor's pussy tighten around his cock as he thrust into her. Her sexy moans fed his desire for her. She tried to get him to quicken the pace, and he responded by telling her to lower her arms out in front of her. When she complied, he drove deeper into her, causing her to tremble with sensual delight. He continued to move within her, coaxing another orgasm before seeking his release.

He pulled out slowly, leaving behind her delicious warmth, and got up to dispose of the condom. He came back with a warm washcloth and gently cleaned her up, as was his habit. He threw the towel in the direction of the bathroom before getting back in bed and pulling her close.

"Good night, Rosebud."

"'Night, Mike," Taylor responded drowsily, barely able to keep her eyes open.

chapter 21

Taylor woke, as the sun was just coming up and Mike's lips and fingers were doing delicious things to her body. She was on her side with her back to him, and her breathing quickened as his fingers delved into her softness. She sighed as he stopped briefly to put on a condom. He lifted her leg and eased into her. She loved morning sex. Along with makeup sex, it was a favorite. She was pretty sure a short nap was in her future after they finished. His steady strokes promised it would be a while before that happened though, and she was totally okay with that.

Later, after showering, Taylor made them breakfast. As she put on the coffee, she thought about the time she'd spent with Mike. Never in a million years would she have thought she would have met someone like him. He was different from any other man she'd been with. He was a little grumpy at times, but he was also sweet and funny. Truthfully, she found him fascinating. The night of the storm, he'd been gentle and understanding. She was sure he'd want nothing more to do with her after finding out about her issues, but she'd been wrong. If anything, he was more attentive to her now than he had been before that night. She loved spending time with him, and the sex was the best she'd had. Not that she had a lot to compare it to, but the few previous relationships had left her wanting. Now, here she was in the middle of her life and on the verge of something unexpected, courtesy of a random act of kindness on an airplane. She was glad Rae was coming. She needed her best friend to help her navigate through this unchartered territory. It was as exciting as it was scary. She knew she was overthinking things but couldn't help herself. She continued her silent musings as she gathered the ingredients for their breakfast. Yes, Rae would help her put things in perspective, but as for now, she'd fix their breakfast and try to reign in her thoughts.

They were eating breakfast when Mike asked, "Are you sure you'll be okay going to the airport by yourself?"

"I'm sure. I have GPS, and I also have a map. I'll be fine. Besides, aren't your kids coming today?"

"Yes, but they'll be here later today, then they're headed out to PJ's. Cheryl and Red are hosting a sleepover for the cousins, including Albee's hellions."

"Why do you call those sweet children hellions?"

"Because they are. You just haven't seen them in action yet."

"Cheryl doesn't mind all the kids?"

"No. She and Red are good friends with Albee's wife, Diane, who'll be there too. Plus, it gives the cousins a chance to hang out together, since they don't get to see each other too often." Mike got up, grabbed the coffee pot, and refilled their cups. "Back to my original question. You sure you're good getting to the airport and back?"

"Yes. I'll text you when I get back. We'll come over to the Red Buffalo this evening, and I'll introduce you to Rae. How does that sound?"

"All right. But promise me if you get lost, you'll call me right away." He looked at her as if he were still skeptical.

"I promise."

They continued to talk as they finished their meal. Taylor found out that the rodeo would arrive in town that day and would have opening ceremonies late in the afternoon tomorrow. The Red Buffalo would be setting up a snack and beverage stand. He told her that they—PJ's family, Denton's, Albee's, the Edwards, and the Hawkins—sat together near his booth every year. Caleb, Davis, and a few others from the saloon helped out. She was surprised to learn that Mike donated 50 percent of the sales from the beverage stand to a local food bank, a land conservation fund, and a fund that provided education and resources to youth in the area.

Mike helped wash the dishes and clean the kitchen, and he was about to join Taylor on the porch when his phone rang. He looked and saw it was his ex-wife calling. He frowned.

"Hello."

"Hello, Michael. How are you today?"

"Fine. What do you want?"

"Since you asked so nicely, I'll tell you."

He ignored her sarcasm. "I'm waiting."

"I need to drop the kids off early. I had to move my flight up, so I have to bring them now. I'll be at your place within the hour."

"And you didn't think to mention this when I spoke to you yesterday?"

"I didn't think it was a big deal. They were coming there anyway. They'll just be a little early."

"Fine. I'll see you in an hour."

"That's all you have to say?"

"Yes. Bye." Mike ended the call and walked out to the porch to join Taylor.

"I'm going to have to leave a little earlier than planned. Suzanne, my ex-wife, just called and said she was dropping my kids off in about an hour."

Taylor smiled, grabbed Mike's hand, and led him back into the house.

"I was saving this for later, but I might as well give it to you now," she told him, reaching into the nightstand drawer beside the bed.

When she turned back around, Mike's T-shirt was off, and he was unbuttoning his jeans. She looked at him.

"What?" he asked, as he continued to get undressed.

"I said I had something to give you, and you're getting undressed?"

"I have something to give you too." He grinned at her. "I thought I'd give you some more of this dick since you like it so well."

Taylor felt herself growing warm and getting wet.

"You know you want it," he teased. Mike was fully naked, stroking himself as he spoke to her.

"I can't lie." Taylor licked her lips. "I do." Taylor quickly removed her clothing, and Mike wasted no time reminding her just how much she wanted it.

After his second shower of the morning, Mike got dressed and went to find Taylor so he could tell her goodbye. He found her in the room she used as a studio. He hadn't spent much time in that room and was surprised by what he saw. There was a worktable set up where she created her designs. Another table held sketch pads, pencils, charcoal, and various other drawing tools. He also saw a picture of a man, a woman, and a little girl. The girl was Taylor. Her features were a mix of both adults in the picture, so he assumed they were her parents.

"Those are my parents," Taylor said softly.

"I can see the resemblance. Your mother was beautiful."

"She was."

"Your father was a big guy."

"I used to love when he'd lift me in the air. It made me feel like I was ten feet tall." Taylor gave a small smile. "I thought my father was the strongest man in the world."

"Looking at that picture, I can see why." Mike pulled her into his arms. "I have to get going."

"I know. But I really do have something for you." She pulled away from him and laughed. She went to the table and picked up a bracelet. Taylor had found a silver medallion with a buffalo etched into it, and she'd attached it to a wide, black leather bracelet and added a closure to it. "I made this for you. I hope you like it."

"You made this?" Touched, Mike took the bracelet and looked it over.

"Yes."

"Wow." He put it on. "I can't believe you made this."

"I did. I hope you like it."

"I more than like it." Mike leaned toward her and kissed her soundly on the lips. "I'll be wearing this tonight."

"You don't have to."

"I want to."

Taylor looked away shyly.

Mike noticed she did that a lot when she was embarrassed.

"I need to get going. Walk me out?"

"Sure."

He stepped aside so she could go ahead of him. When they reached the door, he gave her a sweet kiss. She watched him get in his truck and waved at him as he drove off.

Mike left Taylor's house a little later than he originally planned, and when he arrived home, he saw his ex-wife's car parked in front of his house. He grabbed his duffle and got out, mentally preparing himself for any bitching she was sure to do. The twins jumped out of her car as soon as they saw him walk up.

"Hey, Dad!" they said in unison as they ran toward him and gave him a group hug.

"Hey, Mikey, Kay!" His twins were named Michael Alexander Jr. and Mikayla Ariel, Mikey and Kay for short.

"It's about time you got here. I called and told you we'd be arriving within the hour."

The voice of his ex-wife, Suzanne, grated on his nerves. He couldn't understand how he'd grown to despise someone he'd once loved more than life itself.

"I got here as soon as I could."

Kay, ever the peacemaker, said, "We just got here, Dad."

"Yeah, Dad," Mikey added. "We haven't been waiting long."

Mike ruffled their hair before responding, "I'm sorry I wasn't here when you arrived, Suzanne. I'm here now. Kids, grab your bags and take them to your rooms." Mikey and Kay ran off to do as they were told.

"Where were you, Michael?" She walked over to where he stood.

"None of your business."

"It's always my business when it involves my children."

"Well, since it didn't involve the children, it's none of your business." He hoped she would shut up and leave, but he wasn't that lucky.

"I heard you have a new girlfriend. I don't know who she is, so I don't want her around my children."

"You don't get to come here and dictate your wishes to me. You don't know her, so I *suggest* you keep your opinion to yourself."

"I'm their mother, and I have a say in who they can be around."

"Yes, you are. But I'd never put my children in a harmful situation, so that's a non-issue."

Suzanne looked as if she was about to say something else when Mike interrupted her, "This conversation is over. I'll see you later."

"You don't have to be such a bastard about it." She pouted.

"Yes, I do, because that's all you seem to understand. Safe travels, Suzanne." He turned and walked to the house.

chapter 22

Taylor arrived at the airport a half hour before Rae's plane was due in. She parked in the cell phone lot and scrolled through her emails as she waited. One of them was from her friend Liam—or, as she now thought of him, her not-quite-sure-if-they-were-still-friends friend Liam. He'd sent her an engagement announcement and party invitation. She thought about sending him a scathing email since he'd been avoiding her calls and texts. Instead, she just RSVP'd no to the invite and sent it back. She didn't hate him, but she still thought it was a pretty shitty thing he'd done to Rae. Taylor was sure he knew how Rae felt about him. He could have handled the situation better. The fact that he'd been avoiding her meant he knew that too and was too much of a wuss to do anything about it. His loss. Her phone rang. It was no surprise that it was Liam. She was just surprised he called so soon.

"Hi, Liam."

"Hey, Taylor. How are you?"

"I'm good. You?"

"I'm doing pretty good. Pretty damn good, actually."

"Well, that's nice."

"Yeah, well, it is what it is. But I was calling about the RSVP you just sent."

"What about it?"

"Are you sure you can't come? You're one of my best friends, and I want you to be there."

Taylor closed her eyes and took a deep breath. "Listen, Liam. I can't."

"Why not?"

"You know why not."

"No, I don't."

"Are you going to tell me that you didn't know how Rae felt about you, or was it that you just didn't care?"

"No. I know how she feels about me. But this isn't about her, it's about you."

"It most definitely *is* about her. She's my oldest and dearest friend. You could have at least met with her and told her about your impending nuptials before springing it on her like you did at that party. You hurt her feelings."

"I didn't mean to hurt her," he replied, trying hard to sound contrite.

"Well, *you did*. What are you going to do about it?"

"There's nothing I can do about it."

"You could apologize."

"Why should I do that? She might get the wrong idea."

"I doubt she will."

"If I apologize, will you come to the party?"

"No. But I will come to the wedding. How's that?"

"But I want you to meet Ivy. She's amazing. I know you'll like her if you just give her a chance."

"Not helping." Taylor sighed heavily. "Look, Liam. Here's the thing. You and I go way back. Rae and I go back even further. She's my best friend *and* my sister. If you and I didn't have a history, I wouldn't even come to your wedding. No to the engagement party. Yes to the wedding."

"Okay, if that's how you feel."

"That's how I feel. And you really do need to apologize to Rae."

"What for?"

"For hurting her feelings!"

"Okay. I'll stop by her place on my way home from work."

"You can't do that."

"Why not?"

"Because she's on her way here. She should be landing any minute. If you wait ten minutes, you can call her when she gets off the plane, and you won't have me as an audience to your groveling."

"You invited her without inviting me. That's cold, Tay. How many times have I invited you to visit me?"

"Lots, but this is a different situation."

"All right. I'll call her."

"And even though you broke my best friend's heart, congratulations on your engagement."

"Thanks, Tay. Love you."

"Love you, too. Bye." Taylor ended the call.

Taylor excitedly pulled up along the curbside pickup in front of her best friend-in-the-world friend, cut the engine, and jumped out of the truck.

"I am so happy to see you!" She hugged her best friend tightly.

"I'm glad to see you too!" Rae pulled back and looked at her for a long minute. "Grant was right. You look good. *Really* good. You also look like you might be getting some," she added, and they both started laughing. "This place seems to agree with you."

Taylor blushed and smiled. "Let's just say I like it a lot better than I thought I would."

"I can tell."

"On that note, let's load up and head back."

Rae's suitcase and carry-on were quickly placed in the back seat of the truck cab, and they headed back to Silverton in no time. Just as Taylor had been on her first visit, Rae too, was amazed at the rugged beauty of the area.

"This place is beautiful. Those mountains seem to go on forever and ever. There's no pollution, and the sky is so blue and clear."

"I know, right? I was in awe when I first saw it." As they made their way through the freeway and highway interchanges, Taylor told Rae about some of what she had planned for her visit. "Tonight, we're going to the Red Buffalo. They have a band playing there that I think you'll like. The rodeo arrived in town today too, so there will probably be a lot of cowboys there, just saying . . ."

"I hear what you're inferring. Is that the saloon your boyfriend owns?"

"He's not my boyfriend."

"Okay, is that the saloon your friend with benefits owns?"

Taylor gave her the stink eye. "It's not like that."

"If he's not your boyfriend, it's exactly like that."

"Anyway . . . Tomorrow's mostly free since the opening ceremony of the rodeo isn't until the early evening. Mike's niece, Dana, is singing the national anthem, so we'll need to be there for that. His family is sitting together and invited us to join them."

"That's nice of them. Since we'll probably be the only two Black people there, I'm glad we'll be sitting with some of the town's own."

"That's probably true, but they're good people, and I think you'll like them. Plus, Mike has a booth there so we'll get free food and drinks."

"Sounds like a fun evening to be had by all. I've never been to a rodeo before. It should be interesting if nothing else."

"Neither have I, but I heard it's a lot of fun. Miss Angie said they also have a nice expo. I'm looking forward to that more than the rodeo."

"You didn't mention the possibility of retail therapy. Okay, I'm in."

"Sucker."

"Whatever. Just pay attention to where we're going so we don't get lost."

Taylor texted Mike when they arrived back at her place. He responded with a smiley face emoji and told her he was looking forward to seeing her that evening. He told her to text him when she was on the way, and he'd meet them at the door. She smiled when she read his return text.

"What has you smiling?"

"Nothing. Mike just reminded me to text him when we leave so he can meet us at the door."

"Isn't he sweet?" Rae asked teasingly.

Taylor ignored Rae's question. "Are you hungry? If not, I'll take you on a little of the town and we can eat when we get back."

"I'd like to check out the town. The way you've talked about it has made me want to see it."

"Then that's what we'll do."

chapter 23

After lunch, they decided to walk over to the town square. Taylor pointed out some of the local landmarks and the Red Buffalo, where they would be going later that evening. As they were walking out of a vintage clothing store, they ran into Caleb and Davis. Both men hugged Taylor.

"Hi, Taylor, how's it going?" Caleb said to her as his eyes went to Rae.

"Pretty good. How are you guys doing?"

"The same," he responded.

Davis was openly admiring Rae. At five feet ten inches, she was hard to miss. Her skin was the color of caramel. Her body was long, curvy, and fit. She'd been an athlete in college and regularly worked out with a personal trainer. Her shoulder-length hair was pulled back into a ponytail, which emphasized her high cheekbones. Davis smiled at both women. His eyes held a twinkle, and his deep dimples seemed to pop.

"Who's this with you, Taylor?" Davis asked.

"Davis, Caleb, this is my best friend, Rachel Stephens. Rae, this is Caleb Hawkins and Davis Baker. Caleb is the chef at the Red Buffalo. Davis is a forest ranger."

"Nice to meet you, Caleb Hawkins and Davis Baker."

"The pleasure is *mine*." Davis looked directly at Rae as he spoke.

Caleb rolled his eyes at Davis's response. Rae tilted her head slightly and smiled at Davis as he spoke.

"Are you ladies planning on coming out tonight?" Caleb asked.

"Yes. Mike said Fire Lake is playing."

Caleb nodded. "Nice. I look forward to seeing you ladies tonight then."

"I guess we better get moving. We're doing the booth set-up at the arena," Davis said.

"We'll see you later this evening," Taylor said.

"Yes, you will," Davis spoke to Rae. "Hope you save me a dance." He smiled at her, and then both men walked off.

Taylor and Rae walked over to the ice cream parlor, and the bell above the door rang as they entered.

"I can see why you're looking so happy and content. Do the rest of the men around here look like them?"

"I only know a few, but the ones I've seen have been easy on the eyes. Caleb, Mike, and Davis grew up together."

"Does your Mike look like them?"

"Not quite. His looks are a little more on the rugged side, and his vibe is different."

"How so?"

"Caleb is friendly and has a fun sense of humor. Davis is a flirt and, from what I've observed, a bit of an ass, but a solid friend to those two. Mike is nice but seems like he could go from zero to fifty in less than a second."

"Ooohh, edgy. I like that. I can't wait to meet the man that ended your drought," Rae teased.

"We'll see Mike tonight. His uncle Hawk is the real edgy one. You'll meet him tomorrow at the rodeo."

"It runs in the family, huh?"

"Seems so. And speaking of running in the family, there's Caleb's mother. Try not to drool."

"Wow." Rae's gaze followed her. "I see what you mean. She's beautiful. She looks like a goddess or something."

"I know, right? She's really sweet though. You should have seen Grant when he met her. Come on, I'll introduce you." Taylor introduced Rae to Rainbow, and the three women struck up a conversation as they waited to place their orders.

"So how are you enjoying your visit so far, Rae?"

"I just arrived today, but I like what I've seen so far."

"We're going to the Red Buffalo tonight to hear the band and then to the rodeo tomorrow," Taylor told Rainbow.

"I hate that I'll miss the band tonight. I may be a little biased because my daughter is in the band, but you'll love them." She took her order from the clerk. "It was nice to meet you. I'll be at the rodeo tomorrow, so I'll see you there. Bye, ladies." She smiled and gave them both a hug before leaving.

Rae and Taylor got their ice cream cones and walked along the sidewalk, talking and window-shopping.

"I don't think I've ever met anyone like her before," Rae said.

"I know what you mean. When I first met her, I felt like she was staring into my soul. It's like she's an empath or something."

"I can see that. Maybe she is."

"Her husband is also Mike's godfather. He looks like Jimmy Smits. Not *L.A. Law* or *NYPD Blue* Jimmy Smits but *Sons of Anarchy* Jimmy Smits."

"That's a lot of hotness flowing in one family."

"It is."

They changed direction and headed back to Taylor's house. As they walked, Taylor filled Rae in on her time in Silverton, including details she'd left out during their phone calls.

"If you're up to it, we can walk tonight." Taylor was going through her closet, looking for something to wear, while Rae selected a playlist on her phone and placed it in the speaker dock on the counter.

"It's where we were today, right?" Rae asked.

"Yup."

"We can walk. That way, we can both drink."

"Sounds good to me."

"What are you wearing?"

"I don't know yet. I didn't bring a whole lot of going-out clothes with me when I came here because I wasn't expecting to go anywhere. I was going to order some stuff, but you know how I am about clothes shopping."

"I knew you'd say something like that. Lucky for you, I brought some of the clothes you had at my house. That's why I have so much luggage for such a short visit. Who do you love?" Rae was dancing to the music as she spoke.

"You, crazy. Now, what did you bring me?" Taylor laughed as she started dancing.

"I thought you'd never ask."

After settling on their outfits, they had lunch, then retreated to their rooms to get ready for the evening.

A little over an hour later, both women were ready for the evening. Rae had on black jeans with a leopard print camisole top. Her hair was in a high bun, and she'd rounded out her look with gold sandals, gold drop earrings that Taylor had made for her a few years ago, and bold red lipstick. Taylor had on jeans and a fitted, black, off-the-shoulder top. She had on one of her custom leather bracelets and a few of the rings she'd designed. A circle of beaten gold suspended hung on a leather cord around her neck. She left her locs loose and applied a dark-mauve lipstick that she coated with a nude gloss. Since they were walking to the bar, she opted for her black wedge sandals, which were cute and comfortable enough to walk in.

"How do I look?" Rae turned around slowly.

"Fabulous as always. You sure I look okay?"

"You look great. Mike will definitely notice."

"I'm sure there will be quite a few fellas trying to get your attention tonight. Don't think I didn't see the way you were checking out Davis earlier today."

"He was checking me out, so I returned the favor," Rae smirked.

"It was the dimples, right?"

"Yeah. They're pretty lethal."

Taylor nodded in agreement. "Are you ready to go?"

"I am. Let's take a few pictures before we go."

They snapped a few pictures, grabbed their purses, and left the house. Taylor texted Mike to let him know they were on their way.

"Hey, Taylor," Steve greeted her with a smile.

"Hi, Steve. This is my friend Rae."

"Hey, friend Rae." Steve winked as he spoke.

"Hey, Steve."

"Follow me, ladies, if you please." Both women looked at each other and smiled.

"Look at you, Tay, getting the VIP treatment," Rae whispered to Taylor as they followed Steve into the bar. Steve led them to the end of the bar, where Caleb was standing next to his sister. He hugged Taylor and smiled at Rae.

"Hey, Taylor, Rae."

"Hi, Caleb, Mary. Mary, this is my friend, Rae."

"Hi, Taylor. It's nice to meet you, Rae."

"Mary is the lead singer of the band that's playing tonight. You're in for a treat."

"That's nice of you to say. Glad you came out. I need to get going." Mary nodded in the direction of the stage. "We start the next set in a few minutes." She left to join the rest of the band, who were taking their places on the stage.

"You two ladies are looking lovely this evening. I'm pretty sure there's lots of dancing and free drinks in your future." Caleb leaned forward as he said the last part to them. "And speaking of drinks, what can I get you two?"

"Bourbon."

"Blanton's?"

"That'll work," Taylor answered.

"I'll have the same. And water, please," Rae added.

"Sure. Water for you too, Taylor?"

"Yes, please."

"Have a seat, and I'll get your drinks and let Mike know you're here." Both women took a seat on the barstools and turned to survey the area.

"This is quite the crowd for a town this size," Rae observed.

"They seem to do pretty good business. The first night I came here, there was a good-sized crowd then too. Tonight looks like they might be close to max capacity."

"Looks like there are some good-looking men in this max capacity." Rae's eyes skimmed the crowd. "Damn, these cowboys got it going on in here. They're either strong-looking, sexy, fine as hell, or all the above."

Taylor agreed: those rodeo cowboys were looking mighty good.

"Here are your drinks, ladies."

They turned back to face the bar as Caleb placed their drinks in front of them.

"Care to join us for one, Caleb?" Taylor asked.

"Sure." Caleb poured one for himself. "Here's to good friends, old and new; and to new adventures. May they be better than ever." They clinked glasses and sipped. Caleb talked a bit with them, then excused himself to go back to the kitchen.

Rae leaned toward Taylor and asked, "Which one of them is your Mike?"

"This one," a deep, raspy voice replied, surprising both women. They turned around on their stools and saw Mike standing there.

"Hi, Mike." Taylor laughed.

Mike leaned toward her and gave her a lingering kiss on the lips. "Hi, Taylor." Both looked at each other for a long minute.

Rae looked at Mike and then her friend Taylor. She couldn't quite believe what she was seeing. Taylor had never been one for PDA. She was always awkward and uncomfortable with it. And this Mike, well, he was *very* different from Taylor's norm. She went for the dull, boring types. The ones who were predictable. They may have had different names, but they were all the same guy. But this Mike, yeah, he was different. Rae hadn't believed Taylor earlier when she said he was on the rugged side. Turned out, she was telling the truth. The difference between him and her usual was like night and day. He was tall, muscular, and didn't look like the type of man who would run from a fight. It seemed Taylor had been keeping secrets. *She's going to have to give up some details,* Rae thought as she watched the two of them.

"Ahem." She cleared her throat. Mike, with his arm around Taylor, turned toward her.

Taylor introduced them. "Mike, this is my best friend, Rae. Rae, this is Mike."

"This is the same Rae who thought I was kidnapping you and carrying you off to some hideout?"

"That's her." Taylor nodded with a laugh.

"Oh, you remember that, huh?" Rae winced slightly.

"I do. And I'd be lying if I said the thought hadn't crossed my mind." He laughed. "I've heard a lot about you. It's nice to finally meet you." He smiled in greeting.

"It's nice to finally meet you too." Rae returned his smile.

Davis spotted Taylor and her friend Rae as soon as they walked in. He would have made his way over to them then if he hadn't been delayed by his sister and that coven she hung out with. He probably shouldn't call them witches, but it was nicer than what he really wanted to call them.

"Linda, I don't care how many times you ask me, I'm *not* going to talk to Mike for you. If you have something to say to him, I suggest you tell him yourself."

"I would, but he won't talk to me. He won't answer my texts or my calls. He's always hanging around that Tasha or whatever her name is. Come on, Davis." Linda fixed her mouth into a practiced pout.

Davis was sure that worked on most men, but not him. Shay, the other witch in the coven, was adding her two cents, hoping to convince him to change his mind. He looked at his sister, Mina. "You have something you want to add to this?"

"No." She shook her head. "I'm staying out of it."

Davis took a deep breath and turned to face Linda.

"Look, I get it. You still have feelings for Mike. *But clearly, the man has moved on.* I think you should cut your losses and do the same."

"You know what, Davis? You can kiss my ass! Forget I even asked you to help me!"

"Davis, why don't you think about someone other than yourself for a change? Can't you see how upset this is making her?" Shay placed her hand on his arm as she advocated for her friend.

Davis looked at his sister, wondering for the millionth time why she was friends with these witches.

"I'm done talking to you two." He left and headed to the bar.

There was no way in hell he was going to get involved with Linda's plans to get back with Mike. As far as he was concerned, Mike dodged a bullet when he broke it off with her. She was a spoiled, selfish bitch.

"Mina, why is your brother being such an ass?" Shay asked.

Mina sighed. "You heard me say I'm staying out of this. I meant it. And for the record, I agree with him. Linda should move on. It's clear Mike is done with whatever was between them."

Linda, standing next to Shay, narrowed her eyes at Mina. "Are you serious? You'd rather see Mike with someone else and me with a broken heart? Because if you are, you're not the person I thought you were, and I need to reevaluate our friendship."

Mina looked at the two women she'd been friends with since childhood. Not a perfect friendship, but a friendship, nonetheless. "I *am* serious, and let me save you some time because if you are going to continue to be this petty and ridiculous, you're not someone *I* want to be friends with." Mina left the group and went to join her brother and his friends at the bar.

Linda felt her anger building as she watched her walk away. "This isn't over by a long shot. I'm getting my man back."

Shay, who was messy and thrived on other people's drama, smiled. "I'm with you, girl. Let's go get a drink and not let these assholes spoil our evening."

chapter 24

As Mina approached the bar, she noticed Mike laughing and looking relaxed. He was standing behind Taylor, and she was leaning into him. Her brother, Davis, was laughing and standing next to a woman Mina hadn't seen before. The four of them looked like they were having a good time. *Yes*, she thought, *they look like a better group to spend the evening with than the one I just left.* She saw Caleb come from behind the bar with fresh drinks. Mina had been harboring a crush on him for pretty much her whole life. She always got a little nervous around him, and any conversations they attempted were awkward because she never seemed to be able to make the words that came out of her mouth sound like the ones that were in her head.

"Looks like I found the fun end of the bar." *That sounded kind of lame*, she thought. *But not the worst thing I could have said.*

"Mina!" Mike leaned over and kissed her cheek.

"Hi, Mike." She smiled; her dimples fully present.

"Hey, Caleb," Mina shyly greeted him.

"Mina. You're looking beautiful tonight." He smiled and winked at her.

Mina felt herself blushing and quickly looked away. Davis smirked at her. He constantly teased her about her crush on Caleb. He'd told her he was sure the feeling was mutual, but Mina was too timid when it came to Caleb to explore that possibility.

"Mina, have you met Taylor?" Mike asked.

"No, I haven't. I'm Mina, Davis's sister. It's nice to meet you."

"Hi, Mina, I can see the resemblance. This is my friend Rae. She's visiting for a few days."

"Hi, Mina."

"How are you enjoying Silverton?"

"I just arrived today, but so far, I like what I've seen." Rae looked at Davis as she said the last part. He returned her look, and it was clear the comment was not lost on him.

"Drink, Mina?" Caleb asked.

"I'll have what everybody else is having."

"Bourbon it is." Caleb left to get her drink.

"I don't believe it. Mina, you managed to speak in complete sentences around Caleb," Mike laughed.

"About time too. He was starting to think you didn't like him," Davis added.

Mina, feeling a little embarrassed said, "I need both of you to shut up."

"Just saying." Davis snickered.

"Girl don't let them tease you. That man is fine. I can see how he could make a sista lose her train of thought." Rae held up her hand and high-fived Taylor and Mina, who let out a laugh.

"Hey, hey, why are you talking about him when I'm trying to get your attention?" Davis asked. "I must be doing something wrong."

"Oh no, honey. You're doing *everything* right. Those dimples you and Mina are sporting are dangerous."

"In that case, let's dance, and I'll show you how *dangerous* they can be."

"Sure, why not?"

Davis helped her off the stool, grabbed her hand, and led her to the dance floor.

Taylor watched the two of them as they walked away. She was glad Rae was having a good time. She seemed much happier than she had a few days ago when she spoke with her on the phone.

When Caleb returned with Mina's drink, Mike leaned down and whispered into Taylor's ear. She nodded, and they both got up and went through the doors that led to the kitchen and back offices.

"I wonder where they're going?" Mina said aloud.

Caleb handed her a glass. "I think he wanted to show her something in his office."

"Oh." She felt her face heating up, so she quickly took a sip from her glass and immediately started coughing.

"You okay?"

"Yes, it just went down the wrong way."

"You sure?"

"Yes."

"Have some water." Caleb handed her a glass of water and intentionally let his fingers linger over hers. Surprised, Mina looked up at Caleb.

"Yes, I just did that." He leaned forward. "Consider this notice. I'll give you a little time to get used to the idea." He smiled, then left her standing there with a bemused expression on her face that eventually turned into a smile.

Davis and Rae were laughing when they returned to the bar.

"Where did everybody go, and why are you smiling?" Davis asked his sister.

"Mike and Taylor went back there somewhere." She pointed toward the double doors leading to the back of the bar. "And Caleb will be right back."

Rae's eyes followed the direction Mina pointed. "Taylor went back there with Mike?"

"Yes."

Rae turned toward Davis.

"Okay, what has that cowboy done to my best friend? Her behavior since she's been here is out of character."

He held his hands up in mock surrender. "Hey, I don't know what he did. If it makes you feel any better, Mike's a little different from his usual grumpy-ass self. But if you like, I can show you what, ah, I can do." Davis smirked.

"If I let you, you probably could," Rae responded with a sexy smile.

Mina looked at Davis and Rae. She started to say something when she felt an arm around her waist. She turned to see the owner of the arm was Caleb.

"Let's go dance and leave them to whatever that is they're doing." He pointed between the two. Mina couldn't get words past her throat, so she simply nodded and followed Caleb to the dance floor.

Taylor had barely gotten into Mike's office when she heard the door close and the lock click. The next thing she knew, she found herself against the wall and the recipient of a very hot, carnal kiss. Mike was hard as steel as he pressed his body against her.

"I've been wanting to do this all day. I hope you don't mind." He whispered the words against her lips, then he trailed his own along the side of her neck and to her bare shoulder.

"Ahhh . . ." was all Taylor could manage to get out as he returned to her lips.

Mike grabbed her hair and forced her head back, and she could feel her panties getting soaked. She reached for his belt buckle and undid his pants, slipping her hand inside. Mike pulled away and looked at her.

"Yes," she breathed.

He pulled her from the wall and led her over to his desk. He opened his desk drawer and pulled out a bag. "I guess it's a good thing I bought these earlier today." Inside was a box of condoms. He took one out and threw it on the desk. He rubbed his hands over Taylor's ass before reaching around, undoing the button, and lowering the zipper of her jeans. He turned her around so she was facing his desk, then pulled her panties and jeans down low enough to allow him unrestricted access to her body. He wrapped his arms around her and inhaled her scent while kissing the back of her neck. With one hand, he turned her face toward his, and he hungrily sucked her bottom lip before capturing her sighs with a searing kiss. His other hand skimmed the front of her body and disappeared into the wet, silken folds between her thighs. Finding her more than ready for him, he quickly put on a condom, bent her over his desk, and sank into her sweet center.

Taylor's knees almost buckled as Mike entered her. The fullness of his cock, the feel of his warm breath, and his kisses on her neck and shoulders caused her breath to come in quick, uneven pants. As he thrust in and out of her, she felt the tension build as her pussy grew wetter and wetter. Here, in his office, with her senses highly stimulated, she struggled to keep quiet. Each stroke brought her closer to the edge, and she didn't know if she'd be able to keep it all inside. And right then, being so close, she didn't care.

Each moment Mike spent inside Taylor's body was better than the one before and had him wanting more and more of her. He never expected they would be together like this, and he wouldn't change a thing about it, except maybe have more of her. He felt her body quiver and knew she was close to cumming. He slowed his pace to prolong her pleasure and smiled as she huskily called out his name. *Yeah, she's close,* he thought. And so was he. He covered her with his body as he pistoned into her. He felt her walls constrict around him as she began to tremble. He leaned down and bit her earlobe, then quickly took her mouth just in time to capture her loud moans.

chapter 25

After taking one last look in the mirror, Taylor walked out of the bathroom in Mike's office after cleaning herself up.

Mike looked at her and smiled. "Give me a few minutes, and I'll take you back to the bar," he told her as he went into the bathroom.

Taylor wandered over to his desk and looked at the pictures of friends, family, and staff that decorated its surface. Taylor smiled and closed her eyes as she thought about what just happened. She could still feel the heat of his body pressed into and up against hers.

"I hope that smile is for me."

She opened her eyes and saw Mike standing next to her. "It is."

"Good." He leaned in and kissed her. "Ready?"

"Yes."

Mike opened the door of his office, and she preceded him back to the bar where they had been earlier. There seemed to be more people in there now than before they'd left. Davis was sitting next to Rae and looked over as they approached.

"Look who's back." He leered at Mike and Taylor as if he knew what they'd been doing. Taylor could feel her face growing warm.

"Where did you guys get off to?"

"None of your business."

Davis laughed, and Rae joined in.

Mike kissed Taylor on the cheek. "I need to check on things, then I'll be back. Don't let them give you a hard time." He moved closer and whispered in her ear, "That's my job, Rosebud." He squeezed her waist, smiled at Rae and Davis, and went to find Caleb.

Taylor took her seat at the bar and found herself under scrutiny by Davis and Rae. Davis was still smirking. Rae tilted her head as she looked at Taylor, then reached for her drink and handed it to her.

"Hear you go, Tay. Looks like you might have worked up a thirst while your lipstick disappeared."

Taylor gasped. Davis and Rae laughed. Feeling afterglow and a little embarrassed, Taylor took a drink and tried to look anywhere but at the two people in front of her. Davis excused himself, saying he'd be right back. Rae continued to laugh.

"Damn, girl! Who are you and what have you done with my best friend?"

"You have jokes now?"

"I do. But in all seriousness, I like these changes I'm seeing in you since you've been here. And from the look on your face, Mike must be putting it down."

Taylor laughed. "He's putting it somewhere."

"He needs to keep it up. I haven't seen you like this in a long time. I love it."

"Enjoying yourself?" Taylor changed the subject as she looked around the bar as she spoke.

"I am. More than I thought I would. Everyone's been nice, and Davis is fine as hell *and* funny. He told me a little about the town and what it was like for him, Caleb, and Mike growing up. The three of them were something else."

"From what I hear, they still are."

"I can see why." They looked at each other and started laughing.

"Care to share the joke?" Caleb asked as he rejoined them. Mina had stopped to talk to some friends before going back to the bar.

"No joke, just making observations," Taylor said.

"Well, in that case, how about another drink? Then after that, you two can join me on the floor for some line dancing."

"Line dancing?" Rae asked.

"Yup. The band is about to end their set and take an extended break."

"I don't know how to line dance." Taylor looked at the dance floor and back at Caleb.

"Sure you do. I thought all Black people know how to at least do the 'Electric Slide' and the 'Cupid Shuffle.' Aren't they like wedding reception and family reunion requirements?" Caleb said, straight-faced, with a twinkle in his eye.

"Yes. And don't you think what you just said was stereotypical and a little racist?" Rae asked.

"It's true though, right?" he asked.

Both women laughed. "Boy, if you don't get out of here and get our drinks!" Rae attempted to give Caleb the stink eye but failed. He laughed and went to get the next round.

"I wonder what Black wedding or family reunion his fine ass has been to?" Rae wondered aloud as they watched him behind the bar. "I'm pretty sure wherever it was, the women were on him."

"I know that's right," Taylor agreed.

"You know what's right?" Davis said as he rejoined them.

"Caleb is getting us drinks, and then he says we're going line dancing. Taylor was just agreeing that we both don't know the dances."

"They're not too complicated, ladies. I think you'll pick up the steps pretty quickly."

"If you say so," Taylor said, looking unconvinced.

They continued to talk while they waited for their drinks. Davis was in the middle of telling them about the rodeo when Linda and Shay walked up, bringing tension and bad energy.

"Looks like you're having a good time tonight, Davis." Linda, the blonde Taylor had seen talking with Mike the first time she'd come to the Red Buffalo, spoke first.

"That's what most people tend to do when they go out, Linda," Davis replied.

"Who are your friends?" Shay looked at Taylor and Rae as she spoke.

"This is Taylor. She's a friend of Mike's. And this is my new friend Rachel. Ladies, meet Linda and Shay." Davis looked at them, daring them to say something out of line. Linda looked at Taylor.

"How do you know Mike?" Linda asked Taylor.

"I met him when I moved here last month."

"Would you like to know how I know him?" A fake smile accompanied Linda's words.

Taylor was about to reply when Rae beat her to it. "No, she does not. But she's too nice to tell you that, so I will."

"Excuse me, Linda wasn't talking to you, she was talking to her," Shay added her two cents to the conversation.

Rae glared at Shay as she spoke.

"That's okay, Rae. I got this," Taylor said. "Listen, I don't care how you know Mike, and I don't know why you came over here. Whatever the reason —"

Linda looked as if she was about to say something, but Davis cut her off.

"I think you've said enough, Linda. You and Shay need to go back where you were before you came over here trying to stir up some shit. And if you don't want to go, I can have Steve show you the door, or I can show you myself. Your choice." Davis's tone was calm, but the look in his eyes was anything but.

"Last I heard, it was a free country, and we can be anywhere we want," Shay mouthed off.

Davis raised an eyebrow as he looked at them.

"Come on, Shay. Let's go." Linda, noticing his look, grabbed Shay's arm, and the two women walked away.

"Friends of yours, Davis?" Rae asked. "Inquiring minds want to know."

"Not really. Linda is Mike's ex, and Shay is her bestie. Both are friends with my sister."

"Your sweet sister Mina?"

"Yup, that's the one. They've all been friends since kindergarten. It's a mystery why they're still friends today."

"Well for the record, Taylor and I like Mina."

"Do you like me too?" Davis asked playfully.

"I was going to say no, but those dimples make it hard to lie." Rae laughed.

"Everything okay over here?" Caleb returned with their drinks.

"Yes, why wouldn't it be?" Taylor took her drink from him.

"No reason." Caleb gave Davis a look. Davis nodded his head slightly. "So how about we get these drinks down and get ready to go do some dancing?" Caleb said.

They all raised their glasses in a toast.

Taylor and Rae found out that line dancing wasn't too hard after all, and they had a good time. Caleb, Davis, and Mina lined up on either side of them and talked them through the moves. Mina was between Taylor and Rae. Caleb was on Taylor's other side, and Davis was next to Rae. By the time they got back to the bar, Taylor found she'd worked up a bit of a sweat and grabbed a napkin to fan herself just as Mike joined them.

"Looks like you all were having a good time out there." He wrapped an arm around Taylor's waist.

"We were," Taylor answered. Rae nodded in agreement. Caleb went around the bar and fixed them all another round of drinks. "I didn't expect it to be so much fun."

"Neither did I. Who knew cowboy country had all this going on?" Rae said.

Mike chuckled. "I guess that means you're no longer worried about Taylor being carried off."

"Oh, I don't know about that." Rae smiled as she looked at Davis. "It might be fun."

Davis returned her look and asked if she'd care to step outside for a bit. Rae said yes, so he took her hand to assist her down from the barstool, and the two made their way to the exit.

"Should I be worried?" Taylor asked as she watched them walk away.

"No. Davis is an ass, but he's harmless. By the way your friend was looking at him though, maybe I should ask you the same question."

"Rae can take care of herself."

Mike sat down on the stool Rae vacated.

"I heard what happened with Linda. Are you okay?"

She turned and looked at him. "Yes, why wouldn't I be?"

"Just checking. She can be a bit much."

"It takes more than a few words to scare me," She went on to say, "But what I *am* curious about is why you've never mentioned her."

"I don't know. I guess I didn't think it was necessary. She's my ex for a reason."

"Well, you should have said something. This is a small town, and people talk. From what I gathered from our brief chat, she's heard about you and me and she's not happy about it. It's clear she wants you back."

"That's not going to happen, and I don't give a damn what she *or* this town thinks." Mike sounded as if he was getting angry. "Is this going to be a problem?"

"Maybe. I don't know." Taylor shook her head. "If it is, we need to talk about it."

"Now?"

"Yes, now."

"No need. We're good."

"Are you sure?" Mike sounded unconvinced.

Taylor nodded.

"I need your words, Rosebud."

"I'm sure." Taylor decided to let the matter drop, noting it *would* be revisited at a later time.

"Good. Now, how about a dance?"

She followed Mike to the dance floor, and he pulled her close to him as they danced to a slow song about a man going back home after being away for years and finally getting a chance with his first love. Being with Mike had her doing and experiencing things in a whole new way. Visiting ghost towns, going to a rodeo, sharing secrets, and having the best sex of her life. She was feeling a little off-center with him and hoped it was because of the unchartered territory she now found herself in. She hadn't known Mike long, but she was pretty sure if she wasn't careful, she could easily fall in love with him.

When Mike heard Linda and Shay had been bothering Taylor, he'd gotten angry. He was about to go over and speak to them himself if Mina hadn't stopped him. She told him she was pretty sure Taylor could take care of herself, and if she couldn't, Davis or her friend would step in. He relented and watched them from where he stood near the door. Sure enough, a few minutes later, Linda and Shay stormed away. He had a few words with Steve before going over to join Taylor, Rae, and Davis at the bar.

Now, he was with Taylor on the dance floor, dancing to one of his favorite songs. She felt good in his arms, he thought. Good and right. He was surprised at the depth of his feelings for her. What had been a casual friendship and mild flirtation had grown into something more. He didn't quite understand it or know what it was, he just wanted to be in the moment with her. He was going to have to have a talk with Linda though. He didn't want her interfering with what he and Taylor had. They were just getting started.

chapter 26

"Well, well, well. Look who's finally up." Taylor looked up as Rae strolled into the kitchen, wearing her pajamas and a hair bonnet.

"Hush. No talking allowed until I get coffee."

"Lucky for you, the coffee is ready. The cups are in the cabinet." Taylor pointed to the cabinet over where the coffee pot sat on the counter. Rae grabbed a cup, poured coffee, and sat down at the table, where Taylor sat sipping her coffee and watching her.

"What?" Rae asked, looking anywhere but at Taylor.

"Spill. And don't leave out any details."

"There's not much to say. Davis gave me a nighttime tour of the town." Rae was smiling as she spoke.

"Must have been some tour."

"It wasn't anything special, but it was nice of him to show me around. We got back here just as Mike was leaving. And by the way, I saw that kiss he gave you before he left. Damn, girl. I could almost feel it from where I was standing."

Taylor buried her face in her hands.

"All I have to say is it's about time," Rae added.

"Please tell me Davis didn't see us."

"I would, but I can't. He's the one that saw y'all first." Rae snickered.

"He's not going to let me live that down."

"He probably won't. He seems like a good guy, but he does like to tease."

"So . . ."

"So?"

"What about you and him?"

"We did a little flirting on the tour, then came back here, sat on the front porch, and talked."

"And?"

"And that's it. He went home and told me he'd see me today at the rodeo."

"So, you like Davis, huh?"

"Yeah, I do."

"I hate to change the subject since you're in such a good mood, but I need to tell you something."

Rae looked at her over the rim of her coffee cup. "Tell me what?"

"I spoke to Liam."

"When?"

"Yesterday, when I was at the airport waiting for you."

"What did he have to say?"

"Nothing much worth repeating. I declined the invitation to his engagement party, and he called me. I told him I couldn't go. And I ripped into him a little about how he treated you. He said he understood but hoped I would at least come to the wedding since I was one of his oldest friends. I told him I would."

"I ain't mad at you, sis. He's right. You *are* one of his oldest friends. It would be wrong of you not to support him on his big day."

"No, you're my oldest friend, and if it's gonna hurt you, I'm not going."

"Then I'm happy to tell you I'm okay. Yes, my feelings were hurt initially, but I'm good. I don't think we would have made it anyway. I mean, he couldn't even tell me he was seeing someone. Besides, if things had been different, I wouldn't be here hanging out with you, nor would I have been considering being on the business end of Davis's mouth." Rae smiled.

"So, you're over Liam?"

"Let's just say I hadn't thought about him until you mentioned him just now. So maybe my feelings for him weren't that serious. Maybe I was just lonely, and he was handy." She looked meaningfully at Taylor. "As we both know, loneliness can be a result of being a workaholic. Having someone around who you don't have to put too much effort into is very tempting."

"Then I'm glad this thing with Liam is settled. And whatever this is with Davis, I hope it's fun." Taylor meant the words she told her friend. Rae was her "day one," and she wanted nothing but good things for her.

"What about you and Mike? He seems like a good guy, and I like the way he makes you smile."

"I like him. But I'm not quite sure how he feels about me."

"From what I saw of him last night, he looks like he's into you."

"Yeah, but after last night, I just don't know. I mean, he asked me if I was okay after his ex came over. And I asked him why he never mentioned her."

"What did he say?"

"He didn't say much. I said since Silverton was such a small town, he should have given a sista a warning or something. He got a little angry and said he didn't give a damn about what she or the town thought."

"Well, girl, I think you have your answer. I also think you're overthinking things."

Taylor rolled her eyes.

"Hear me out. You *do* tend to overthink things. I think this thing with Mike has pulled you out of your comfort zone, and as much as you hate to admit it, you like him more than you expected. You're used to those boring, predictable, bland-as-hell men. Mike has you running scared." Rae reached across the table and grabbed Taylor's hand. "Tay don't let that heffa steal your joy. Mike seems like he's his own man. If he wanted her, he'd still be with her. Enjoy him and see where this goes."

"I know, you're right. I do need to get out of my head. I know one thing though, if his ex and her scrawny friend come at me again, it's going to be a problem."

"Don't worry. I got your back. Hopefully, she's not that stupid. Otherwise, she'll get a little R&R." Both women laughed. "R&R"—Rosamunde and Rachel—was what they called themselves in elementary school, where they got into trouble more than once.

chapter 27

Never having been to a rodeo, Rae and Taylor were excited about going. Mike told her to pick up their tickets at the will-call window when they'd spoken earlier and reminded her to text him when they arrived he'd come to get them. They got to the arena an hour and a half before it started, so they'd have time to check out the booths at the expo. Taylor was particularly interested in seeing the jewelry displays. She'd been toying with some designs she thought might be of interest and wanted to see what some of the local artisans were doing. While they waited for Mike to meet them, they stood talking and people-watching. There were quite a few people there, and Taylor assumed they'd come from the neighboring counties.

"How're you ladies doing this afternoon?" Both women turned to see two men standing to the right of them.

"Fine, thanks," Rae said.

"You must be new around here. I don't think I've seen you before." The man who spoke smiled, but it didn't reach his eyes.

"Fairly new," Taylor confirmed.

"You look familiar, have we met?" He took a step closer to Taylor.

"No, we haven't." Taylor moved away from him,

"I *definitely* would have remembered if I'd seen you. My name's Jason, and this is my friend Amos." The other man said as he eyed the women appreciatively.

"Hi Jason, Amos. I'm Rae, and this is Taylor."

"Nice to meet you. What brings you to the rodeo?"

"We were just in the area and thought we'd check it out," Taylor answered. The man and his friend seemed nice enough, but there was something about them that was slightly off-putting.

"Well, if you'd like some tour guides, we'd be happy to show you around."

"Thanks, but we've got it covered," Taylor replied.

"That's too bad. There's a party in the square tomorrow night. Maybe we'll see you there."

"Maybe," Rae said in a noncommittal tone. She looked over at Taylor and then smiled when she looked past her to see Davis walking toward them. Jason and Amos didn't seem too pleased at his arrival.

"I'm here to keep you two out of trouble." Davis gave a hard look at the two men as he spoke to Taylor and Rae jokingly. "Taylor, Dana needs your help. Why don't you girls come with me, and I'll take you to her." Glad to see him, the women quickly said goodbye to Jason and Amos and walked away with Davis. None of them saw the hardness in Jason's gaze as he watched them leave.

"New friends?" Davis asked.

"Hardly. They came up while we were waiting for you," Rae responded, walking between Davis and Taylor. "They offered to show us around, but we told them we had it covered. There was something *off* about them."

"Off like how?"

"Nothing real obvious, just a vibe I got."

Davis had a similar read on the two men. "There's a lot that goes on around here, and unfortunately, there are some unsavory people who show up at events like this. Be careful, and if someone gives you trouble, come get one of us."

Taylor and Rae looked at each other. "We will," Rae said.

"I'm serious."

"Okay. I said we will."

"Good. Now that we've got that covered, I'll take you over to the booth and the section where we'll be sitting. Mina's there, and she'll show you around and take you over to Dana."

Mike's booth was larger than expected. In addition to beer and soda, they sold brown sugar lemonade, nachos, and house-made potato chips with various seasonings. They also gave away free bottles of water to anyone who wanted them. Mike was talking with Mina and Caleb as they made their way over. Taylor watched his movements as he talked. He had on jeans, and his T-shirt was wet with just enough sweat to hint at his solid body underneath. He was wearing sunglasses and a cowboy hat. His grown-man sexy was in full force. He smiled when he saw them approach and walked over to them.

"Hey, Rae," he said. Then he bent to place a kiss on Taylor's lips. "Hey, Rosebud."

Taylor felt her face heat up, and she was pretty sure her panties were getting damp. Mike only called her that when they were alone together.

"Thanks, Davis," he told his friend.

"No problem."

"How're two doing today?"

"Pretty good, and you?" Taylor said.

"Now that we pretty much have everything in place, I'm good."

Mina exited the booth and came to greet the ladies. She had a drink carrier in her hand.

"Hi, Taylor, Rae. I thought you'd like to try the brown sugar lemonade. It's a little tart but perfect for a hot day." She gave each of them a drink.

"That's pretty good," Taylor said.

"Better than I expected," Rae added.

"Cool. Well, if you're ready to go, I'll show you where everything is."

"Hold on a minute. I got chips." Caleb handed each of them napkins and cones filled with freshly made potato chips.

"Caleb, I hope you're giving out bigger servings than these to the customers. This small size is just a tease." Davis watched Rae eat a few chips and then lick the salt off her fingers.

Mike fed Taylor chips from his cone. His were sprinkled with chili lime seasoning instead of sea salt like hers were.

"Like them?"

"I do." She purposely licked his finger when he fed her another chip. Rae snickered, and Taylor realized she'd seen them. "We, ah, should probably get started on that tour."

Mike smiled at her. She was pretty sure if he didn't have sunglasses on, she would see in his eyes what she was currently feeling. He whispered in her ear, "Enjoy the tour." Then he kissed the side of her neck.

Taylor nodded because she didn't seem to be able to speak. She took a sip of her lemonade and turned to find Rae and Mina grinning at her.

"Shall we?" Mina asked, and Rae chuckled.

"Let's go," Taylor turned away, trying to ignore them both.

Davis, Caleb, and Mike stood watching them walk away. Davis smiled appreciatively.

"Damn, that's a lot of ass."

"You shouldn't be looking at your sister's ass, Davis."

Mike laughed at Caleb's comment.

"You know who I'm talking about."

"I know, but you made it too easy, and I couldn't resist. And for the record, there's nothing wrong with Mina's ass."

"Watch it, man, that's my sister. We're friends, and I know you like her, but I'll still fuck you up."

"Whatever. But you're right about the ass."

Mike was watching Taylor's jean-clad legs walk away. All he could think about was getting her out of them later that night. Davis interrupted his thoughts with his next words.

"Two guys were talking to Taylor and Rae when I went to get them. I've never seen them before, but there was something about them. They seemed a little too smooth and a little too helpful. Taylor and Rae picked up on it too. I told them to be careful and to come get one of us if they ran into any trouble."

Mike felt his body go tense. "What did they look like?" Davis described the men, and Caleb and Mike said they'd keep an eye out.

Taylor enjoyed the expo. In addition to jewelry, clothes, and boot displays, there were exhibits on any and everything rodeo-related, including information on rodeo clown schools—*much* to Rae's displeasure. Mina introduced them to some of the vendors she knew and told them stories about some of the rodeos she'd attended in the past. Rae and Mina engaged in some good-natured teasing of Taylor as they browsed the different booths. Rae said she was going to have to get some pictures of her with Mike Because she was sure no one back home would believe her without evidence.

"I mean, come on, Taylor. The guys you dated in the past were all the same person."

"No, they weren't." Taylor rolled her eyes at Rae.

"Yes, they were. Mina, if you saw them, you'd agree with me. They were all boring. They all dressed in the same style—a cross between an accountant and a science teacher, circa 1970."

"They weren't that bad, Rae."

"I beg to differ. Remember the one who lived with his mother? She made him break up with you because she thought you kept him out too late. Or what about the one who was a closet sub and tried to get you to go all dominatrix on him?"

"Okay, I'll give you those two. But in my defense, I didn't know Alan lived with his mother. And when Donald asked me if I liked to take charge now and then, I thought he meant something else. Although truth be told, I might have given it a try if he hadn't sprung it on me the way he did." All three women burst out laughing.

"Mina, girl, you should have seen it. Tay and I had just come back to her place after shopping. I went with her to her bedroom with some of the stuff she was intending to hang up. And there he was, lying naked on the bed with a blindfold and a collar, his hands secured to the bedpost. Lying next to him on the bed was a paddle."

"A paddle?" Mina asked, laughing.

"Yup, a paddle for spanking that ass," Rae smirked.

"Oh my word!"

"I know, right? I mean no one would have ever guessed Mark had a kink, much less that one."

"So, what did you do?"

"Much as she wanted to stay and see what happened next, I made Rae leave," Taylor said. "I went back in and talked to Donald about his little surprise, and he said he was a little disappointed, as he'd always wanted to get dominated by two women. I couldn't say anything in response to that, so I undid his hands and told him to get dressed and leave."

"So, did you see him again?" Mina looked at Taylor, clearly curious to know how the story ended.

"No. I thought about it, but there was something about my best friend seeing my scrawny-ass boyfriend spread-eagle and naked on the bed that wouldn't let me," she admitted, sending them into another round of laughter.

"I somehow don't think that would ever happen with Mike, Taylor," Mina said.

"I don't either," Rae agreed. "But from the way you've been smiling and blushing since I've been here, and not to mention how you get all flustered when he gets close to you, *something* is happening."

"It's not what you think." Taylor knew it was true, even as she denied it.

"Girl, you are the worst liar, so don't even try it."

"Okay, enough about me. What about you and Caleb, Mina?"

"Ooohh, yes. Do tell," Rae added.

"There's not much to tell. I've had a crush on Caleb since I was little. He was always dating someone and never showed any interest in me that way. Plus, I think the fact that he and Davis are friends had something to do with it." Mina blushed a little as she spoke.

"Most guys don't like their friends dating their sisters." Rae glanced at Taylor when she spoke. "Taylor and I had the same problem growing up. I didn't have any brothers, but as far as everyone was concerned, Taylor's brothers were mine too, so hardly anyone ever approached us."

"Everything changed a few months ago when we were at the wedding of a mutual friend. I didn't notice it until my friend—well, former friend—Shay, said something about how the only reason he asked me to dance was because I was his friend's sister. Now that I think on it, I think they thought he was doing the fat girl a favor." Mina frowned.

"Mina, you are *not* fat." Taylor couldn't believe Mina thought of herself as fat. Yes, she wasn't as slender as her former friends, but no way was she overweight.

"Compared to Shay and Linda I am."

"No, compared to them, you are normal and healthy, and they are skinny bitches." Rae continued, "Them making comments like that makes me think they were probably jealous of you."

"I don't know about them being jealous, but they can be mean sometimes—more so now that Mike and Linda broke up. Shay has always liked Davis, but he can't stand her. Both Linda and Shay don't like Caleb because of his mother. They hate her because she's beautiful and half the men in town are in love with her."

"I've seen his mother, and she *is* beautiful," Taylor said.

"Yes, well, she doesn't like them either, so the feeling is mutual."

"So, with all that hating going on, how did you two manage to connect?" Rae asked.

"Since the wedding, Caleb seemed to be around a lot. He'd always been nice to me, but then he started flirting and teasing me, and he'd never done that before. Listening to Shay and Linda, I was beginning to agree with them and thought maybe I was reading him wrong. The other night, he let me know I wasn't."

"Ahh, the joyful feeling of a new relationship," Rae smiled.

"Like I said, it's early going."

"From what I know of him, he's nice. Funny too. And the man can cook. If he can handle his 'other' business"—Taylor did air quotes with her hands— "like he cooks, you might have yourself a keeper."

Mina giggled and blushed as Taylor and Rae laughed in agreement. They continued walking until they arrived at the building that had been converted into the dressing rooms for the rodeo queen, her court, and Dana.

When they entered Dana's dressing room, they found Cheryl consoling a very upset Dana. She looked relieved to see the other women.

"Do you need us to come back later?" Taylor asked.

"No, but I could use your help. Dana's friend, who was supposed to do her hair and makeup, flaked on her."

"Oh, sweetie, I'm sorry to hear that," Taylor told a tearful Dana.

"I'm thinking she's not much of a friend if she flaked on you at a time like this," Rae added. Both Cheryl and Dana looked at her. Taylor side-eyed Rae.

"Cheryl, Dana, this is my best friend, Rae. She can be a little blunt."

Rae winced. "I'm sorry. But I do think that was a messed-up thing to do. Nice to meet you two, by the way," she ended lamely.

"Nice to meet you too. And I agree." Cheryl smiled.

"What am I going to do, Mom? This is the most important day of my life, and I wanted to look my best. I have no clue how to do my hair and makeup for an event like this. This isn't the same as singing in Uncle Mike's bar." Tears fell from her eyes as she spoke. Cheryl handed her a tissue.

"I can help with your hair, honey, but I'm not that good with makeup. I was hoping Taylor or Mina might be able to help with that."

Mina shook her head. "Lip gloss and tinted moisturizer are pretty much all I know how to do. Anything else, and I might have you looking like a rodeo clown." They all laughed.

"I'm not much better, but Rae is pretty good with makeup," Taylor said. "I think between all of us, we can get you ready."

"Miss Rae, would you do my makeup?"

"Sure, Dana. I'd be happy to."

"See, honey, I told you it would be okay." Cheryl hugged Dana and mouthed a thank-you to Taylor, Rae, and Mina.

chapter 28

Two hours later, Cheryl, Mina, Rae, and Taylor left the dressing room where a happy Dana was doing a vocal warm-up. After a short discussion, they'd decided on a faux-hawk French braid and a natural look with a hint of glam: winged eyeliner, lashes, bronzer, and a matte red lip. Dana let out a squeal of delight when she looked in the mirror after Rae finished.

"Oh my goodness, is that me?"

Rae smiled. "That's all you."

"You look beautiful, honey." Cheryl's eyes were a little misty.

"Rae, I'm going to need you to give me a few tips before you leave town," Mina said as they made their way to their seats.

"Thanks again. I don't know what we would have done without you ladies." Cheryl expressed her gratitude for what they'd done.

"I think you would have figured something out. And, honestly, I'm glad we could help. Dana is a sweetheart." Taylor smiled as she spoke.

"She really is. She's worked so hard for this opportunity. I swear if I see her so-called friend tonight, I just might slap her."

"We'd be happy to help you make that happen. I mean, what kind of friend does that?" Rae added.

"A jealous one," Mina replied.

"You girls want to grab a drink before we take our seats?" Cheryl asked.

"That sounds like a good idea."

They went to the Red Buffalo booth and got beer and a few orders of nachos before joining the rest of the Knight family and friends. When they got there, Red and Denton were sitting with Albee and his wife, Diane, the Hawkins, and the Edwards. Davis, Mike, and PJ were handing out drinks and hot dogs to the younger kids. Taylor recognized Albee's three children, Matthew, Matilda, and Angelica, and PJ's two youngest sons. The others, she didn't know. Two had red hair and looked to be about the same age as Albee's kids. She thought they might be Red and Denton's. The other two were Mike's twins. She recognized them from the pictures she'd seen at his home. They were on the bench below where the adults were sitting.

When they finished passing out the food, they came over to join them. PJ asked Cheryl if everything was okay. She told him that thanks to Taylor and Rae, Dana was ready. Davis sat down next to Rae. Taylor noticed he rubbed his hand along Rae's back when he sat down, and she scooted a little closer to him. Mike sat next to her, leaned over, and kissed her cheek.

"How was everything?" he asked.

"It was good. I saw a lot of cool stuff."

"Nice. After the kids get finished eating, I'll introduce you."

"Okay. I can't believe how much they look like you," Taylor observed.

Mike chuckled. "Much to my ex-wife's displeasure. According to her, they not only look like me, but they also act like me."

"So, they're grumpy little people?"

"Yeah, something like that." He laughed. They talked as they waited for the kids to finish eating, and then Mike called them over.

"Mikey, Kay, this is Miss Taylor. Taylor, this is Mike Jr. and Mikayla."

"Nice to meet you, Miss Taylor," they responded in unison.

Taylor smiled. "Nice to meet you as well. Are you having fun so far?"

"Yes, ma'am. We—" They were interrupted when Matthew, Matilda, Anjelica, and two other red-haired children came over to join them.

"Miss Taylor! We didn't know you were coming!" Matthew said excitedly.

"Hi, Matthew, Matilda, and Anjelica! How nice to see you. Who are your friends?"

Matilda answered for all of them, "This is Denny, and this is Mandy. Mandy, Miss Taylor is the fairy princess we told you about." Angelica moved closer to Taylor and pointed to Rae. "Is she a fairy princess too?"

Taylor laughed. "That's my best friend, Rae." Hearing her name, Rae turned toward Taylor.

"Kids, meet Miss Rae. I've known her forever, and she came for a visit. Tell her your names." Each of the children introduced themselves. Mike told them to take a seat as the opening ceremony was about to start and it was almost time for Dana to sing. They excitedly sat on the bench in front of Mike and Taylor.

"Ladies and gentlemen, welcome to the fifty-first annual Silverton rodeo," A booming voice said over the arena's loudspeaker. The Range Riders Riding Club set the pivots and took their position for the invocation and the presentation of the colors. The color guard entered, followed by Dana.

"Please rise for the national anthem, sung by Miss Dana Knight."

Everyone watched as Dana closed her eyes and took a deep breath. She opened her eyes, raised the microphone in her hand, and began to sing a cappella. Dana's voice was rich and soulful, each note was in perfect pitch, and each word was enunciated clearly. When she finished singing, Dana glowed as the crowd clapped and roared with appreciation. PJ had a huge smile on his face as he held Cheryl, who was crying happy tears. Taylor thought it was the cutest thing when he reached into his pocket and pulled out a handkerchief, kissing Cheryl on the cheek as he wiped her tears.

The grand entrance followed the singing of the national anthem. The Silverton County events committee, the rodeo queen, her court, and the contestants entered the arena. Next, an empty horse saddle served as a tribute to the memory of all the cowboys who had passed on. It was brought in and placed on a podium in the center of the arena floor.

Later, Jamie, PJ and Cheryl's oldest son, and his friend joined them in the stands. They were both members of the riding club that set the pivots earlier. Dana joined them shortly after.

"There's the lady of the hour," Jackson announced. "You did an amazing job tonight!"

"You sure did, honey! I'm so proud of you!" PJ stood and hugged her. Red kissed her on the cheek and congratulated her. The rest of the group commented and complimented her. Dana, beaming shyly, thanked them. She hugged her mother, then made her way to Taylor and Rae and gave them each a heartfelt hug.

"Thank you both so much for everything. I appreciate it."

Rae, never one to hold back, said, "Why didn't anyone tell me you could sing like that?" They all laughed. "Your voice gave me chills."

Angie gave her a bottle of water, and she sat down with the rest of the group to watch the show.

chapter 29

Later that evening after the day's events ended, Taylor and Rae went back to Taylor's house to freshen up and fix a light meal. The younger kids were staying with the Edwards, who were hosting a pool party and sleepover for them, and Davis, Caleb, and Mike were coming to Taylor's later after taking care of the booth and stopping by the pool party. She and Rae were in the kitchen trying to decide what to fix for a late supper.

"Do you think the guys will bring Mina with them?" Rae asked.

"I don't know. But I'll text Mike and have him ask her if she wants to join us." She shot off a quick text. He responded a few minutes later saying that she would and that she'd probably get there before the rest of them did.

"That's settled. Now, what do we do for a meal?"

"What do you have that's quick and easy?"

"I have stuff to make chicken lettuce wraps, fresh spring rolls with dipping sauce, and some fruit I can toss together for a dessert."

"Sounds good to me, Tay. I can take care of the stuff for the lettuce wraps, but you're on your own with the spring rolls."

"You might be able to do them. Now, how about we open a bottle of wine, turn on some music, and get started?"

Taylor grabbed a bottle from the wine rack and two glasses from the cabinet. Rae placed her phone into the speaker dock and pressed play. They drank and danced as they prepared the food. They almost didn't hear the doorbell, as Taylor was laughing at Rae, who was having a harder time than she should have making the spring rolls.

"I'll see who that is and come back and check your progress." Taylor had left the front door open when they came in and saw Mina on the other side of the screen door.

"Hey, Mina! Glad you could make it!" Taylor unlocked the door to let her in. "Rae's in the kitchen." Taylor relocked the screen door.

"Hi, Rae," Mina said, following Taylor into the kitchen.

"Hey, Mina. You wouldn't know how to make a spring roll would you?"

"No, but it can't be that hard, can it?"

Taylor started laughing and pointed to Rae's sad attempt.

"Apparently, it is. She's been working on that same spring roll for the last five minutes."

"I may need to rethink this friendship. Abuse because of my inability to roll vegetables in rice paper is not a good look on you, Tay." Rae playfully narrowed her eyes at Taylor.

"Yeah, yeah, that's the wine talking. And yeah, you *do* suck at this. Speaking of wine, Mina, would you care for some?"

"Yes, please."

Taylor poured her a glass and set about showing her how to construct a fresh spring roll.

"See, that wasn't so bad, was it?" Taylor asked Mina as she looked at the rolls she'd done.

"Nope, I got the hang of it in no time. They taste pretty good too."

"See, Rae," Taylor teased. "It's not that hard."

"Yes, well, if I were the Black Suzy Homemaker like you, I'd be able to do it, but I'm not."

Mina snorted, then laughed. "Oops, sorry," she said quickly.

Taylor and Rae looked at her.

"Girl, why are you apologizing?" Rae asked. "I thought it was funny too, that's why I said it."

"I was apologizing for snorting. I didn't mean to do it."

"No need to apologize. It happens. And if you do it again, so what?"

"Trust me. No one's going to notice you snorting because they'll be too busy staring at your smile." Taylor refilled her wine glass.

"How about we show you a few of the line dances we know?" Rae suggested. "It may be a bit before the guys get here." They all grabbed their glasses and went into the living room where there was more space for dancing.

Taylor, Rae, and Mina were doing the "Cha-Cha Slide" when they heard Caleb's voice call through the screen door.

"Hey! What's going on in there? I've been knocking for five minutes!"

Rae went to the door and saw Davis and Caleb standing on the other side of the screen door.

"Maybe you should have tried ringing the doorbell. I know you have them out here in the country."

"Cute *and* funny. Open the door, and I'll show you what else we have out here in the country," Davis responded with a smile.

"Good one, man," Caleb chuckled and gave Davis a fist bump.

"Whatever, *man*," Rae said as she unlocked the screen and walked back into the living room. Davis and Caleb followed behind her.

"Hey, Mina, Taylor. Mike will be along in a few. What were you all up to?" Caleb was looking at Mina when he spoke.

"Not much. Drinking. Dancing. Cooking," Taylor answered. "Do you guys want to wait for Mike, or do you want to eat now?"

"We'll wait."

"Cool. Can I get you guys to go to the back porch and grab some extra chairs?"

"Sure."

"Just go straight down the hallway through the back room."

The men went to retrieve the chairs. Rae turned down the music and followed Mina and Taylor into the kitchen. Mina helped Taylor add the leaf to the table to expand it. Rae took dishes from the cabinet and started setting the table.

"Taylor, is that all your work in the back room?" Davis placed the chairs he was carrying around the table.

"Most of it is. Some of it is my parents' work."

"You're pretty good," Caleb added.

"Thanks."

"Maybe you can tell us a little about some of the pieces after dinner." Caleb wandered over to the counter and looked at the food the women had prepared. "What's on the menu, ladies?"

"Something light and filling. Lettuce wraps, fresh spring rolls, and fruit salad for dessert. And there's beer and wine. Would you care for a drink?"

Caleb nodded. "I'll have a beer."

"Same," Davis said.

There was a knock on the screen door.

"Rae, will you get the beers?" Taylor asked as she went to answer the door.

"You made it!" she exclaimed when she saw Mike.

"I did." He opened the door and gave her a quick kiss.

"It's about time you got here. I was about to suggest we start without you. As good as this food looks, there might not have been any left by the time you got here," Davis said.

"In that case, let's get started." They all sat down at the table. Caleb said grace, and they began to pass the food around. Plenty of conversation and laughter accompanied the meal. It had been a long time since Taylor had entertained someone other than Rae or her family members.

After dinner, they cleaned the kitchen and adjourned into the back room that Taylor used as a studio. She showed them some of the jewelry she'd made and some of the sketches she'd done since arriving in Silverton. She also showed them the wooden keepsake box her father had made and a copy of the portrait her mom had made of the three of them before she died.

"Is everyone in your family creative?" Mina asked.

"My father was a carpenter, and my mother was an artist. The Sawyers were my parents' best friends who adopted me after my parents died. Mimi, my mother, is a whiz in the kitchen, and Poppy is a former athlete and all-around brainiac. My older brother is a surgeon, and you've met Grant."

"Your Mimi taught you how to cook?" Caleb asked.

"She did." Taylor nodded.

"I think I need to meet her."

They went into the kitchen and refilled their drinks, then went to the back porch and talked for a while. By now, it was around 11:00 p.m., and the evening came to an end. Tomorrow was a big day, with the rodeo and the party in the town square. Mike held Taylor's hand as she walked with him to the front door.

"Are you coming out tomorrow?" he asked.

"I think so. I'm not sure what time we'll get there."

"Text me when you're on your way, and I'll meet you at the will-call booth."

"Okay."

"I'll look forward to seeing you tomorrow. I hope you save me a dance tomorrow night." He wrapped his arms around her and pulled her close.

"Definitely."

"Good." Mike lowered his head and kissed her. When he ended it, he leaned his forehead against hers. "Goodnight, Rosebud."

"Goodnight, Mike." He gave her one more squeeze and a peck on the lips, then got into his truck. He waved as he drove away. Taylor returned his wave, went back into the house, and sat down on the couch next to Rae, who handed her a glass of wine.

"Thanks." She took the glass and raised it to her lips.

"You look a little dazed there, my friend. Did the grumpy man do something to you out on the porch?"

"No. And why are you calling him that?"

"Because he is. He's a nice guy and all, but you have to admit it's true."

"He is a little bit, but that's part of his charm."

"Whatever. But he does seem to like you and doesn't care who knows it."

"What do you mean?"

"Last night at the bar, today at the rodeo, and tonight. And you seem to be enjoying it."

"I am. He's a good man." Taylor took a sip from her glass. "I didn't tell you all of what happened the night I went over to his place for dinner, did I?"

"There's more than what you told me?" Rae looked surprised.

"Yes. I left some things out when we talked. Mostly because it took me a while to process it all."

"What happened?"

"Mike cooked, and we ate and shared more about ourselves. Everything was going fine until a summer storm happened unexpectedly."

"Oh no." Rae knew about Taylor's history with storms.

"I couldn't sleep, so I got up to find something to drink to help settle my nerves. The thunder was so loud it scared me, and I screamed, then I went into a full-blown meltdown as Mike came into the kitchen. He took me back to the bedroom, then made me something to drink, and I ended up telling him my story. I was sure after seeing all of my crazy, he was going to excuse himself and go back to the den where he'd been sleeping. But he didn't. He moved up on the bed to sit next to me and held me while I cried. The next thing I knew, I woke up and found myself still in Mike's arms." Taylor teared up as she told Rae about that evening.

"Oh my God, Taylor. Wow. Who would have thought that Grumpy Smurf had it in him." Taylor looked at Rae for a beat, and then they both laughed.

"I mean, you know I'm right."

"Mike may not be Mr. Bubbly, but he has a lot of good qualities. And I will admit, I was surprised he didn't run when he got a glimpse of my issues."

"Real men don't run from issues, Tay. They either fix them or help you get through them. I like you with him."

"I like me with him too."

"I'll drink to that," Rae said, and they clinked glasses.

chapter 30

The next morning, Mike rose early to go pick up his children from his uncle's house. His manager was overseeing the booth operations at the rodeo today, so there was no rush to get to the arena for the day's events. As he made his way along the highway, he thought about the previous night. He'd enjoyed the evening. Taylor was an unexpected addition to his life that he truly enjoyed. The shadows he'd seen in her eyes when they first met were fading, and she seemed to smile more. When he broke up with Linda, he was convinced he was ready to take a pause on relationships. Now, somehow, he'd found himself with Taylor. They hadn't put a label on what was between them, but for all intents and purposes, it was a relationship. And he was perfectly fine with that. He hoped Taylor felt the same. He couldn't imagine himself being the only one feeling this way.

As he pulled in front of the Edwards' home, he saw his uncle Jack talking with Albee, his wife, and their children.

"Hey, Uncle Mike!" Anjelica called as he got out of his car and joined them.

"Hey, sweetie. How are you? Morning, folks."

"Morning. How're you doing today?" Albee asked.

"I'm good. How about you?"

"We're good. Just came to pick up the kids. Kids, say thanks to Uncle Jack so we can get going."

"Thanks, Uncle Jack," they replied. "See you later."

"You're welcome, kids."

Albee and his wife put their kids in the car and drove off. Mike stood next to his uncle and watched as they drove away.

"How was it?"

"Not too bad. They pretty much behaved. I think it's because they were afraid if they didn't, they wouldn't get any pizza." Jack chuckled. "But I have to say, that youngest one of Albee's has a set of lungs on her. That little girl uses screaming like a superpower."

"I would have to agree with you on that."

"So how are you doing, Mike?" His uncle asked him while looking him over. "I have to say, you seem to be in a pretty good mood these days. Would it have anything to do with Silverton's newest resident?"

"I'm good, Uncle Jack. And yes, I have been spending time with Taylor."

"I like her. She's a sweetheart."

"Yes, she is. Uncle Jack, do you ever wonder why Pop decided to leave the house to her?"

"I did initially when he had me add it to his will. But when he told me why, I understood."

"Why did he do it?"

"Well, he said he was touched by the kindness she showed him. He also said she had an air of melancholy about her, and it made him want to do something nice for her. I don't know if you knew this or not, but that day at the airport, she changed her connecting flight to a later time so she could wait with Preston until PJ arrived because she didn't want to leave him alone. He said she never said a word about it, just excused herself for a few minutes and came back with coffee and snacks."

"I didn't know that." Mike was about to ask his uncle another question when the front door opened, and Mikey and Kay ran toward him.

"Hey, Dad!"

"Hey, kids! Were you guys good for Aunt Angie and Uncle Jack?"

"Yes, sir."

"Good. Let's go get your backpacks so we can head home." Mike and Jackson followed them back into the house.

Taylor and Rae decided to skip the rodeo and hang out at the house before going to the party in the town square later that evening. They'd slept late, then fixed brunch. While they were cleaning the kitchen, Mimi Face Timed Taylor.

"Hey, girls! How are you?"

"We're doing fine, Mimi. How are you doing?"

"We're doing good. The reason I'm calling you is because Liam's mother has been blowing up my phone. She's upset that you two aren't going to his engagement party. Is that true?"

Taylor and Rae looked at each other before Taylor answered. "Yes, Mimi. It's true. But we are planning on attending the wedding."

"Why aren't you going to the party?"

"Rae has a conference, and I got a big project due around the same time."

"Are you sure? Because Tara seems to think you don't like the bride-to-be."

"No, that's not it. We just can't make it."

"Okay. I'll let her know. Between you and me, I don't think Tara likes her future daughter-in-law. She seems to be more concerned about you two not going to the engagement party than getting to know her. I think she was secretly hoping one of you would be Liam's intended. I know you girls are close to him, but honestly, as much as I love that boy, I don't think he's man enough for either of you. I'm glad neither of you was foolish enough to hook up with him." Rae elbowed Taylor, warning her not to say anything. Her mother continued, "And one more thing. Your dad and I are going to Las Vegas next week for one of his reunions."

"That should be fun. You guys always have a good time at those things."

"Thanks. And, Rae, your folks are going with us."

"I hope you guys behave, because I don't want to have to fly to Vegas and bail y'all out, plus Mama and Daddy," Rae said.

"Where's the fun in that?" They all laughed. Then Mimi asked, "Rae, how are you enjoying your visit?"

"I'm having a good time, Mimi. Since I've been here, I've been to a saloon, a rodeo, and done some country line dancing."

"Have you met Mike? Don't bother lying for Taylor. Grant told us about him."

"I have, and he's pretty nice."

"That's good. It's a shame I had to hear about my daughter's new man from everyone but her."

"Mimi! That's not true. It's still early going. I was just waiting a bit."

Her mother looked at her. "Uh-huh. Somehow, I'm finding that hard to believe. Anyway, what are you two getting into today?"

"We're just hanging out right now, and later we're going to the party they're having in the town square. Supposedly, it's a tradition held at the end of the rodeo."

"Sounds like it might be fun. Watch out for drunken cowboys."

"We will."

"I gotta run, girls. Take care of yourselves and have fun."

"We will. Love you, and tell Poppy I said hi."

"I will. Love you, too. Bye."

"So, Mimi thinks Miss Tara doesn't like Liam's fiancée, huh? That's interesting." Rae voiced the same thought Taylor had when she heard that bit of news.

"Yes, it is. I also found it interesting what Mimi said about Liam."

"I know, right? But you know what? I'm going to agree with her on this one."

"I'm going to have to go with her on this too. Honestly though, if she would have said that before, I might not have. But now, I'd say she's spot-on."

"Enough about him." Rae got up from the table. "Why didn't you tell Mimi about Mike?"

"Because I don't know what this is between us. I think I might be a little in love with him, and I'm scared that it might be too soon, it might not be reciprocated, or he might not be over his ex. Then there are his kids. They seem nice enough, but what if they don't like me?"

"Damn, girl, really? Why are you torturing yourself like this? That man is definitely into you. Y'all might not have a label, but this *is* something. Stop worrying about what might happen and enjoy the moment." Rae put her hands on Taylor's shoulders and looked directly at her. "Tay, I get it. Mike is very different from the guys you normally date, and that scares you. I'm saying this again: don't let your fear keep you from finding out where this could go." She pulled her in for a hug. "Besides, I don't think I could take another double date with one of those weird-ass men you always seem to hook up with." They both laughed. Rae pulled back. "Promise me you'll at least think about living in the moment and giving this a try."

"I promise." Taylor nodded.

"Good. Now, I'm going to turn on some music. We're going to pick out our outfits for tonight, have a mini spa day, and indulge in a little day drinking. How does that sound?"

Mike finished the sandwiches he was making for lunch and added chips and pickles to the three plates before carrying them to the table where his children waited.

"What's for lunch, Dad?" Kay asked.

"BLTs, chips, and some of Red's pickles."

"I love her pickles."

"I do too. Mikey, why don't you say grace so we can eat."

"Okay, Dad." The three of them joined hands, and Mikey blessed the food. Kay ate a couple of pickles before picking up her sandwich, and Mikey added some chips to his sandwich before taking a big bite.

"You guys want some lemonade?" Both kids nodded.

Smiling, Mike rose to go to the refrigerator to get the lemonade. The twins often answered questions in unison, finished each other sentences, or made the same gestures. He couldn't recall doing that with his brothers while growing up. He found their twin actions, as he thought of them, funny and cute. Mikey and Kay were good kids, and despite having endured a messy divorce, they still maintained sunny dispositions *and* their innocence, which were often casualties for children of divorce. Mike filled their glasses, grabbed a bottle of water for himself, and sat back down at the table.

"Dad, did you break up with Miss Linda?" Kay looked at him.

"Why do you ask?" Mike had not been expecting that question.

"Mom said you had a new friend, and Miss Linda didn't sit with us at the rodeo."

"Miss Linda kept looking over at our section last night. She didn't look like she was happy," Mikey added.

"New friend?"

"The lady you introduced us to. I forgot her name."

"Her name is Taylor. And yes, I did break up with Linda."

Kay took a bite of her sandwich and chewed thoughtfully before looking across the table at Mike.

"Mom said Miss Linda said you broke up with her because of Miss Taylor. Is that true?"

Mike found himself getting a little angry at hearing that his ex-wife was discussing his love life with his kids. He would have to talk to her about that.

"No, that's not true. Linda and I stopped seeing each other right after Pop passed away. I met Taylor a couple of months ago when she moved here."

"Oh," both twins responded.

"Do you like her?" Mikey asked.

"Yeah, I do. Is that okay with you two?"

"She seems nice," Kay replied. "Plus, I heard Aunt Cheryl say she made Dana's outfit and she and her friend helped with her hair and makeup when Dana's friend didn't show up. She would have to be nice to do that."

"Is that right?" Mike smiled. "She is nice. She also knew Pop."

"She knew Grandpa Preston?" Mikey and Kay looked surprised.

"She did. She met him on a plane." Mike went on to tell them how Taylor and his father had met.

"Wow, she really is nice," Mikey said. "I think I like her. Plus, she's pretty."

"Yeah, Dad, she *is* pretty," Kay agreed.

"You two okay with me and Taylor being friends?"

"Yeah, Dad, it's cool. We didn't really like Miss Linda all that much anyway," Mikey said.

"Why didn't you say something?"

"We didn't want you to be alone," Kay told him.

Up until that moment, Mike hadn't realized just how much attention his children had been paying to his life. He'd been lonely for a long time after the divorce. He'd started dating Linda to ease the loneliness. Mikey and Kay were much more observant and wiser than he'd given them credit for. He wouldn't make that mistake again.

"I love you two." He reached over and grabbed their hands.

"We love you too, Dad."

The conversation turned to last evening's pool party and tonight's party in the town square. There would be a special area for those under the age of eighteen, with games, music, movies, and food. Mikey and Kay were looking forward to hanging out with their cousins again, as well as some of the other children they knew and only got to see when then they were with Mike.

chapter 31

After spending a fun afternoon pampering themselves, eating dinner, and drinking a couple of glasses of wine, Taylor and Rae got dressed and walked over to the town square, where the party was in full swing. Taylor wore a burnt-orange maxi dress, topped with a denim jacket. She had on flat gold sandals and a small matching crossbody bag that held her phone, lipstick, a credit card, some cash, and ID. She left her hair loose and added some loc jewelry. She had on large gold hoops and a brown leather cuff on her wrist that had a disk with an etching of the sun on it. Taylor had switched out her nose stud for a small gold ring, and on her neck, she wore a gold chain with an infinity symbol. The necklace had been her birth mother's and was one of her favorite pieces.

Rae wore a brown tank dress that stopped just at the knee. She paired it with a matching cardigan and leopard print flats. She washed her hair and wore her natural curls loose and wild around her face. She wore gold earrings, a necklace with amber-colored stones, and two rings Taylor had recently made. Just before leaving the house, Taylor texted Mike to let him know they were on their way. He'd offered to come to get them, but they decided to walk instead.

"Did you think about what I said earlier, Tay?"

"I did."

"Well?"

"Well, what?"

"Don't make me smack you. Friend or not, I'll do it."

Taylor laughed. "I've decided I'm going to talk with Mike. That's as far as I'm willing to go."

"Okay, that's progress."

"And you could never hurt me. No one else would be willing to be your best friend."

"Whatever. But you're probably right." Rae gave her the side-eye.

They were both laughing when they spotted Mike and his twins standing near the entrance of the town square.

"Girl, there's your man and those twins who look like he gave birth to them instead of their mama."

"I know right? It's like she didn't have anything at all to do with their creation."

"Those are some *strong* genes," Rae whispered as they got closer to them.

"Hey, ladies. Glad to see you made it safely." Mike kissed both women on the cheek.

"Oh, so you know me like that now, huh?" Rae asked, grinning.

"Yeah, I think I do." Mike chuckled.

"Okay. You do."

Mike whispered in Taylor's ear. "And I definitely know you like that, Rosebud." Taylor giggled. Rae looked at her in surprise and started laughing. "Say hi to Taylor and Rae, kids."

"Hi, Miss Taylor. Hi, Miss Rae." As was their habit, both Mikey and Kay spoke in unison.

"Hi, Mikey and Kay. I can't get over how much you two look like your dad," Taylor said.

"We get that a lot," Mikey said, while Kay whispered in Mike's ear.

"Taylor, Kay was wondering if she could ask a favor of you," Mike said.

"Sure, Kay. What is it?"

"I liked the way you braided Dana's hair, and I was wondering if you could braid mine."

"I'd be happy to." Taylor looked up at Mike.

"We can go to my office, and you can do it there."

"Is this going to take long? I want to get to the gaming station," Mikey asked.

"No, it won't take long at all."

They walked along the sidewalk to the back entrance of the Red Buffalo. During the short walk, Kay talked with Taylor about how she wanted her hair. Mikey walked behind them alongside Rae. Rae, who also enjoyed gaming, asked Mikey about the gaming station. Mikey was excited to discuss his favorite hobby with someone who seemed to like it as much as he did.

When they reached the office, Kay pulled a brush and some elastics out of her small backpack and handed them to Taylor.

"What did you kids do today?" Taylor asked as she brushed Kay's hair.

"We went horseback riding. It was fun. What did you do?" Kay asked.

"Rae and I had a mini spa day."

"Oh wow, I bet that was fun," Kay said excitedly.

Mikey looked confused. "What's a mini spa day?"

"Son, that's a day when women get together, do beauty treatments, eat tiny, pretty sandwiches, and drink water with slices of cucumber in them." Mike was smiling as he saw the frown form on his son's face.

"Why would you want to do that?" Mikey asked.

"Because it's fun and what girls do," his sister replied.

"Maybe while you're here, we can have another one. We can invite your aunts and cousins and make it a girls' day," Taylor said.

"That sounds gross." Mikey's frown deepened.

"He even frowns like you," Rae told Mike, laughing.

"Sometimes it's like looking in a mirror at my younger self." Mike shook his head and laughed with her.

While the others talked, Taylor finished Kay's hair.

"Your dad has a mirror in the bathroom, so why don't you go take a look and see if you like it."

Kay rushed to the bathroom to see her hair. She ran back out and hugged Taylor.

"Miss Taylor, I love it! Thank you!"

"You're welcome. I'm glad you like it." Taylor laughed and returned her hug.

"Dad, can we go now? I don't want to miss all the fun," Mikey said impatiently.

"Yes, I'll take you over. Both of your phones charged?"

"Yes, sir," they answered.

"Good. Let's go." He turned to Taylor. "I need to check them into the under-eighteen area then come back here to check on a few things. I'll catch up with you right after."

"All right. See you in a bit. Have fun kids!"

"Yeah, have fun. And Mikey, don't forget what I told you about the Sorcerer's Revenge game," Rae said.

"I won't."

"Thanks again, Miss Taylor! Bye, Miss Rae!"

chapter 32

Taylor and Rae wandered around the square and ate samples from some of the different food booths before making their way to the beverage tent. Taylor was waiting at the beer bar for Rae to return from the bathroom when one of the men they'd met yesterday at the rodeo joined her.

"Good evening, pretty lady. Nice to see you here."

"Oh, hey, uh, Jason, is it?"

"Yes, it is Jason. I'm flattered you remembered me." Taylor didn't know what to say to that, so she smiled and took a sip of her beer.

"You remember Amos?" Jason looked past her.

Taylor, feeling the presence of someone behind her, set her plastic cup on the bar, turned, and saw the other man from yesterday.

"Yes. How are you?"

"Better now that I've seen you."

Taylor attempted a small smile at that lame comment and turned back to her beer, hoping Rae would hurry up and get back.

"Are you enjoying the party?" Jason asked.

"I haven't been here that long, but so far, it's not bad."

"We'll just have to make sure you have a good time tonight, right, Amos?" Jason smiled, and like last time, it failed to reach his eyes.

"Right. It would be our pleasure." Amos chuckled.

Taylor was beginning to feel a little uncomfortable standing between the two men. She felt as if they were intentionally crowding her. While she sipped her beer and made up her mind to go find Rae rather than wait for her there. Thankfully, when she looked in the direction of the restrooms, she saw her and Davis walking toward her.

"There's my friends. We're going to visit a few more booths. I hope you fellas have a fun evening."

Jason grabbed her elbow as she turned to go. "Aww, leaving us so soon? How about a dance later?"

"I can't promise anything. I don't know how long I'll be out tonight." Without waiting for him to respond, she pulled away from him and went to join Rae and Davis. Both were frowning.

"What took you so long, Rae?"

"Were those guys bothering you, Taylor?" Davis asked.

"No, not really. He and his friend were saying hello. One of them was asking me for a dance when I saw you guys."

"Be careful. Sometimes folks can get a little drunk and out of hand. Let me know if anybody bothers you," Davis told her.

"We will." Rae turned toward Taylor. "Davis said they have carnival games. You want to go check them out?"

"That sounds like fun. Maybe he can win you a giant bear or something."

"Or maybe she can win *me* a giant bear or something for me." Davis smiled.

They had been walking around the carnival area for about half an hour when Taylor stumbled. Rae grabbed her arm.

"Now I know you haven't drunk so much you can't walk straight," Rae joked. When Taylor swayed unsteadily on her feet, Rae became concerned.

"Taylor, are you okay?"

"No, I'm feeling a little weird. I think I need to sit down."

"Davis, do you see a bench or something? Taylor needs to sit down."

Davis looked closely at Taylor. "You don't look so good. How do you feel?"

"Not good."

"Rae, why don't you take Taylor over to the saloon? I'll go get my truck, meet you around back, and take you both home."

"All right. Taylor, come on." *Thankfully*, Rae thought, *the Red Buffalo was right down the block.* As they slowly walked toward the bar, Rae asked Taylor what was wrong.

"I don't know. I just started feeling dizzy."

"When we get to the bar, I'll get you some water while we wait for Davis."

After they arrived at the back entrance of the Red Buffalo, Rae told Taylor to go to Mike's office and wait for her there. Taylor carefully made her way to Mike's office. She thought she heard him talking as she approached the door and assumed he was on the phone. She knocked briefly and then turned the handle. She gasped in surprise as she saw a skimpily dressed Linda kissing Mike. Hearing her, they broke apart. Taylor, unsteady on her feet, walked as fast as she could to the back entrance and down the steps. She heard Rae calling her, but she refused to turn around. She felt tears sting her eyes and blur her vision, as the dizziness increased. She wasn't sure if it was from being sick or from seeing Mike with his ex. Intent on getting away from the saloon and not paying attention to her surroundings, she ran directly into a wall. A human wall. It was Jason, the man she'd met at the rodeo and spoken to earlier that evening.

"Well, well, well. Where are you off to in such a hurry, hon? Coming to give me that dance you promised me?"

"No, I'm going home. I don't feel well." Taylor's words were slightly slurred.

"Sorry to hear that. Why don't you let me take you home?"

"No thanks. I can get there on my own."

"Oh no, I *insist*." Jason grabbed her arm and pulled her close to him. "I think I can help you feel better."

"No, I'm going home." Taylor tried to pull away from him, but he just gripped her tighter and walked faster toward the parking area.

"No! Let go of me!" she repeated weakly. She stumbled and tried to pull away, but her limbs felt like lead.

"Hey! Hey! What are you doing? Let go of her!" Taylor heard Rae yelling. "Help! Somebody, help!"

Taylor felt like she was in a vacuum. She could hear Rae, and she tried to call out to her.

Rae continued yelling as she ran toward Jason, who picked Taylor up and carried her to a waiting SUV. She grabbed his arm and tried to stop him as he was putting her in the back seat.

"Put her down!" She swung at him, hitting him on the side of the head with her fist.

"Bitch!" he shouted, and he gave her a hard push away from him.

She continued screaming and hitting the man, as she tried to get to Taylor. Seeing that she wasn't going to give up trying to save her friend, the man shoved Taylor farther into the truck. Then he turned and punched Rae, the force of it knocking her to the ground. He quickly got into the truck before it sped away. She pulled out her phone, and focusing on the tag, she snapped a picture. Because of the darkness, she couldn't see it very well and hoped the picture was able to capture what she couldn't see.

Caleb and Mike ran out of the backdoor to where Rae was getting up from the ground. Both men helped her up.

"What the hell happened? Where's Taylor?" Mike asked anxiously.

"They took her!" Rae cried.

"Who took her?" Mike's voice was heavy with urgency.

"I don't know. She wasn't feeling well, and I told her to wait for me in your office. When I didn't see her in there, I came back out here to look for her. I saw a man carrying her toward the open door of a waiting truck."

Davis pulled up to the small group and saw Mike standing in front of Rae with his hands on her shoulders.

"What's going on?"

"Someone just grabbed Taylor and took off," Mike told him.

"Get in!" The three of them got in the truck.

"Rae, which way did they go? Did you get a good look at the vehicle?"

"That way." She pointed straight ahead, which led to the main highway. "It was a dark-colored SUV. It had dark windows, and it looked like a Suburban."

"Did you get a look at the man holding Taylor? Or the driver?" Mike asked.

"No, I didn't. But I did get part of the license plate number. I also got a picture of it as it drove off."

Rae was seated between Davis and Mike in the front seat of the truck. She felt her breathing quicken and felt her tears as they flowed from her eyes nonstop. She was also beginning to feel the pain from the hit she'd received.

"Oh my God! I should have stayed with her! What if we can't find her?" Rae was on the verge of a panic attack.

Mike grabbed her hand. "We'll find her, Rae. But right now, I need you to breathe."

Davis quickly got them out of town limits and drove at top speed down the highway. His expression was grim as he concentrated on the road ahead. Mike asked to see the picture, and then he took out his phone and called his uncle Jack and PJ to let them know what happened and have them get in contact with the sheriff. Caleb, who was sitting in the back seat of the cab, reached forward and placed his hand on Rae's shoulder.

"Rae, do you remember seeing Taylor's purse on the ground at all?"

"No, why?"

"Is there a possibility she might have her phone with her?"

Rae closed her eyes as she continued to take deep breaths. "She had a crossbody bag. Her phone was in it."

Davis's phone rang. He hit the speaker button. "This is Baker."

"This is Sheriff Anderson. Jack Edwards just called me. What's your location?"

"We're on Highway 22, heading east."

"I'm running a check on the tag. Hopefully, we'll have something shortly."

"Her friend says she thinks she might still have her phone. If we give you the number, do you think you might be able to ping it?"

"Maybe. If it's still on and in range. What's the number?"

Davis looked at Rae as she recited the number. He removed one hand from the wheel, placed it on her thigh, and squeezed gently. He knew this was hard on her.

"We got a hit on the tag number. It's a rental. Looks like it was rented to Amos Chandle. Does the name ring a bell?" Sheriff Anderson asked.

"No. I got nothing," Davis replied.

"Same," Mike said.

"Nothing," Caleb added.

Rae asked the sheriff to repeat the name. "Oh no! Please God, no!"

"What's wrong?" Davis asked.

"Amos is the name of one of the men we met yesterday. We saw them earlier this evening. Remember, Davis? They were at the bar talking to Taylor."

"His name was Amos?"

"Yes."

"Do you remember his friend's name?"

"I think it was John or Jason."

"Davis, how far are you from Whitestone?" the sheriff asked.

"About another ten miles, why?"

"When you get there, go to the sheriff's office. I'm going to run a check on this Amos Chandle and see if anything comes up. I'll see if we can get a hit on the vehicle, since most rentals have tracking devices, and see if anything comes up on the cell phone. I'll send what I get to Sheriff Macon."

"Thanks." Davis ended the call.

"What happens now? They could be anywhere," Rae said to no one in particular.

"We go to the sheriff's office and hope they have something," Davis replied. "We'll find her."

Mike listened as Davis reassured Rae. He felt helpless as he replayed the events of the last hour in his mind. He was angry at Linda for being in his office, and he was even angrier at himself for not kicking her out as soon as she walked in. He'd grabbed her arm with the intent of turning her around and forcing her out the door. She'd had other ideas, as she reached up and kissed him. It was at that moment that Taylor had shown up. He'd seen the hurt look in her eyes before she turned and disappeared. He pushed Linda aside and went after Taylor. He heard Rae yelling as he was leaving his office. He hoped and prayed Taylor was okay.

They arrived in Whitestone shortly after ending the call with Sheriff Anderson. Davis parked in front of the sheriff's office. Davis held Rae's hand and Mike and Caleb followed them inside.

"We're here to see Sheriff Macon," Mike told the clerk.

"Are you here about the missing woman?"

"Yes."

"Right this way. She's expecting you."

The clerk led them to a conference room where a man and woman were seated and appeared to be discussing the papers that were spread out on the table. The woman stood up and walked over to them as they entered. She was tall, with blonde hair. Her eyes were blue and hard looking. She looked at the group, then at Davis and Rae's joined hands.

"Hi, Davis, Mike, Caleb." To Rae, she said, "I'm Sheriff Ali Macon, and this is Deputy Spiers."

"I'm Rachel Stephens."

"Do you have anything for us, Ali?" Mike asked impatiently.

"Yes, but first, I need to get some information from Ms. Stephens. Please have a seat."

They each took a seat at the table. Davis sat next to Rae and continued to hold her hand. She was grateful for his warmth and strength. Mike sat on the other side of her. His body was tense, and he looked angry.

"Ms. Stephens, from what I understand, you were a witness to the alleged abduction. Is that correct?"

"Yes, I was. And it wasn't alleged." Everyone there, especially Rae, noticed the tone the Sheriff used when she asked the question. "I *saw him* grab her and force her into that truck. I tried to stop them, but they drove off."

"How many were there?"

"I don't know. I just saw the one who had her. I don't know who else was in the truck other than him and the driver."

The sheriff nodded to the deputy, who placed a picture of a man in front of her. Rae gasped and put her hand over her mouth. "Do you recognize this man, Ms. Stephens?"

"Yes."

"Do you know his name?"

"I'm not sure. He's either Amos, John, or Jason. We met him and another guy yesterday at the rodeo. They were at the town square tonight."

"How well do you know him?"

"I don't know him at all. I already told you that. I met him yesterday when he and his friend came up and spoke to us."

"What about your friend? Did she know him?"

"No, she didn't," Rae answered as tears started down her cheeks again.

"Thank you, Ms. Stephens. I know this is difficult for you, but we'll do whatever we can to figure this out," Sheriff Macon said with fake compassion before sliding a box of tissues toward her.

"Are you going to tell us what you have?" Mike asked the sheriff.

"I was getting to that," the sheriff answered. Her displeasure at his tone was evident in her response.

"We were able to ping Ms. Sawyer's phone and get a location. We were verifying the coordinates when you arrived. It looks like they're at the Reynolds Creek Ranch just north of here. This ranch is about a fifty-thousand-acre spread. The signal from the phone was weak and sporadic. It may be because of the lack of cell towers or because the battery is low. It could also be because they found the phone and tossed it."

"Have you pulled up a satellite picture of the coordinates?" Davis asked.

"No, we haven't. We're trying to access the database, but it may take a while."

Davis grabbed the paper with the coordinates. He snapped a picture of it with his phone and then sent a text message.

"I just sent this to a buddy of mine. He'll be able to get it for us."

A few minutes later, his phone dinged. He read the text and then looked at the picture.

"The coordinates show what looks like a cabin or an old line shack on the southeastern boundary of the property."

"I don't suppose you would be interested in helping with retrieval?" the sheriff asked. The three men were on their feet instantly. "I thought so. Let me get you some gear." She motioned to the deputy. The sheriff then turned to Rae before continuing, "Ms. Stephens, I'm going to need you to stay here. I know she's your friend, but it's better if you remain here in case she tries to contact you." Rae slowly nodded her understanding. Mike and Caleb followed the deputy and the sheriff as they left the conference room.

Davis went to his truck to get his gear. As a ranger, he knew there was always the off chance that trouble would arise, be it animal or human. He set his duffle in one of the conference room chairs and unzipped it as he looked at Rae. He placed his bulletproof vest and the night vision goggles on the table and walked over to where she was standing.

"What happened to your face?"

With all that had been going on, Rae hadn't much thought about it. She pressed her lips together as tears fell from her eyes.

"The guy that took Taylor hit me when I tried to stop him."

Davis pulled her close. Gently touching the bruised area, he said, "You need to get some ice on this."

"I will."

"I know this is hard for you, but you can't give up hope. We'll find her. And then maybe I can get you to give me your phone number before you go back home." Rae looked up at Davis and smiled weakly through her tears. Davis held her for a minute longer, then he moved back to put on his vest.

"Do you think you'll need that?" Rae asked worriedly.

"I don't know, but it's better to have it and not need it."

She watched him as he put on his vest, and then he pulled a 9mm Glock and a rifle out of the duffle and checked their readiness. Next, he pulled out a small backpack and filled it with two boxes of shells and bullets, a flashlight, a knife, and a first aid kit. As he zipped it closed, Mike, Caleb, and Sheriff Macon returned, each wearing vests and carrying weapons.

The deputy spread out a map on the table. He pointed out the coordinates and access points that would be the best options for approach without being seen. He handed out earpieces to be used for communication and night vision goggles.

"Any questions?" he asked as he finished handing out the gear. Hearing none, he stated they would be taking two vehicles. He tossed a set of keys to Mike, who caught them in midair.

Mike walked over to Rae, placed his hand on her shoulder, and squeezed it gently. "We'll bring our girl back."

Rae nodded and fervently hoped he would.

Caleb slowly rubbed her back. "We'll get her." Then he and Mike left the conference room.

Davis pulled her close and hugged her tightly. "We'll contact you as soon as we have her. I promise." He pulled back and placed a soft kiss on her forehead, then he smiled, his dimples popping out as he lowered his head to whisper in her ear. "I'm saving a real kiss for when we get back and you give me your number. Now get some ice for your face." He winked at her and left the room.

Rae watched him walk out.

"Ms. Stephens, Deputy Spiers will be here and will be monitoring communications. I expect you to cooperate fully with him," the sheriff said.

"Why wouldn't I?" Rae frowned.

"I'm just letting you know in case you've forgotten to tell us anything. Spiers, call me if you have any problems." The sheriff looked at Rae as she spoke. Her eyes seemed colder than when they first arrived. She left without saying anything else.

Rae looked at her retreating back and then at the deputy, who shrugged his shoulders and avoided looking her in the eye. Rae didn't know what that bullshit was about, and she didn't have time to try to figure it out. She just hoped it didn't interfere with finding Taylor. She sat down and tried to calm herself. She didn't know how long she would be there, so she needed to get a handle on her emotions. Closing her eyes, she took a few deep breaths and tried to focus on finding stillness. When she opened her eyes, she saw the deputy coming toward her with a cup of coffee and an ice pack.

"For your face," he said quietly, then he left the room.

She picked up the ice pack and gently pressed it to her lower left cheek, which had begun to throb in earnest.

chapter 33

Mike and Caleb stored their gear in the back seat and walked over to join Davis, who was standing outside the entrance to the sheriff's office. Caleb spoke first.

"Ali didn't look too happy to see you, Davis. Matter of fact, she looked downright pissed."

Davis looked at the serious expressions on the two men's faces. "Yes, well, whatever is bothering her, she'll get over it."

"Glad you think so, because you're riding with her," Mike added. "And, Davis, I didn't care for her attitude in there. She acted almost as if she didn't care that Taylor had been abducted. If something happens to Taylor because of her lack of urgency, sheriff or not, I will deal with her."

"I hear you, and I'd do the same. We'll get her back, Mike."

Sheriff Macon came out. "Let's go."

Davis and Sheriff Macon got into her SUV and took off, followed by Mike and Caleb. After riding for a few minutes in silence, Caleb looked over at Mike. "We'll find her."

"I hope so. I feel like this is all my fault."

"How is this your fault?"

"She came into the office and saw Linda kissing me."

"Aww man, I thought you two were done?"

"We *are* done. Didn't you hear me? *She* was kissing *me*, not the other way around. Although I'm sure that didn't matter to Taylor because as far as I could tell, all she saw was my half-dressed ex kissing me in my office. She didn't say anything. She just looked at me and hightailed it out of there."

Caleb sighed heavily. "What happened after that?"

"I went after her. I was almost at the back door when I heard Rae screaming. If I had gotten there sooner, I would have been able to stop them from taking her."

"You can't know that for sure. From what Rae was saying, Taylor wasn't feeling well. That might be why she wasn't able to put up much of a fight when they grabbed her. It's not your fault."

"It is my fault. We need to find her."

Caleb understood why Mike felt the way he did. He would feel the same way. He sent up prayers on Taylor's behalf. Both men were silent as they followed the sheriff to Reynolds Creek Ranch.

"Was that your new girlfriend, Davis? She doesn't seem like your type."

"No, Ali, she isn't."

"Are you sure? Because that's what it looked like to me."

"I'm sure. And what you saw was me comforting a woman whose best friend was abducted earlier this evening, which you don't seem to care too much about."

She turned from the road and looked at him. "What are you implying?"

"I'm not implying. I'm stating."

"Look, I was just doing my job. Lots of women go out and hook up with strangers. They don't always tell their friends what they're doing."

"Yes, that may be, but that's not what happened here, and you know it."

"Like I said, I was just doing my job. How are you all involved in this anyway?"

"Taylor is new to the area, and she doesn't know that many people. The only reason she was there in the first place is because Mike invited her."

"Which goes to my point. You don't know her, so you can't be sure she didn't go willingly."

Davis didn't know Taylor all that well, but he wasn't about to tell Ali that. He was sure, however, she wasn't the type to disappear without telling her friend where she was going.

"I'm pretty sure she didn't. Her friend said she's not the spontaneous type."

"I don't recall her saying that."

"Too bad. You know what? Why don't you just drive? You seem to have a bug up your ass about something, and I'm not in the mood to deal with your shit."

"You really are an asshole, Davis."

"Tell me something I don't know.

Taylor felt like she was having an out-of-body experience. She could hear sounds around her, but she couldn't see anything, and she couldn't move her arms or legs. She was trying to make sense of what she was feeling, but her mind seemed to be in a fog, and she couldn't seem to clear it. Where was she? What was happening? Minutes later, with her mind no clearer, she felt herself being lifted. She heard a slamming noise that she couldn't quite make out, and she felt cold.

She heard a man's voice say, "Shit, she's heavy. Help me lift her."

She opened her mouth to speak, but nothing came out. She couldn't figure out if she was dreaming or awake, but she knew something was wrong. She continually tried to move, but her efforts were unsuccessful.

"Let's set her down on the bed, and I'll get the heater going." The voice was unfamiliar to her. She heard another voice and strained to hear it. Suddenly, the darkness disappeared, and she was squinting at the brightness that replaced it.

"You're awake." Her eyes slowly adjusted to the light, and a man's face filled her vision. She tried once again to speak but couldn't.

"She's awake."

"Good. Let's have a drink and get to it." The man in front of her smoothed her hair from her face and touched her cheek. She flinched as she tried to move away from him. "I know you feel a little strange right now, but don't worry, it'll be okay."

The look she saw in his eyes was communicating a different message. She didn't know what was about to happen, but she was sure it wasn't going to be good.

chapter 34

Mike pulled up beside the sheriff's truck and rolled his window down. Davis rolled his down as well.

"We're about a half mile south of the cabin. We'll have to walk from here so they don't hear us."

Sheriff Macon leaned forward so she could see the men in the other vehicle. "I think we need to go a little closer. We won't be able to see much without additional light."

Caleb looked out of the front windshield. "I think this is good. The moon's almost full and should give us enough light."

They got out, checked their weapons, grabbed the rest of their gear, and took off toward the cabin. Mike and Davis were in front, followed by Caleb and the sheriff. Caleb had been right about the moon. It illuminated the path they were on eliminating the need for night vision goggles. They moved swiftly up the path, and upon their arrival at the cabin, they saw a black Suburban parked next to it. Caleb walked up to it. He first checked the license plate and then placed his hand on the hood.

"It's still warm. I don't think they've been here long." He spoke quietly as he rejoined the group. "Let's look around and see if there's a back door or any other windows. There doesn't seem to be much light in there, and I didn't hear anything." The others nodded. "Be careful. We don't know what we'll find once we get inside."

Davis and Ali quietly trekked around the cabin to see if there were any other points of entry, he on one side, her on the other. While the cabin wasn't large, there was a window on one side of the cabin and a back door. They were able to see inside the dimly lit cabin through the screened back door. The side window was covered by a screen. The inside window was raised.

Ali looked in the side window and saw a man removing a whiskey bottle and glasses from a cabinet. When he finished pouring, he picked up the glasses and handed one to another man, who stood at the counter next to him. She was about to turn and walk back to join the others when she thought she saw a flash of color out of the corner of her eye. Careful not to make a sound, she got as close to the window as she could without giving her position away. The color she saw was a piece of orange material. Remembering the missing woman had been wearing an orange dress, she quickly went to find the men and let them know what she'd seen.

The man who had spoken to Taylor earlier sat down beside her on the bed. Another man was with him. He stood next to the bed, smiling as he leered at her.

"Don't look so scared, sweetheart. We won't hurt you—that is, unless you want us to." Both men laughed. "This is going to be fun. Don't worry. We'll take *real* good care of you."

Taylor looked at both men and felt fear welling up inside her as she lay there unable to do anything. She was barely able to get her limbs to move.

"No. Please, no," she said as she tried to move.

The man sitting on the bed lifted her upper body and removed her purse and her jean jacket. The other man tied her wrists together, leaned down, and rubbed his cheek against hers. He took a deep breath as he inhaled her scent.

"You smell good. I can't wait to fuck you," he whispered in her ear, then ran his tongue lightly around its shell. He pulled back and helped the other man move Taylor to the middle of the bed. She felt the bed dip as the other man sat on the bed. He sat against the headboard and shifted Taylor so her back was pressed against him. He lifted her hair and kissed her neck and exposed shoulder. The other man raised Taylor's dress and began to run his hands along her exposed legs. Taylor squeezed her eyes shut against the assault and felt tears escape her eyes as she was overcome with fear and helplessness. She tried to move to fight off the terror she was experiencing, but she was unable to stop what was happening.

"I think the woman might be inside. I saw two men. I didn't see her, but I did see something orange hanging down from what might be a couch or a bed."

"Taylor was wearing an orange dress," Mike said quietly. It felt like he lost the ability to breathe because his heart was beating so erratically.

Sheriff Macon looked at each man. "I couldn't see what was going on in there, but I don't think we should wait too long to get in there. I didn't see any weapons, but that doesn't mean there aren't any. We have the element of surprise, so that can be used in our favor. We can enter the front and rear doors as well as the side window. I'm going to call for backup," Sheriff Macon said as she stepped farther away from the cabin to use her radio to call it in.

chapter 35

"I don't have a good feeling about this. I think we should go in now," Caleb told both men. They agreed with him.

"Caleb, take the window. I'll take the front door. Mike, you go in through the back," Davis said quickly. "When you're in place, Caleb, make one of those bird calls or animal sounds or something, and we'll all go in at the same time."

Mike walked to the rear of the cabin, where he could see into the back half of it through the screen door. He cautiously checked the door handle. Finding it locked, he stepped back a few paces and waited for Caleb's signal. When it came, Davis kicked the front door open, sending it back on its hinges. At the same time, Mike punched a hole in the screen, reached in to lift the lock, then opened the door. Not knowing what he would find, with his gun raised, he walked as quietly as he could toward the front room.

Caleb knocked the screen in and climbed in through the window. One of the men rushed toward him. Caleb fired, and the man grabbed his leg as he went down. Caleb walked toward him and stood over him with his foot on his chest and his gun pointed at his face.

The first thing Davis saw when he entered the cabin was both men on the bed with Taylor. One jumped out of the bed and ran at Caleb. Davis faced the remaining man with his gun drawn. Mike's vision morphed into a red haze of anger immediately after entering the room, as he saw a man drag Taylor from the bed and press his forearm against her neck.

"Let her go," Davis said quietly. He saw Taylor's hands were bound as she struggled against her captor. Her movements were slow and clumsy.

"I don't think so," the man said. "I think I'll hold on to her a little longer to make sure I get out of here in one piece."

"Think again, fucker," Mike hissed as he pressed his gun against the man's temple. "Let. Her. Go. Now."

The man let his hands fall to his sides, then turned quickly and tried to knock the gun from Mike's hand. Mike responded by slamming the gun against the side of his head and knocking him out. He stood over the man's prone body, more than willing to put a bullet in it should he get up. Through the fog of his rage, he heard Davis calling him. Hearing his name, he turned and saw Davis removing the ropes from Taylor's wrists.

Mike ran to her, picked her up in his arms, and moved over to the couch, where he sat down with her on his lap. He could feel her shaking as she began to sob. He felt his rage return as she buried her face in his shoulder and cried. He slowly rubbed his hand along Taylor's back and whispered softly to her, telling her she was safe. She tried to talk but couldn't seem to stop crying.

"Shh, it's okay, Rosebud. I got you, baby."

"How is she?" Davis asked.

"I think she's in shock."

Davis took a quilt off the bed and gave it to Mike, who quickly wrapped it around Taylor.

"Oh my God, Mike. I've never been so scared in my life." Her slurred words were barely above a whisper.

"I know, baby. We'll get you out of here." He adjusted the blanket around her and looked over at the two men. One was handcuffed, and the other, whom Caleb had shot, was lying on the floor, unable to move due to Caleb's foot still firmly pressed to his chest. Mike called out to Davis and tossed him the keys to the truck. He gave the man on the floor one more look, then left to get the truck.

Sheriff Macon entered the cabin, looking first at Davis as he walked past her then the others in the cabin. "Is that her?"

"Yes," Mike answered.

"How is she?"

"She's in shock. Other than that, she seems to be okay. Looks like we got here just in time."

The sheriff walked over to the couch where Mike sat holding Taylor. She looked questioningly at Mike, and he nodded.

"Ms. Taylor-Sawyer, I'm Sheriff Ali Macon. Is it okay if I ask you a few questions?"

Taylor looked up. She saw the concern in the sheriff's eyes and said yes. Her voice was barely above a whisper.

"After you give us your statement, I'd like to get you to the hospital to get checked out."

Taylor looked at the sheriff and then at Mike. He gave her a gentle squeeze. Taylor felt safe and comforted in the warmth of his big body.

"Okay," she said quietly.

"Can you tell me what you did this evening?"

"My friend Rae and I went to the party in the town square. Mike and his children met us on the corner just outside of the square. I remember braiding his daughter's hair then walking around the square with Rae, checking out some of the booths."

"Do you remember the two men who were here in this cabin?"

"I met them yesterday at the rodeo. I saw them again tonight in the square."

"Do you remember coming to this cabin?"

"No, I don't. I remember being in the dark, being scared, and not being able to move. I didn't know if I was awake or in the middle of a nightmare."

"What else do you remember?"

"I think my head must have been covered at some point, because I remember suddenly seeing blinding light. One of the men told me it would be okay, then I heard them both laughing."

"So, Taylor, what you're saying is that you met these two men yesterday and again this evening, and then you came to this cabin with them?"

"No," Mike said angrily. "That's not what she's saying!"

The sheriff looked at him and then back at Taylor. "I need to hear it from her."

Taylor could feel Mike's body tensing as she struggled to sit up. "No, that's not what happened. I'm telling you I met them yesterday and ran into them again this evening. I did *not* come here with them." Taylor was feeling confused and attacked. She didn't understand why this sheriff was treating her as if she'd willingly put herself in a dangerous situation with two strangers.

"Are you sure?" The sheriff sounded as if she didn't quite believe her.

"That's enough, Ali!" Mike shouted.

"No, it's *not*, Mike. I'm trying to get all the facts while they're fresh in her memory."

"If that's your intention, you're doing a piss-poor job. This interview is over. Go wait outside, and don't bring your ass back in here."

"I'm the sheriff, and I'll conduct this investigation as I see fit."

"I don't give a fuck who you are. Get the fuck out!"

"She'll still need to get checked out by a doctor."

"I'll take her." Mike glared at her until she got up from where she'd been sitting and left. "It's okay, Rosebud," Mike gently reassured her. "I've got you, baby. You're safe now." He held her close and gently kissed her forehead as they waited for Davis. When he heard the truck pull up out front, Mike carried her outside and put her and himself in the back seat, pulling her close to him. Caleb told Davis he'd meet him back in town and for him to bring Rae to the hospital. He got in, started the truck up, and headed toward the road.

chapter 36

The staff at the hospital had been alerted that Taylor was being brought in. They worked quickly and efficiently. She was examined, and blood was drawn for lab tests. The attending emergency room physician told Mike that, based on his initial examination, he suspected Taylor might have been drugged. A tearful Rae arrived just as the doctor was finishing up. The doctor told Taylor he would return as soon as he got the lab results back. Mike exited the room with him to give the two women some privacy.

"I'm okay, Rae. You can let me go now," Taylor said as Rae hugged her after rushing into the emergency department exam room.

"No. I'm never letting you go," Rae said through her tears.

"Really, I'm fine. If it wasn't for you, they wouldn't have been able to find me as fast as they did."

Her friend continued to hug her tightly.

"Seriously, Rae. Let go. You're squeezing too tight."

"I'm sorry." Rae reluctantly let her go.

"No need to be sorry." Taylor reached for her hands. "Thanks, sis. I mean it."

Rae nodded and started to cry again. She wiped her eyes. "What did the doctor say? Are they going to let you go home, or are you going to have to stay?"

"The doctor said I could go home once he gets the lab results but emphasized that I should see a doctor for a follow-up in a few days. He suspects I might have been drugged."

"Drugged?"

"Yes. I'm trying to figure out when that could have happened, but I can't remember. I can't remember anything past being at the bar, talking to those two guys we met yesterday while waiting for you to come back from the restroom."

"Wow."

"The next thing I knew, I was with them in that cabin. I remember being terrified, especially when I wasn't able to move."

"Oh my God, Tay!" Shocked, Rae looked at her with her hand over her mouth. "They didn't . . . did they?"

"No." Taylor shivered. "But they would have if Mike, Davis, and Caleb hadn't gotten there when they did. The sheriff was with them, but she didn't do much."

"I'm not surprised. I wasn't impressed with her. She acted like we were bothering her when we showed up at her office."

"She practically insinuated that this was all my fault. Mike stopped the interview and told her to go wait outside. She tried to argue with him, going on about her being the sheriff and it being her investigation, but he wasn't hearing it. She was pissed, but she left. I haven't seen her since."

"I saw when she and Davis came back to the station. She came in and spoke to the deputy but didn't say a word to me."

"Not too terribly surprised to hear that. I don't know what her problem is."

Dr. James "Jim" Slater and Mike were acquainted with each other, as they'd attended the same college, and their paths crossed from time to time.

"Mike, can I talk to you for a minute?" Dr. Slater asked.

"Sure."

"Let's get some coffee."

Mike followed him to what looked like the staff break room. The doctor handed him a cup, took another for himself, grabbed the coffee pot, and filled both cups. He walked over to a table, and he and Mike sat down.

"As I mentioned earlier, I think Ms. Sawyer was drugged. She's the fifth woman in the past few months to come in with a similar story. The memory loss, fatigue, and disorientation are the same as the others; however, she's the only one who wasn't violated."

"And by violated, Jim, you mean raped?"

"Yes. After the women had been examined, it was clear they'd been with a man, and after speaking with Ms. Sawyer, possibly two men. But they had no recollection of meeting anyone or having sex."

"Does the sheriff know about this?"

"Yes, she does, but she thinks they may just be a series of coincidences where the women were out partying, drank too much, and made poor choices."

Mike cursed. "Based on the way she was talking to Taylor; she's thinking the same about her as well. Were these other women drugged?"

"My gut tells me they were, but the lab tests didn't reveal anything. We also didn't see any of them until almost two to three days after they were assaulted. That, along with the memory loss, doesn't give us much evidence to prove anything."

"This occurred this evening. Maybe something will show up."

"I'm hoping so," Jim responded.

Mike saw Caleb and Davis as he went back into the waiting area. They stood up as he walked over to them.

"How is she?" Caleb asked.

"Jim Slater is her doctor. He thinks she may have been drugged, but other than that, she's okay."

"Drugged?" Davis repeated.

"Yes. He's waiting for the lab work to come back now. He's hoping the tests will show something."

"Damn, Mike. How could that happen?" Caleb asked.

"I have no idea. Something else Jim shared was that Taylor's story is not all that unusual. There have been other women in the past few months who he thinks may have been drugged as well; however, nothing showed up in their system. Like Taylor, they had memory loss. He also said there was evidence that they'd had sex, but the word he used was *violated*. Especially since the women had no memory of it ever taking place."

"Why are we just now hearing about this?" Davis asked angrily.

"Because Ali seems to think it was a string of coincidences and that the women got drunk and slept with whomever. In other words, their risky behavior was responsible for what happened to them, and they should have made better choices. I have to say, after the way she spoke to Taylor, she's thinking the same about her as well."

"Seriously?" Caleb thought this was incredulous.

"I would never hit a woman, but I wanted to slap the shit out of her when she insinuated that Taylor had willingly gone to that cabin with those two fuckers," Mike said.

"Ali's always been a bitch, but her actions tonight have been out of line," Davis said.

"Mike, before I forget, Uncle Jack called. He said Dana took Mikey and Kay home with her, and he wants you to give him a call in the morning," Caleb told Mike.

"Thanks." Mike looked toward the doors leading back to the emergency exam rooms and saw them open. Taylor was sitting in a wheelchair being pushed by a nurse, with the doctor and Rae walking next to her.

"I'll go get the truck and meet you outside," Davis told them as he moved toward the exit.

"I'll go with you," Caleb said, going to catch up with him.

Mike walked over to Taylor, knelt in front of her, and gently took her hand. "Ready to go?"

She squeezed his hand and nodded. He stood up and looked at the doctor, who gave a small nod.

"Ms. Sawyer has her discharge instructions. If she has any problems, give us a call or have her contact her primary care provider." He gave his attention to Taylor next. "Take care, Ms. Sawyer. Goodnight, Ms. Stephens. Mike." He nodded. "I'll be in touch." He shook hands with Mike and went back through the doors.

"Let's go." Mike walked next to Rae as they followed behind Taylor to the hospital exit.

When they got outside, Davis was waiting. Mike got Taylor settled in the back seat of the truck cab and then joined her. Rae sat in the front between Davis and Caleb. Davis started the truck and pulled out onto the highway. Mike pulled Taylor close to him, and she snuggled into his side. The ride back to Silverton was quiet. Everyone was grateful that the evening had had a good outcome, but they were also tired.

chapter 37

Davis pulled up to Taylor's house and Caleb got out to open the back door of the cab to help Mike get an exhausted Taylor into the house. Davis followed them onto the porch. Rae unlocked the door and Mike carried Taylor into the house. Caleb hugged Rae, said goodnight, and went back to the truck.

"Are you okay?" Davis pulled Rae close.

"I am."

"Try to get some sleep. I'll talk to you tomorrow." He kissed her on the cheek. Then he jogged down the stairs, got in his truck, and drove away.

Rae locked the door and placed her and Taylor's purses on the table. She got a glass from the cabinet, filled it with water, and took it, along with the bag containing the pills the doctor had prescribed, back to Taylor's room. Taylor was sitting on the edge of the bed.

"Here're your meds."

"Thanks."

The sound of water could be heard coming from the bathroom.

"Need anything?" Rae asked.

"No. I'm going to take a bath then try to get some sleep."

"Sounds like a good idea. I think I'll do the same." Rae turned to go to her room.

"Rae?" She walked back over to where Taylor sat. "Thanks again. Love you, sis."

"Love you, too." She hugged Taylor, then she stood up as Mike came out of the bathroom. Before leaving the room, she walked over to Mike and hugged him. "Thanks for bringing our girl back." She smiled at Taylor as she went to her room.

Mike sat next to Taylor, pulled her close before placing a gentle kiss on her temple.

"Let's get you in the bath so we can get you to bed." He took her hand and led her into the bathroom. He removed her clothes, grabbed an elastic band, pulled her locs into a ponytail the way he'd seen her do many times before, and helped her into the steaming, lavender-scented bathwater. Taylor sat back, closed her eyes, took a deep breath, and let the warm water cover her.

"Stay in here as long as you want. Let me know when you're ready to get out."

"Please don't leave." She opened her eyes and turned her frightened gaze to Mike.

Mike lowered himself to the floor on the side of the tub. Taylor reached out and grabbed his hand, closed her eyes, and began to cry. Mike felt both helpless and angry as he listened to her sobs. He rose from the floor, removed his clothes, and climbed into the tub behind her. He wrapped his arms around her, trying to absorb her pain and comfort her in any way he could. He softly whispered soothing words to her and held her until she was ready to get out of the tub. He gently dried her off and rubbed lotion over her body. He helped her put on a nightgown and pulled back the covers for her to get in bed.

"Do you want to take your meds now?"

Taylor shook her head. "The doctor told me they're to help me sleep, but I don't want to take them."

Taylor rolled over onto her side as Mike slid into bed. She felt a soft kiss on the side of her neck as he spooned her. Finally, the horrific nightmare that began earlier that evening was over.

A few hours later, Taylor woke with a start. She was having trouble breathing and, in the darkened room, couldn't figure out where she was. Mike immediately woke up and turned on the bedside lamp. He thought Taylor might be having a nightmare when she began to toss and turn and cry out in her sleep.

"Taylor. Taylor, look at me. Look at me."

She opened her eyes and looked at him. Her eyes slowly began to focus. Then realizing where she was, her tears returned.

Mike wrapped his arms around her. "It's okay, Rosebud." He gently pulled her over so that she lay on top of him. The contact and the warmth of his body comforted her. He felt her tears as they fell onto his chest and tried to keep his anger at bay. Taylor woke up a few more times before exhaustedly falling into a deep sleep.

chapter 38

A habitual early riser, Mike woke up and, after making sure Taylor was sleeping soundly, got out of bed. Having some things at Taylor's, he took a quick shower, got dressed, and headed to the kitchen for a much-needed cup of coffee. He was surprised to see Rae in the kitchen. She was sitting at the table with a cup in front of her.

"Morning. Coffee's ready if you want some," she said.

"Thanks. How're you doing?"

"I'm okay. Last night seems surreal."

"It does." Mike poured a cup of coffee and joined her at the table. "Was Taylor able to sleep at all?"

"She woke up a few times, but she seems to be sleeping now."

"Does this kind of thing happen a lot around here?"

"No, it doesn't."

"Taylor told me about the sheriff. Does she think Taylor willingly left with those men?"

"Honestly, I don't know what she's thinking. But I plan on talking to our county sheriff today about what happened. I hate the thought that this might happen to someone else."

"Hopefully, he'll be more helpful than that other one."

"I'm sure he will." Mike took a drink from his cup. "I didn't ask last night, but did you contact Taylor's folks about what happened?"

"No. I would have if she hadn't been found as quickly as she was. They're very protective of her, and I didn't want to worry them. I'll leave the telling to her." Rae looked over the rim of her cup at Mike. "Do you mind if I ask you a question?"

"Sure, go ahead."

"Last night, I told Taylor to meet me in your office while we waited for Davis. Did she not come to your office?"

Mike took a deep breath and paused for a minute. "She did, but then she left."

"She left? Why?"

"She left because Linda was there."

"And?"

"And Linda was kissing me."

"You were kissing your ex-girlfriend in your office?"

"No, *she* was kissing *me*. I was about to go find you two when she came into my office. I'd just told her to leave when she kissed me. Taylor walked in at the same time. She left and I immediately went after her." He sat his cup down on the table and raked his fingers through his hair.

"Does Taylor remember any of that?"

"I don't know, but I don't think so. I feel terrible about this whole thing. If I'd left sooner instead of stopping to deal with Linda, this could have been avoided."

"It's not your fault, Mike. There is no way you could have known this would happen. It *is* your fault, however, that your ex-girlfriend is still trying to get back with you."

"How is that my fault?" Mike couldn't believe she said that.

Rae just looked at him as if he should know the answer to her question.

Mike looked back at her and shook his head. "It is over between us. It was over before Taylor arrived. I haven't given her any reason to think otherwise."

"Just make sure she stays away from Taylor. I leave in a few days. I'd hate to have to beat her ass before I go. And that goes for her bony-ass, shit-stirring friend too."

Mike laughed. "Damn, I didn't know college professors had such potty mouths. Don't worry, I'll take care of Linda."

"Earth science is my specialty. In case you didn't know, a little dirt goes with the profession." She laughed as she refilled her cup.

Rae was a good friend to Taylor, and a funny one at that, Mike thought. The two of them were opposites, but he could see they genuinely loved and cared for each other. She also seemed to have a dark side. He wondered if Davis knew it. He probably did. Davis always went for the crazy ones.

"I need to go talk to the sheriff, then I have to go pick up my kids. I'll be back later this afternoon. If you need me, give me a call."

Rae put his number in her phone and shot off a text to him so he'd have her number as well.

"Will do. Do you want anything to eat before you go?"

"I'll grab something later."

"Do you want to use the truck?"

"No, mine is parked in the back of the saloon. I'll walk over and get it." He drained his cup, walked to the sink, rinsed it out, and set it on the counter.

He went back to the room where Taylor slept. He knelt beside the bed and watched her sleep. Careful not to wake her, he leaned over and gently kissed her cheek. She wrinkled her nose, but other than that, she remained asleep. He got up, said goodbye to Rae and left the house. After checking on things at the saloon, he planned to go talk to Sheriff Anderson.

When Mike arrived at the saloon, he saw Caleb's jeep parked next to his truck near the back entrance. He let himself in.

"Morning, Caleb."

"Hey, Mike. How's it going?"

"All right, I guess."

"How's Taylor?"

"She's doing okay. She was sleeping when I left."

"What about Rae?"

"She's fine."

"Good." He handed Mike a cup of coffee. "I was about to make myself some breakfast before the madness starts. Want some?"

Mike was about to say no when his stomach growled loudly. He hadn't eaten since early yesterday afternoon.

"I'll take that as a yes," Caleb said, chuckling, and he went about fixing breakfast.

Caleb set a plate of pancakes with a side of bacon in front of Mike and sat down with a matching plate of his own.

"What brought you in so early? I wasn't expecting to see you here today," Caleb asked.

"I needed to get my truck, and I wanted to talk to the sheriff."

"You going to talk to him about last night?"

"Yes, and I want to talk to him about Ali."

"Andy's a good guy, but sometimes these law enforcement types stick together. Maybe you ought to test the waters a bit first. Tell him about how she handled things with Taylor, see how he reacts, then see if he knows about the other women."

"Good idea. I've been thinking about how I want to approach that." Mike ate another forkful of pancakes, deep in thought as he chewed. Caleb looked at him from across the table. "What?"

"Why was Linda here last night? After you made your rounds in the bar, you said you were going to meet up with the ladies."

"I did say that didn't I?"

"You did. Did you know she was here?"

"At the time, I didn't. I was about to go find Taylor when Linda showed up. We had some heated words, no different than usual. When I told her to leave, that's when she kissed me." Mike paused. "And for the record, I was not expecting that, nor did I kiss her back."

"So, you weren't expecting her?"

"I wasn't." He was starting to get annoyed with Caleb's questions. "What are you trying to say? Why don't you just spit it out?"

"I like Taylor. A lot. I also think she's good for you. I thought you and Linda were done. From what happened last night, it sounds like maybe she still hasn't gotten the message that it's over between the two of you. Please tell me you are not considering getting back with her," Caleb said angrily.

"No, I'm not. If you had been listening, you would have heard me say, I didn't invite her to my office. And again, *she* kissed *me*." Caleb gave him a blank stare. "I pushed her away from me, and that's when I saw Taylor standing in the doorway. She was there for a moment, then she was gone."

"Damn, Mike."

"Yeah, tell me about it. I can't help but feel responsible."

"It's not your fault. But I know you, so I know there's no way I can convince you otherwise."

"Do you know if anyone else knows about what happened to Taylor?"

"I don't think so. The kitchen was closed last night, so everyone was out front. The music was pretty loud, and honestly, the only reason I heard Rae at all was because I just happened to be back here when you came running out."

"Good. The fewer people who know about it, the better. I want to try to keep this as quiet as possible. Taylor has enough to deal with."

"I agree."

Mike finished his meal, stood up, took his plate to the kitchen, and set it in the sink. Caleb did the same.

"Thanks for breakfast. I'm going to go on over and see the sheriff now."

"Let me know how it goes."

chapter 39

Sheriff Anderson was talking on his phone when Mike arrived at the station. He nodded at Mike and pointed to the phone. After his call ended, he reached over and shook Mike's.

"Hey, Mike, how goes it?"

"I'm all right, Andy. And you?"

"I'm good. I'm guessing you're here to talk about last night."

"I am."

"Let's go in my office." Sheriff Anderson unlocked the door, and Mike followed him inside. "Have a seat." He pointed to a chair and asked, "Care for any coffee?"

"No thanks."

"How's Ms. Sawyer doing?"

"As well as can be expected."

"I just got off the phone with Ali Macon. She says you all hijacked her rescue operation and then interfered with her investigation."

"I don't remember it quite that way."

"How *do* you remember it, Mike?"

"We got to her office, and she didn't seem too interested in helping us find Taylor. She inferred that Taylor had probably gotten drunk and went with those guys. She had an attitude towards Taylor's friend Rae, too, but I suspect that was because of Davis."

"What does that have to do with anything?"

"You know Ali's got a thing for Davis."

Andy chuckled. "Yeah, I forgot about that. What about the interview? She said you stopped it."

"I'll admit to that. I also told her to leave the room." Mike felt his anger returning as he recalled the events of the previous night.

"Sounds like she was out of line."

"She was, and I don't understand why."

"Oh, I can tell you why. She's been taking some heat regarding her handling of some recent missing person cases. The families of the missing have lodged complaints because they think she should be doing more to find them."

"What do you think?" Mike looked at Andy.

"On the record? I don't know. Off the record? I think the complaints may be valid."

"Good to know. Off the record, I need to tell you something." Mike told him about his conversation with Dr. Slater.

"Was there anything in the lab work?"

"Yes, there was. Jim's going to try to stall the release of the report. I asked him to do it so I could talk to you first."

"Who else knows about this?"

"Other than you? Jim, Davis, and Caleb."

"Be careful who you share this with. Ali has a lot of friends around here."

"Are you one of them?"

"She is a colleague, but she's not someone I would call a friend."

"Is there something that can be done about this?"

"Maybe. Let me look into a few things and get back to you."

"I appreciate this, Andy." Mike stood up.

"Don't thank me just yet." He made clear he wasn't making any promises as to what he might or might not be able to find out. "I'll be in touch."

Mike left the sheriff's office and got in his truck to go to PJ's to pick up his kids. On the way there, he called them to let them know he was on his way.

"Hey, PJ."

"Morning, Mike. How are you?"

"I'm fine. How's everyone there?"

"Good. The kids are still sleeping. How's Taylor?"

"She was sleeping when I left. Her friend is with her."

"Damned sorry to hear what happened to her."

"Me too. I'm on my way and should be there shortly."

"I'll get the kids up."

"Thanks. See you when I get there."

"Yup. Bye."

After ending the call with his brother, Mike called Rae.

"Well, hello there, Mike."

"Rae. How's Taylor?"

"She seems okay. She got up not too long ago. She's in the shower. You want me to get her for you?"

"No, I'll call back."

"Okay. Talk to you later."

"Bye." Mike ended the call. He had a lot on his mind. He was worried about Taylor, and the fact that this didn't seem to be a random occurrence was gnawing at him. He hoped Andy came through with some information.

"Dad, did something happen last night?"

Mike looked in the rearview mirror at his son, who'd asked the question. "Why do you ask?"

"Because Dana said you needed to help the sheriff with something."

"Yes, something did happen, but it was taken care of."

"Did you help the sheriff?" Kay asked.

"Yes, I did. Dana took you guys with her last night because I didn't know how long it was going to take."

"Did you have to shoot anybody?" Kay asked.

"What? Why would you think that?"

Kay shrugged her shoulders. "I don't know. There were a lot of people around last night. Maybe the sheriff needed you to cover him, like in the movies."

"No, I didn't shoot anyone." Changing the subject, he asked them if they had fun last night at the party.

"It was a lot of fun, Dad. I also got to try that game Miss Rae told me about. I didn't do too good, but I liked it." Mikey went on to tell him about the game.

"What about you, Kay?"

"I had fun. I got to hang out with my friends, and they liked the way Miss Taylor did my hair. I was the only one there with a braid like that."

"I'm not surprised. It did look pretty on you." Mike smiled at her in the mirror.

"You're just saying that because you're my dad."

"Nope. I'm saying it because it's true." Mike came to a stop in front of his house. "Grab your stuff, kids, and I'll make lunch."

"Yay!"

chapter 40

Taylor sat at the kitchen table with Rae. Rae was leaving the next day, and Taylor didn't want her friend to go. She was trying to talk her into coming back for the summer.

"Aww, come on. You're not teaching any courses this summer, and I know for a fact you don't have any travel planned."

"I know. The reason I was keeping my options open was because I was hoping I'd be able to talk Liam into spending some time with me and maybe taking a trip together," Rae said sadly. Taylor reached over and squeezed her friend's hand. "That didn't work out so well for me did it, Tay? I mean, he knew how I felt, but he didn't choose me."

"It's his loss, Rae. And, honestly, I think he may have done you a favor by showing you his true colors before anything went further."

"You're right, but it still pisses me off."

"All the more reason for you to come spend the summer here." Taylor looked at her and smirked. "Plus, I'm sure Davis wouldn't mind it either."

"There is that." Rae smiled.

"Just think about it. It would be so great to have my bestie here."

"I'll give it some thought."

"Good."

I think she's going to do it, Taylor thought happily. Smiling to herself, she got up from the table and grabbed her phone off the counter to check her messages. Mike was making plans to take Mikey and Kay to a museum near the airport. Taylor told him she was taking Rae to the airport and asked him if they'd like to meet for lunch. He said yes, but he insisted on driving and said he'd pick them both up in the morning. He'd sent her a text to confirm the time. She sent a text back to confirm and asked if he had plans for the evening. He said he didn't. The kids were visiting their maternal grandparents, and the saloon was closed for a few days to give the staff a break after working at the rodeo and the town square party. She told him she wanted to have a going away dinner for Rae and asked if he would let Davis, Caleb, and Mina know. He said he would, but he'd get Caleb to do the cooking because he didn't want her overdoing it. Taylor told him she was fine and she could do it, but he wasn't having it, so she relented. He sent her a smiley face emoji and told her that Caleb would be in touch and that he'd see her later that evening. She was smiling as she put her phone down.

"You must be texting Mike," Rae said as she got up to refill her coffee cup.

"Why do you say that?"

"Because you always get that goofy smile on your face whenever you hear from him."

"I do not."

"You do. Prove me wrong."

"Whatever."

"Just like I thought."

"Anyway, I didn't mention it earlier, because I didn't know what everyone's availability was, but we're having a little dinner for you this evening."

"We are?"

"Yes, we are. Mike said Caleb will take care of the food."

"That's sweet of him."

"Do you feel like making a peach cobbler?"

"Sure, I can make one."

"Good. I'll make some vanilla ice cream to go along with it."

"So, uh, who all is coming? I mean, so I'll know how big of a cobbler to make."

"I think the question you meant to ask is 'Will Davis be able to make it?'" Taylor looked at Rae.

"No, it's not. But since you brought it up, will he?"

Taylor laughed. "Mike is going to call him. If he's off, I'm sure he will."

"I guess we better get started then."

The homemade ice cream was in the freezer, and the cobbler was on the counter cooling when Caleb arrived. After bringing the grocery bags in and setting them on the kitchen table, he reached into one of the bags and pulled out a bottle of wine.

"Join me for a drink before I start cooking, ladies?"

"Are you sure you don't mind cooking?" Taylor opened the cabinet to get the glasses.

"Of course not. Even though I do it for a living, I enjoy it much more when it's for people I like."

"Thanks, Caleb."

Rae walked into the kitchen. "Hey, Caleb! What we drinking?"

"A little birdie told me that, like your friend here, you have a fondness for Pinot Noir."

"And that little birdie would be right." She looked at the bottle. "Haven't had this one before."

"I think you might like it," Caleb said as he opened the bottle of wine and poured it into the glasses Taylor had placed on the counter.

"You were right," Rae said after taking a sip. "This is pretty good."

Taylor nodded in agreement. "I'm guessing you didn't let Mike pick this one?"

"Of course I didn't," he confirmed.

"Come on, he's not that bad," Taylor remarked, laughing.

"Yes, he is. He's pretty good with beer and spirits, but wine, not so much. That's why he lets Josh over at the wine store make the selections we serve."

"I'm going to tell him you said that."

"Well, if you do, you might miss out on all this good food, and I *know* you're gonna want some."

"I'm hungry, Tay. Don't do that. What's for dinner, Caleb?"

"Glad you asked. I thought I'd do comfort food. Since you're leaving us tomorrow, consider it a hug."

"I like the sound of that."

"I'm doing my special fried chicken, mashed potatoes, gravy, steamed veggies, and homemade biscuits. I also have some of my mom's honey. It tastes amazing on biscuits."

"That sounds delicious. It will go nicely with the dessert we made," Rae said.

"What'd you make?"

"Peach cobbler and vanilla ice cream."

"That'll go great."

"Can we help with anything?" Taylor asked.

"Sure, you can peel the potatoes and prep the vegetables while I get started on the buttermilk batter for the chicken and the biscuit mix."

Rae pulled up a playlist on her phone, which was in the speaker dock on the counter.

"A little mood music. Let's get started."

The three of them set about preparing dinner. After getting the vegetables ready as Caleb had requested, Rae and Taylor did more drinking and dancing than cooking. There was a lot of laughter going on in the kitchen as well. Caleb gave them the first piece of chicken he removed from the cast-iron skillet, and both women swore it was the best chicken they'd ever tasted.

chapter 41

While they were praising Caleb's culinary skills, the doorbell rang. Taylor went to answer it and returned to the kitchen followed by Davis and Mina. Both were holding bouquets.

"Something smells mighty good in here," Mina said. She handed the bouquet she held to Taylor.

"I agree," Davis added, his eyes on Rae. "These are for you."

"Aww, thanks." Rae blushed as she accepted the flowers from Davis.

"Thanks, Mina." Taylor inhaled the scent of the flowers. "These are beautiful. Let me get something to put them in."

"Would you two like something to drink?" Rae asked. "We have wine, whiskey, and beer."

Mina asked for wine, and Davis a beer.

Mike arrived a few minutes later.

After getting the food on the table and saying grace, everyone began to pass the serving dishes around and filled their plates. Davis proposed a toast.

"Here's to good food and good friends, old and new." He winked at Rae as he said the last part. They all raised their glasses and smiled. The dinner was delicious, and just as Caleb had said, it was like a nice hug. The conversation was fun and easy. Rae and Taylor told the others the story of how they met and shared some of the things they got into through the years when they were younger. Rae asked Mike how he, Caleb, and Davis became friends.

"Caleb and I were born on the same day, in the same hospital. According to our parents, we've been friends since the nurse placed us next to each other in the nursery." Mike answered.

Caleb continued the story. "We met Davis in first grade. He'd gotten into a fight with some older boys, and we decided to help."

"Aww, that was sweet of you," Taylor said.

"No, it wasn't. We missed recess because of him. He didn't even thank us for our trouble. Even back then he was an ass," Mike said.

"Whatever, man," Davis interjected, making them all laugh.

"We've been friends ever since. Although sometimes I wonder why." Caleb finished jokingly.

"Mina, what was it like growing up with these guys?" Rae asked. "I'm an only child, but Taylor's brothers used to scare off any boys who tried to talk to us."

Mina smiled as she recalled similar happenings. "It was pretty much the same for me. I also had to contend with girls wanting to be my friend so they could get close to them. They were a little scared of Mike, and Caleb had this mysterious aura about him, but it didn't stop the girls from wanting to be with them. This one"—she pointed to Davis— "was a kind of a jerk, but he'd pretty much just smile and get away with everything. Even the teachers let him get away with stuff."

"Remember the librarian who had the hots for your dad?" Mike added.

"I'd forgotten about her." Caleb and Davis laughed at the memory.

"Davis looks pretty much like our dad did back then," Mina explained to Rae and Taylor. "He was a single parent, and a lot of the unattached ladies here and in the next county were trying to get his attention. They were always doing stuff for us, baking cookies, cooking casseroles, and making clothes for me. There was this librarian, though, who had it bad for him. Dad went out with her a few times."

"What happened?" Rae asked.

"We didn't know what was going on at the time, but after they stopped seeing each other, she kept calling the house," Davis said, picking up where Mina left off. "Dad never said anything about it, but he started screening the calls, letting them go to the answering machine before picking up. I guess she got tired of him ignoring her calls because she started showing up at our house. One time, she showed up drunk and crying. Dad took her home. He drove her car and had me follow him so he'd have a way back. On the way home, I asked him if she was okay. He said something about her being upset but didn't go into any details."

"Years later, I was out with Dad, and we ran into her. She was pleasant enough to me, but you could tell she wasn't all that happy to see him. Dad said something about her not letting things go. I asked him what he meant. He said that she was holding a grudge because, and I quote"—Davis did air quotes— "he hit it and quit it." They all laughed.

"Dad said she was a little different, which he didn't mind, but as it turned out, she was batshit crazy, and that was something he didn't want to deal with."

Rae looked at Davis. "Sounds like your daddy was a bit of a player."

"The ladies loved him, that's for sure. After what happened with Ms. Burke, the librarian, he decided to go after the woman he wanted."

"Did he get her?" Taylor asked.

"He did," Mina answered, smiling. "But it wasn't easy. The woman was our housekeeper, and she knew all about his reputation with the ladies. It took him a while to convince her he was serious about her, but he finally did."

"How nice."

"*No*, I wouldn't call it nice," Davis said.

"Why would you say that?" Taylor looked confused.

"Yes, Davis, why *would* you say that?" Caleb repeated the question.

"You know why." Davis frowned. Mike and Caleb snickered. Mina's face turned pink with embarrassment.

"I'll tell you why," Mike said, trying hard not to laugh. "Let's just say that once the two of them got together, they spent a *lot* of time getting busy."

Davis rolled his eyes. "I don't want to talk about my folks getting busy or the kinky shit they're into. Can we change the subject please?" Everyone but Davis laughed.

"Oh, so in addition to being a reformed player, your daddy has a little freak in him?" Rae looked at Caleb and Mina, then Davis. "Does it run in the family?" she asked, causing more laughter from the others.

"On that note, let's move this to the porch for coffee and dessert." Taylor got up from the table to go into the kitchen and start the coffee. Mike came up behind her, wrapped his arms around her, and kissed her on the side of the neck.

"How are you feeling?"

"I'm okay."

"Good. But take it easy. I don't want you overdoing things." He kissed her again.

"Hey, hey, break it up. We have work to do." Caleb came into the kitchen carrying empty serving dishes, followed by Rae and Davis, who carried the plates, glasses, and silverware. Mina was close behind with the remainder of the glasses. They quickly loaded the dishwasher and cleaned up the kitchen. By the time they finished, the coffee was ready. Rae poured the coffee into a carafe and set up a tray with cups, cream, and sugar. She walked out to the porch, followed by Davis, who carried the tray. Taylor removed the ice cream from the freezer and set it on the counter next to the cobbler. Caleb served up the cobbler, and Mike added a scoop of ice cream to each dish. Mina grabbed spoons and napkins. Between the four of them, they carried the dishes outside to join Davis and Rae.

The night was warm, and the scent of the flowers permeated the air and reminded Taylor of her Mimi's garden. She paused for a moment to take it all in. If someone had told her last year that she would be in a small town in Wyoming, of all places, enjoying a pleasant evening with friends, she would never have believed it. If they had told her that one of those friends would also become her lover, she would have called them crazy. Those types of things always happened to others but never to her. Hearing the banter going back and forth between everyone warmed her heart.

"Why are you so quiet, Taylor?" Caleb, who was sitting next to her, nudged her knee.

"I was just thinking of what I'm going to say to Rae on the way to the airport tomorrow to convince her to come back for the summer." She answered, wanting to keep her true thoughts to herself.

"You're thinking about coming back?" Davis asked.

"I'm not teaching any classes this summer and haven't made any travel plans, so I'm giving it some thought." Rae looked back at Davis, who gave her a lopsided grin in return.

"What time is your flight?"

"Noon."

"Taylor, would you mind if I took Rae to the airport? I think I might have an offer she'll find hard to refuse." Davis spoke without taking his eyes off Rae.

"Oh, really?"

"Really." He smiled, dimples in full force.

Taylor looked at Davis and then Rae, who seemed to be engaged in a staring contest.

"That would be great, Davis. Thanks." Neither acknowledged her comment.

Mike cleared his throat. "Now that we've got that settled, I'll pick you up at ten o'clock, since Rae has a ride to the airport."

"Where are you two going tomorrow?" Mina asked.

"I'm taking the kids to the science museum. Taylor's coming with us."

"The interactive museum?"

"Yup, that's the one."

"That should be fun. I took my class last semester, and they loved it. I did too. It was much better than I thought it would be."

They continued to talk for another hour or so, then the party broke up. Mina and Rae helped Taylor take the dishes back into the kitchen and put them into the dishwasher. Afterward, they returned to the porch.

"I guess we'll get going," Davis said. He and Mina had ridden together.

"Davis, I can drop Mina off, since I have to go past her place anyway." Caleb looked at Mina as he spoke. "That is, if it's okay with you."

Mina blushed and nervously pushed her hair behind her ears. "It's okay."

"Let's get out of here before your brother tries to cockblock," Caleb whispered in her ear.

Mina giggled and left the porch with him. Mike held the screen door open for Taylor and followed her inside, leaving Davis and Rae on the porch.

Davis was sitting next to Rae on the bench, and the two remained when the others left.

"How is Taylor doing?" Davis asked.

"She's had a few rough nights. Other than that, she's okay"

"I'm glad to hear that."

"I am too. I don't know what we would have done without you guys."

"Thankfully, we'll never have to find out." Davis looked at Rae. "Barring that night, how has your time here been?"

"It's been good. I will admit, I was a little nervous about coming out here though."

"Why were you worried about coming here?"

"Well, it is a small town in a state with more land than people."

"And?"

"And it's not known for its diversity. Even though Taylor said pretty much everyone she's met has been pretty nice, I didn't fully believe her. I thought she was just saying that to keep us from worrying about her."

"I can understand that." He turned to look at her, his whiskey-colored eyes looking directly at her. "How do you like us now?"

Rae felt her heart rate quicken a bit. "I like you just fine."

"Good." He leaned forward and touched his lips to hers. Not meeting any resistance, he deepened the kiss. "That's the kiss I promised you. Now I need your phone number."

"My what?"

Davis smiled and repeated himself. "Your number. So I can text you when I'm on my way over in the morning."

Feeling a little embarrassed at her reaction to his kiss, Rae looked away from him as she gave him her number. She and Davis had been flirting with each other since they first met. He'd told her just before he left to search for Taylor that he was going to kiss her and get her number. She thought he'd been just trying to cheer her up. She hadn't seen him since that night they rescued Taylor. And tonight, he'd treated her pretty much the same as before, so she hadn't expected the kiss. When it happened, she was surprised at how good it felt. She was glad there wasn't much light on the porch, so he couldn't see just how much his kiss affected her.

Like his father, Davis was a bit of a ladies' man. He pretty much enjoyed them all and often showed his appreciation for them through smiles and light, sometimes flirtatious banter. His father had been the same way. But as popular as he'd been with the women, he always treated them with respect and taught Davis to do the same. He also told him he'd only ever loved two women—his first wife, Davis and Mina's mother, who'd been killed by a drunk driver, and his current wife, Priscilla, or "Cici" as he called her.

Davis liked Rae Stephens from the moment he met her. She was a solid friend to Taylor. She was also intelligent, sexy, and a little crazy; a mix he found very appealing. He was surprised and impressed when he found out that she was also into earth sciences. He was hoping Rae decided to come back for the summer. He wanted to ask her help with a project he was working on, and because he genuinely liked her and wanted to get to know her better.

"I would love to stay out here a little longer with you, but it's getting late, and we'll need to get an early start in the morning." Rae nodded in response. Davis leaned in and captured her lips once more.

"I'll be by to get you between 7:15 a.m. and 7:30 a.m. I figure we can have breakfast at a place I like near the airport. Is that okay?"

"Yes, that's fine."

"Good. How about you give me a kiss goodnight before you go inside?"

Instead of waiting for her answer, he held her a little tighter, and what started as a single goodnight kiss turned into him leaving the porch half an hour later, overheated and highly aroused. He adjusted himself as he walked to his truck. He got in, started it, and waved at Rae, who was still standing on the porch where he'd left her. He was pretty sure she was in the same condition as him.

Rae waved at Davis as he drove off. She was feeling out of sorts from the kisses they'd shared, and she found herself wondering what would have happened if he had come inside instead of going home. She was kidding herself. She knew exactly what would have happened had he come in. Neither Liam's kisses nor those of her on-again-off-again booty call boyfriend Bobby moved her like Davis's. She was glad he didn't stay. As much as her body wanted to, she wasn't ready to go there with him. Somehow, he must have sensed it. She saw understanding in his eyes when he told her goodnight.

She needed to sort out her feelings. Bobby was just someone to fill in the gaps, but she still had some residual feelings for Liam that she had to deal with. She hadn't told Taylor, but she planned to see him when she got back home. Liam had wanted to meet with her to apologize face-to-face for not telling her about his engagement. She wondered if he would also apologize for sleeping with her while he'd been dating his now fiancée. Rae doubted he would. Whatever the case, she felt she needed to see him and get resolution, closure, or both, before deciding whether she'd spend the summer in Silverton—and if she'd see where things might go with Davis.

To be continued . . .

EMERGENCY RESOURCES

The list below has contact information for anyone experiencing crises, having an emergency, or needing help.

Experiencing or witnessing an emergency – Dial 911

988 Suicide and Crisis Prevention Lifeline – Dial 988

Veterans Crisis Line – Dial 988 then press 1

National Suicide Prevention Lifeline – 1-800-273-8255 (TALK)

National Human Trafficking Hotline – 1-888-373-7888

Text "HELP" to "BEFREE" (233733)

Email: help@humantrafficking.org

ACKNOWLEDGMENTS

Thank you, God, for this story. Writing has been an interesting and exciting journey. I want to thank the following: Tori—the best hype woman ever, sister-cousin, and friend. Forever friends: April, Devany, Demetra, and Melerie. Brian—I appreciate your insight. One More Glance Editing, All That's Wright LLC. and Tenth Muse Enterprises. A heartfelt thanks to the authors in the romance community who encouraged me, answered my questions, and connected me to resources to help bring my writing to life. Your kindness is greatly appreciated. And most important of all, thank you to the readers of my stories.

ABOUT THE AUTHOR

Harper Black's love of reading and curiosity about the world was stirred at an early age. That curiosity, a desire to get a college education, and a sense of adventure, led Harper to enlist in the U.S. Navy. Harper's military career took her to intrepid and romantic destinations, embarking on a journey to achieve her professional goals while navigating the ebbs and flows of international romance. Her travels included memorable experiences in Scotland, Italy, and England. Her experiences in traveling and dating inspired her to write. In her stories, Harper crafts romantic adventures that reflect diverse cultures and explores some of the many places and ways love can happen.

Website: www.HarperBlackWrites.com
Instagram: @harperblack10writes
Email: harper.black10@gmail.com

www.ingramcontent.com/pod-product-compliance
Lightning Source LLC
LaVergne TN
LVHW091713070526
838199LV00050B/2386